Born in the Southern United States, Diana Reed Morris has traveled extensively and lived in Italy, Spain, and Canada. Her works include *Treasures of War* and *Flower of the South*. She resides near family in North Georgia where she is collecting material for her next novel.

To Jack

Diana Reed Morris

A NIGHT IN MONTERREY

AUSTIN MACAULEY PUBLISHERS™

LONDON • CAMBRIDGE • NEW YORK • SHARJAH

Ordering Information
Quantity sales: Special discounts are available on quantity purchases by corporations, associations, and others. For details, contact the publisher at the address below.

Publisher's Cataloging-in-Publication data
Morris, Diana Reed
A Night in Monterrey

ISBN 9781685623005 (Paperback)
ISBN 9781685623012 (ePub e-book)

Library of Congress Control Number: 2023905825

www.austinmacauley.com/us

First Published 2023
Austin Macauley Publishers LLC
40 Wall Street, 33rd Floor, Suite 3302
New York, NY 10005
USA

mail-usa@austinmacauley.com
+1 (646) 5125767

For inspiration, education, and encouragement, I am grateful to family and friends who live in Houston, Beaumont, and Galveston, Texas. Similarly, I am grateful to those whom I encountered during my years of service at the University of Texas Medical Branch, people who told stories that highlighted connections between Texas and Mexico.

Thanks to the residents of the Norgarden in Sidney, BC who supported my writing efforts. Special acknowledgement is given to Shirley Patton who lived in Mexico for many years and advised me about the post-revolution land ownership system.

Thank you to my capable reader and critic, William J. Reed, my brother and lifetime friend. Huge thanks to my kind, indulgent husband Jack for many hours of listening patiently to rewrites.

A night in Monterrey is a work of imagination. None of the characters is real. All errors, alas, are mine.

Preface

The towheaded cowboy of about eight or nine years old pulled his toy pistol from its holster and aimed it at his playmate. His playmate, however, had beaten him to the draw.

"Bang, bang, you're dead," said the playmate, blowing pretend smoke from the stick that served as his weapon.

"No, I'm not," said the towhead.

"Yes, you are," insisted the playmate. "I shot first."

"My house, my yard, my game. I get to say who is dead. I say you're dead," replied the towhead, each word louder than the last. "Fall down. Dead people fall down."

"How do you know what dead people do?" The playmate threw his stick to the ground and lowered his knees to the soft grass that served as front yard to the ranch.

"Because I'm the prince of the house and I know everything. Someday I'll be king." The towhead hoslstered his gun, and ran in circles around his playmate.

"King, king, I'll be king and you'll work for me," the towhead taunted.

"Cowboys aren't kings," said the playmate, turning onto his stomach, planting his elbows in the grass and lifting his upper body off the ground so that he could see the world around him.

The towhead halted his running and sat down beside the other boy. He stretched his legs and flexed his feet in turn, admiring his hand-tooled boots.

"I can be both. My dad says I can be anything I want because we are rich." The little boy lifted his chin and by moving only his eyes, looked down at his playmate mimicking a facial expression of his father, a smug expression of superiority and disdain.

"My father says I can be president of Mexico, if I want," retorted the playmate.

"I'll be president of the world," said the towhead. Correcting himself, he added, "King of the world. I'll be king." He jumped up and dashed around the yard, yelling in staccato, "King, king. I'll be king."

Part 1
1942

Chapter 1

Jeananne Cameron stepped out of the shower lowering her eyes to avoid seeing her naked body in the mirror hanging on the back of the door. She reached for the frayed thin once brilliant blue towel and covered herself with it as best she could.

She was 17 ½ years old. The half was important to her because she would have freedom in just six months. Eighteen was the magic age when she could do as she pleased.

She had shoulder length red hair and blue-green eyes, a translucent teal that immobilized the observer. She was taller than many of the boys in her class, had a narrow waist and a small bosom.

After she dressed in a heavy white cotton nightgown, she knelt by her bed and prayed to rid herself of the sins of pride and of the flesh. She fervently wished to avoid sin, not solely for reasons of devotion but to avoid the wrathful punishments of her father, Pastor Early Cameron.

Pastor Cameron frequently preached about sin at home and at meeting. In addition to his wife and daughter, he enjoyed a small but loyal following, mostly Okies who came east to escape the dust and stayed because it was easier to stay than to leave. The Okies were enthusiastic about his subject matter believing that someone must have sinned pretty mightily to create the great Dustbowl and the poverty of the Depression.

They did not wish to be thrown into the more citified religious denominations, preferred separation and called themselves Lambs of the Lord, or Lambs, for short. None had ever seen a real lamb.

With Pastor Cameron as their shepherd, the lambs convened every Sunday morning in the concrete block structure that served as the administrative offices of the Arkansas Traveller Motor Inn and Park. It was located in the northwest part of the state where land was green and catfish were plenty, swimming along the bottoms of rivers just waiting to be lured to the frying pan.

During the service each week, Mr. and Mrs. Joyner led the singing. The group could not afford an organ but Mrs. Joyner had perfect pitch. Janice Thompson, who had a full set of teeth and the best reading voice, second only to the pastor, read the scripture. Jeananne and her mother passed the collection plate, actually a round tray that had once held hot sauce, salt, and pepper at a roadside barbecue stand outside Little Rock.

As Jeananne pulled the sheet up to her chin, the Bible verse and sermon were still ringing in her head. Proverbs 16:18. Janice Thompson read the entire verse from the King James Bible. "Pride goeth before destruction and a haughty spirit before a fall…Yea, all of you be subject one to another, and be clothed with humility: for God resisteth the proud, and giveth grace to the humble." Pastor Cameron said it was the first part of the verse that mattered most.

"Pride goeth before a fall." He repeated that phrase several times during the course of his sermon. "Cast down your eyes and do not offend God. Be humble."

It was those words that reverberated in Jeananne's head. She did not want to be the proud person who was condemned to hell for eternity. Jeananne's picture of hell was the one her father painted. It would be sort of like an enclosed bonfire with little imps prodding people who were suffering and screaming.

She did not want to offend God or her father and at times she confused the two. She wanted to be a good person who did good deeds. She also did not want to suffer painful consequences of bad thoughts and bad behavior, consequences that could be wrought by either God or Pastor Cameron.

Jeananne was modest in appearance, wearing clothes made by her mother, dresses that were always large so that she could grow into them. She fit in with the other children who grew into their teen years during an era of deprivation. They talked of cities and movie stars and cars and had hopes but no money to support their dreams. They dreamed, nevertheless.

In her senior year in high school, in December, 1941, she and her classmates heard the radio announcement of war declared by President Franklin Delano Roosevelt. The boys were excited and talked incessantly about signing up and becoming soldiers. Jeananne had no experience of war.

14

Camerons had fought in the War Between the States and in the Great War but that was long ago, before she was born. She knew war was serious and that people would be killed. In her prayers, she spoke to God, pleading for the safety of all of those who were fighting and in faraway places.

Talk of war at home was limited as her father did not want to discuss violence. He said it was always better to focus on something godly. Before his flock, he expressed the view that the war would bring jobs for people who needed them and change would come. He prayed for peace and for good jobs for the Lambs and generously, for everyone else he knew. He also prayed that death and destruction would come to the enemy.

Pastor Early advised Jeananne to think about working as soon as school was out in May. He spoke as though Jeananne knew nothing of work. This puzzled Jeananne because she was already working for Aunt Faye Farris on Saturdays and afternoons after school. She had been saving the money she earned in a fruit jar hidden in a box beneath her bed. She wasn't sure how she would spend it, but she knew she needed money for her escape.

Aunt Faye was a retired school teacher, a spinster whose sole purpose in life was to take care of her aged father. She had found Jeananne by consulting with the school's principal, explaining that she wanted to hire a student to work for her after school hours. The principal had sent three girls to meet Aunt Faye and of the three, she took an immediate liking to Jeananne. When she hired Jeananne, it was with the understanding that she expected timeliness, cleanliness, and a willingness to work. Jeananne would do the dusting, wash dishes and do housecleaning, and she would help with the care required by Aunt Faye's father. There might be other duties as needed and in return Jeananne would be paid in cash weekly for the hours worked at an agreed upon rate.

Generally reticent about "putting herself forward," Jeananne was quiet and as taught by her father, spoke only when spoken to. After several weeks on the job, she and Aunt Faye became increasingly comfortable with each other. They began conversing more, at first about everyday household and care giving matters. Their talks expanded and became more personal, with Aunt Faye encouraging Jeananne to talk about herself, her friendships, her schoolwork and, eventually, her dreams.

"What would I do without you?" she would say to Jeananne. "You bring sunshine into my life." To these sorts of compliments, Jeananne would say a polite thank you and look down at her feet, hoping to remain humble and filled with humility.

In the spring of 1942, as the end of Jeananne's senior year approached, Aunt Faye asked her to stay late, to sit with her in the parlor and visit. This was a rare occurrence. Usually they talked while in action and normally Jeananne left when she finished her tasks. Jeananne cleaned the parlor but never enjoyed relaxation in the room with the velvet upholstered settee and chairs.

This particular evening in the formal parlor, Aunt Faye sat, legs crossed at the ankles right over left, hands folded in her lap. She opened the conversation. "You are such a beautiful young girl, Jeananne, and so kind. You must know how much my father and I enjoy having you around. Now that you are finishing high school, what do you intend to do with your future?"

"I don't really know. My father says there will be work for me at a munitions plant. Factory work."

Aunt Faye adjusted herself in her over-stuffed living room chair crossing her left ankle over her right. "Is there no boy that you dream of? No, I guess not. Forgive me, they will all be signing up, I suppose."

"My father would not allow it."

"Let's have a cup of hot tea, or I suppose you would like lemonade. I want to talk with you about some ideas I have. Would you get it while I sit for a bit and think?" Aunt Faye was not actually Jeananne's aunt but she was related somehow on her mother's side. Not everyone called her Aunt Faye because she was formal in the manner of an educated woman of her generation and preferred to be called Miss Farris. Only relations called her Aunt Faye. Jeananne's mother had explained to Jeananne the complicated details of her familial relationship to Faye Farris, thus entitling Jeananne to call her Aunt Faye.

Once comfortably served, stirring her tea, Aunt Faye spoke again. Jeananne listened intently, sipping on her cold lemonade, refreshing in the evening heat of late spring in the South.

"I have an idea. It affects both of us, something I want you to think about."

While Jeananne didn't know what to say, her posture spoke for her. She automatically sat up and looked directly at Aunt Faye, not exactly directly into her eyes. That would have been rude, but close enough.

Chapter 2

Aunt Faye reached for her shawl and removed it from her shoulders. The room was warm. Sensing that her shoulders were rounded, she adjusted her posture, straightening her back. She smiled at Jeananne and placed her teacup and its saucer on the lamp table next to her chair.

"I have a widowed sister in Houston, Texas," she said. "Martha is living alone in a large house and would very much like me to come live with her. Of course, I cannot. I have our father to take care of and I am set in my ways, unlikely to enjoy being removed from my routines."

"Is that your sister's picture?" Jeananne pointed to a framed picture of a smiling couple dressed in fancy clothes. They looked to Jeananne like movie stars.

"Yes, that was taken many years ago. They were celebrating one of their wedding anniversaries."

"They look very happy."

"They were. And now Martha is by herself. She is not very happy living by herself. She and our sister Miriam live in the same city, not far from each other. Nevertheless, Martha writes that she is lonesome."

Jeananne frowned, furrowing her eyebrows. "Yes, I can understand that it would be difficult for a woman after her husband dies. Does she have any children?"

"No. Miriam has one son. He's in the Armed Forces, doing his duty. Miriam worries about him all the time. We never know exactly where he is or how he is doing."

"You must be worried about your sisters. I'll pray for them and for your nephew."

"That would be kind of you, my dear. You are such a kind young girl, but you are growing into a young woman and we need to think of your future."

Jeananne, feeling uncomfortable about the compliment, noticed the empty teacup and jumped up saying, "Let me put that cup in the kitchen. I'll wash it before I go. And my glass."

"Don't go yet. I have more to say to you. Dishwashing can wait."

Jeananne returned to her seat sensing Aunt Faye's unease and determination. Her curiosity both interested and frightened her.

Aunt Faye, aware that she had Jeananne's attention, continued, "Since you are finishing high school soon and have no definite plans, I wondered if you would like to go to Houston to live with my sister. There, I've said it."

"Do you mean Martha? The one who is a widow?"

"Yes."

Jeananne flushed with excitement. "You mean live in her house and work for her? What would I do? Would she pay me? I have to earn money. What is her house like? I'm sure she is a nice person because she's your sister, but does she want me? She doesn't know me."

Jeananne's nervousness was apparent as she blurted out questions and thoughts. Suddenly she had an unexpected option, an alternative to a continuance of her life with Pastor Early, an alternative to work in a munitions factory.

"I want to escape. I don't mean escape. My parents want me to live the rest of my life at home with them. They don't approve of boys. They don't approve of my being on my own. They don't approve of my having a life. Honor thy father and mother. I do, but I need something. I don't even know what I need, but it isn't living at home for the rest of my life." Tears were falling from Jeananne's eyes.

Aunt Faye felt sorry for Jeananne. "I think it must be overwhelming for you. You are young and have little experience. My sister is upstanding and respectable, and Christian. I think your parents could accept her. They accepted me."

"What about work?"

"Martha has many friends. She could help you find work. After all, you have a skill. You took typing, didn't you?"

"Yes, and shorthand. I'm not great at shorthand but I can type sixty words per minute."

"Good. You will be able to earn a living as a secretary, or a clerk, working in an office."

Jeananne perked up. "You mean I wouldn't do housework?"

"No. Martha already has someone who does the housework."

"She must be rich." Jeananne was beginning to imagine the rich sister in the fancy clothes living in a big house.

"Martha's husband was successful and she is what we call 'well-fixed'. That is not your concern. She will help you find a job and you would live in her house, like a companion. Do you think you might consider going to Houston?"

Aunt Faye was beginning to think that Jeananne might accept the proposal, but she knew she needed to be patient and answer questions and help Jeananne overcome her fears and obstacles.

"How would I get to Houston? What about my parents?" There was doubt in Jeananne's voice.

"I will talk with your parents. I think they will agree that it is a great opportunity for you. If you decide you want to go, we will find a way to pay for the trip. You might go to the library and consult an atlas to see where Houston is located. You would get there on a bus. That would be an adventure, wouldn't you agree?"

"You were right when you said it is a lot to think about. What about your sister? She doesn't know me. Are you sure she wants me?"

"I am absolutely sure." Aunt Fay did not reveal the letters that she and her sister had exchanged regarding the matter. The letters had been going back and forth for the past three months. The two women were emotionally close despite their physical distance. Throughout their adult lives, they maintained their relationship by letter and in recent years, by telephone on special occasions.

Jeananne did not realize how much Aunt Faye cared for her, thought about her problems and wanted to help her. If asked, the never-married Aunt Faye might have said she viewed Jeananne as a granddaughter. Linking two people she loved, Jeananne and Martha, seemed a simple and obvious solution to the problems of each.

As Jeananne left Aunt Faye's home and began the short walk to the trailer park, it was that part of the day when the light makes all the leaves and plants take on a soft greenish gray hue. Along her path, she began counting lightning bugs.

In that gentle calmness, Jeananne began to envision herself in a new life, away from her parents. She tried to imagine herself in a real bedroom with a window and maybe a chair and her own closet. She imagined herself in the clothes she had seen actresses wearing in movie magazine pictures, suits with straight skirts and jackets with peplums, high heels. Maybe she would even own a fancy gown like the one Aunt Faye's sister was wearing in the photograph.

By the time Jeananne arrived home, in her imagination, she had already moved to Houston and begun a new life of glamour.

Pastor Early Cameron noticed something different about his daughter, a look that he did not understand but did not like.

"Whatever you're thinking, you should cleanse your mind."

Chapter 3

Aunt Faye studied the houses on either side of the sidewalk, noting other Victorian style family-sized homes similar to the one she shared with her father. Dressed in her standard black skirt and white high-necked blouse, the stately Faye Farris, her black leather pocketbook in hand, was a determined figure aiming for the entrance to the Arkansas Traveller Motor Inn and Park. She knew that Jeananne's parents had no automobile. No bus travelled through the old neighborhood. She had no other choice but to walk.

Since Aunt Faye was the supplicant, she insisted they meet on Cameron territory. She had a university education, a strong will and a solid plan. What lay ahead would be a battle, and she was prepared to win.

It was a warm afternoon. Mrs. Cameron had placed a pitcher of sweetened iced tea on the center of a round metal table that Pastor Cameron had positioned outdoors on the shady side of the trailer.

"Walk on up to the street to meet her," Mrs. Cameron urged her husband. "It is bad enough that she has walked alone in this heat, and at her age."

"She wants something from me, she can come to me," the pastor said, but he turned and walked toward the entrance to the park as his wife had requested.

Jeananne was not present at this high-level meeting where strong disagreement was anticipated. She stayed with old Mr. Farris who could not be left alone.

The dark interior of the house was cooler than the outdoor temperature. Before she left, Aunt Faye had turned on a fan that oscillated around the old man's bed. Jeananne sat in front of the fan and read aloud from <u>Robinson Crusoe</u>, lulling her listener to sleep. She watched him for a moment but bereft of written words to occupy her mind, she began to fantasize about the conversation taking place between her parents and Aunt Faye.

Her entire future depended on the outcome. She desperately wanted to accept the offer made by Aunt Faye and her sister Martha. When she presented the possibility to her parents, her father had barely allowed her to complete her plea before he said no in such an adamant voice that Jeananne feared there would be complaints in the trailer court. She had made subsequent pleas and, in the end, resorted to begging. All efforts were fruitless.

Jeananne did however have her mother on her side. Her mother was persuaded that this was Jeananne's big chance, her opportunity to make something of herself.

Sitting next to Aunt Fay's sleeping father, Jeananne felt both hopeful and terrified. At the door to adulthood, she wanted both to move forward and backward. She picked up the book and tried to read to herself but could not concentrate.

Aunt Faye returned with Mrs. Cameron at her elbow, Aunt Faye's complexion pale and Mrs. Cameron red with the heat. Jeananne rushed to the entry hall when she heard the door opening. She could hardly contain her excitement.

"What happened? Am I going to Houston?"

"We have to sit and cool off first. Aunt Faye needs some water, as do I," said Jeananne's mother. Both women seated themselves in the parlor. Something about the velvet upholstery made the room seem even hotter.

Jeananne had never seen her mother in a home this grand, and she was surprised that her mother seemed comfortable and was taking command.

"If there is a fan, get it. Get a damp cloth. Get two. We both need damp cloths. Cold."

Jeananne hurried with her tasks trying to hide her disappointment. If the news were good, surely they could have come in laughing and eager to talk to Jeananne. The signs were not good.

Waiting while Aunt Faye and her mother recuperated from their walk in the heat, Jeananne's head filled with her own screams. No, they cannot tell me no. Her body limp; she sat defeated, looking down and trying to affect a humble attitude.

"Don't look so glum," her mother admonished her as a cool manufactured breeze swept across her face. "You are getting what you want."

Jeananne wasn't sure she heard correctly. "I'm going to live in Houston?"

"Yes," said her mother. "I feel well enough now to walk back home. Your father will want me there. You stay here and help Aunt Faye. She'll tell you what happened. No one needs to show me the way out. I can find my own way."

Aunt Faye smiled at Jeananne, a smile that started small, became a grin and ended up as laughter. Jeananne began laughing too. She dashed into the kitchen, ran cool water over the washcloth that she had given her mother earlier, and whisked it across her own forehead as if to awaken herself to her new reality. She poured two glasses of water, hurried to the parlor, handed one to Aunt Faye forgetting that she already had one, and sat down on the floor at her feet.

On the outside Jeananne tried to appear calm, but inside her heart was beating rapidly. She tried to be patient waiting for the story to come from Aunt Faye's lips.

"I am recovered. The meeting went very well," began Aunt Faye. "Your parents were kind and gracious."

"Aunt Faye, surely they were not exactly…" Jeananne could not find the right word to express her thought.

"Agreeable?"

"Yes. My father surely wasn't agreeable."

"He came around. He was persuaded to see the good in my sister's offer." Aunt Faye moved at her own pace, too slow for Jeananne who wanted to know everything at once.

"But he told me I could not go. You're saying he changed his mind."

"It was not easy. I assured him that Martha was a fine Christian lady and that she wanted a companion. She will pay you with room and board and will give you an allowance, as though you were her relation. As a matter of fact, you are a distant relation. I reminded him of that. The Farris family and the Camerons were related long before the war." Aunt Faye did not mention which war but continued, "Your father said he wants you to have a respectable job that pays well so you can contribute to the family."

"That sounds like him. What did you say?"

"I told him that you would make enough money to support yourself so that he and your mother would not have the expenses associated with your needs. They would not be buying food and clothing for you. You would be independent and not rely on them. That would free up their money to be used solely for themselves."

"He liked that idea?"

"Yes. I think it is important, Jeananne, that you are financially independent. Do you know what that means?"

"That I do not need their money?"

"Yes, and they do not need yours." She paused to let that thought float in the air.

"I had not thought of that. And he agreed?"

"He insisted we allow him to accompany you on the bus to Little Rock. I think he believes his parental responsibility is to see to your safety. So be it."

"I am truly shocked. I never thought he would agree. I hoped. You are an angel, Aunt Faye."

"My dear, I think the $500 that I contributed to the church building fund helped."

The smile returned to Aunt Faye's face. "Money may be the root of all evil but it sometimes can buy happiness."

Chapter 4

After dinner as the temperatures were decreasing outside, Jeananne and her father sat under an awning attached to the trailer. Pastor Cameron said, "Aren't you afraid to travel alone on the bus all the way from Little Rock to Houston? Who knows who could sit next to you? Could be the devil himself tempting you or worse, a big hairy fellow who might want to eat you or steal your money."

Pastor Cameron was sipping a cold beer, his third or fourth of the evening. Jeananne hated times like this when her father began slurring his words and he said crazy things.

Tonight he was frightening her. Her experience of the world was limited to school, church meeting, and the immediate neighborhood. She had never been on a long trip by herself and she began imagining the scary scenes her father described. She knew she would not have much money for a big hairy man to steal. She doubted anyone on the bus would want to eat her but she was not comforted.

From the school library she had consulted an atlas and saw that the distance on the map between northwest Arkansas and Houston was several inches. With the librarian's help, she had converted those inches to miles and learned about maps and map keys in the process.

She told herself it seemed every day that she was learning some new detail about life. She was hesitant to admit the pride she felt, afraid of the fall to come.

Four hundred thirty-five miles from Little Rock to Houston, she wrote on a notepad kept under her mattress. She added another two hundred miles, the distance from nearby Fayetteville to Little Rock. Altogether she would be travelling 635 miles. She would talk to Aunt Faye about how she would get her ticket.

"Is that letter for me? It's been opened." Jeananne was disappointed. She rarely received mail and never had she received a letter from someone in another state. It was from Aunt Faye's sister Martha and addressed clearly to Jeananne.

"It's addressed to you, isn't it? That means it's for you." Pastor Cameron was standing inside the curtain that served as a makeshift door dividing Jeananne's private space from the rest of the trailer. Jeananne reached for the letter but Pastor Cameron wasn't giving it up.

"Did you read my letter?" She couldn't help herself. Her father had no right to read her mail.

"While you are living under my roof, you will speak to me with respect. I won't stand for any sass. I will not be accused in my own home."

Jeananne was afraid he would hit her. She didn't want to back down but she didn't want to provoke her father. She was counting days – fourteen more days until she would have her freedom. Plus, she wanted to read the letter.

She had her bus ticket. Aunt Faye had in some unknown way managed to get it for her. The bus left Fayetteville on Wednesday, a day of fellowship for the Lambs. Pastor Cameron chose to stay to conduct the service. He would say good-bye to his daughter at home, not in the Little Rock bus station. He reasoned, if she was old enough to leave home, she was old enough to travel alone.

Jeananne politely agreed with her father about all matters, particularly now. She did not want to stir up trouble. She was eager to read the letter from Martha. She knew now, after spending hours questioning Aunt Faye, that Martha and Miriam Farris had married two brothers. Aunt Faye called them the Wilkins boys but Jeananne knew they could not be boys now.

Wendell Wilkins had married Martha. Sam Wilkins married Miriam. Two sisters had married two brothers. They had all moved to Houston where the men had found oil and formed an important company.

With her father standing so close, Jeananne stood absolutely still looking down at her feet lest her father think she had a bad attitude. He took a step backwards through the curtain and handed the unsealed letter to her.

"She doesn't say much. She says someone will pick you up at the bus station in Houston. You might as well read it. She'll be your boss soon enough."

"Thank you."

Jeananne took the letter from her father's proffered hand and read it after he left. She studied the envelope and noted the address which would be her address someday. The information inside was complicated but Jeananne memorized the details. When she arrived at the Houston bus station, she would be met by a man who worked for Miriam Wilkins. His name was Edo and he was a tall, thin man but Jeananne was not to worry about finding him because he would find her. He would hold up a sign with her name on it just in case there was any confusion. Edo would drive her to Martha's home.

Martha said Jeananne should not worry about her clothing, just bring whatever she wore to school or to church, that there are plenty of shops in Houston that sell clothes. She said Jeananne's room was ready for her, that it was decorated in yellow and was girly and she hoped Jeananne would like it. She said Jeananne would be free to put her own items in her room and could bring photos or sentimental items with her.

"I am looking forward to meeting you. Faye says you are a lovely, kind girl. I know we will get along well. Several people here are looking forward to meeting you. Faye told me you took typing and shorthand in high school. I have a job here waiting for you." Jeananne read and reread these words. Who would want to meet her? What would the job be like? How much money would she make?

About her belongings, Jeananne had already decided she would pack everything she owned. She had one big suitcase and a travel case. These were combination high school graduation and birthday gifts from her parents. Both events had occurred in early June. Jeananne would never forget her father's comments on the morning of that 18th birthday. "You're an adult now. You can have your breakfast here but you are on your own for dinner." He had said it seriously. She had been so dumbfounded that she was unable to reply.

He had responded to her blank look with "I'm only kidding. That's what my daddy said to me and he meant it. But with girls, things are different. Besides, you'll be leaving soon enough."

Jeananne thought she would never be able to shake off the feeling that her father was pleased to see her go.

Returning to the letter, Jeananne read *Yours truly, Martha Wilkins.* She realized she had been calling her Martha but maybe that wasn't appropriate. What would she call her new boss? Martha, Miss Martha, Aunt Martha, Mrs. Wilkins were all possibilities. She would ask Aunt Faye.

Chapter 5

After drinking a Nehi orange at the first stop and a Nehi Grape soda when the bus stopped in Texas, Jeananne's fifty-dollar fortune had dwindled to forty-nine dollars and fifty cents. The sack of food she carefully prepared in the small kitchen of the trailer was now empty.

The bus trip to Houston took fourteen hours, eleven hours of travelling and three hours in transfers at Little Rock and Texarkana. With the United States in full war mode, the more direct bus route from Fort Smith to Texarkana was cancelled to save gasoline and rubber tires. All bus transport went through, started, or ended in the state's capitol city. From Texarkana to Houston there existed only one direct route and the bus took it.

En route no big hairy man brought evil to Jeananne and no one tried to steal her purse. She was not, however, without a little excitement. Her on-bus adventures included a whiskey drummer who wanted her to taste his wares (she declined), an old woman who passed round pictures of her son who had enlisted and was fighting in Europe. She got the entire bus to pray for him.

At Texarkana a tired mother of three exited the bus leaving her baby in Jeananne's arms. Jeananne had to yell to the bus driver to let her off. She chased the mother into the terminal thrusting the baby into its mother's arms then dashed quickly back to the bus to resume her journey.

During most of her travels, Jeananne sat by a window. As the bus travelled further from her home, she missed the forests of the northwest part of Arkansas.

When she arrived in the middle part of the state, she was shocked to see how big Little Rock was. The bus passed the state capitol building as it made its way to the depot in the center of town. Its magnificent dome took her breath away. She had seen plenty of rivers in northwest Arkansas, but never the wide Arkansas River that skirted the big city. To that moment Fayetteville was the largest city she had seen and she was sure that Little Rock was much larger, had more houses, more tall buildings and more people.

She was disappointed that she had been unaware of leaving Arkansas and entering Texas. She had expected some indication that she had moved from one state to another. It seemed that the bus entered Texarkana, Arkansas, then without any fanfare pulled into the depot in Texarkana, Texas.

Once in Texas, Jeananne looked for cattle and oil wells but didn't see any until the bus stopped to let a family off in Conroe. Close to the road was a herd of cattle bigger than any herd Jeananne had seen before. She started counting but the bus resumed its journey before she could get to one hundred.

The Houston bus station was on the north side of town. It was bustling with soldiers, sailors and airmen, all handsome in their uniforms, some with the look of intent on their faces, others jovial in denial of their mission. While the driver removed stowed suitcases, cardboard boxes and sacks stuffed with belongings for passengers to identify and retrieve, Jeananne gawped at the men who walked hurriedly and purposefully past her. The driver nudged her saying the obvious, that they had arrived in Houston, she should pick up her suitcase and move on.

"Which way?" Jeananne planted her feet solidly and twisted her head from one side to the other looking for a sign of direction.

Taking pity on her, the driver, who had a daughter of his own about Jeananne's age, pointed toward the waiting room inside the corrugated building that expanded Houston's pre-war smaller terminal.

Jeananne walked slowly inside carrying her train case and suitcase. A tall, thin man in blue jeans and a cowboy shirt and hat approached her and asked if her name was Jeananne Cameron.

The tall man, his complexion dark, said, "Miss Miriam and Miss Martha sent me to pick you up." He reached for Jeananne's cases. She held back her train case but allowed the man to take her larger suitcase.

"My name is Eduardo. Everyone calls me Edo. You can call me Edo. You've never been to Houston." This last comment he made as a statement, not a question.

"Suddenly eager to talk, Jeananne gushed, "I've never been anywhere. I can't believe I'm here. Houston is big. I read that Texas is big, the biggest state in the Union. Everything here is supposed to be big. Are you from here? Have you always lived here? How far is it to Miss Martha's home? What's it like? Do you live there?"

"Slow down, Miss," Edo laughed. "Follow me, we'll be on our way." He led her to a car parked nearby, a long dark car with whitewall tires. He opened the front passenger door and indicated she should get it.

"Ride up front with me, Missy," he told her. She obeyed.

The area around the bus station was busy with people walking and standing around in groups and a few soldiers hitching rides. Here and there was a single-story building but in between were large empty stretches of overgrown weeds. They passed a hardware store recognizable from the goods in the window. They passed another store that advertised its wares with a wooden bull on the sidewalk.

"We have cattle in Arkansas, real cattle," she informed Edo, forgetting the cattle she had seen earlier in the day. Looking out her car window and seeing only flat land, she added, "…and mountains."

"No mountains here. Where I come from, there are mountains. In Mexico, but not in Houston. It's pretty flat here and you'll see cattle. This town, though, is big on oil. It's growing now and pretty soon will be as big as…," he puzzled over how to end the sentence. "Everything is big in Texas."

"Yes, I heard that before." Jeananne was getting the message that people in Texas liked to talk about everything being big.

She craned her neck looking out the car window as their route took them through downtown. She saw proof of Edo's claim about Houston growing. Twice Edo had to take detours because dump trucks were stalled in the roadway.

"There are a few new stores down here that the ladies like." Edo pointed to a store larger than any Jeananne had ever seen.

"Does Miss Martha shop here? It certainly is fancy. Tell me about her, please. I don't know much about her except I will be living with her."

"Yep. Miss Martha and Miss Miriam are sisters. They live in big houses not too far from each other. The one you're going to live with is a widow. Her husband Wendell (everyone called him Win) died not too long ago. My sister Marva does for her, cooking and cleaning. Miss Miriam's husband is still living. I work for him, Mr. Sam. Some days he has me help out the ladies, like today, picking you up at the bus station."

"How did you get here? You said you came from Mexico." Jeananne was puzzled about how a person from another country would be in her country. She knew Okies were from Oklahoma. She had even crossed the state line into Oklahoma to go to a rodeo. It was no trouble to go from one state to another, but she couldn't imagine how a person could go from one country to another.

"Mr. Sam owns a ranch in Mexico, in my home, Monterrey. I've been living on that ranch most of my life except one day when he was down there, he said he wanted me to come with him to Houston. We have a regular habit now, Houston most of the winter, and Monterrey in November before Christmas and sometimes for Christmas. Miss Martha never goes to the ranch so I don't know if you'll be going down there."

Jeananne could not imagine going to Mexico. "You said you have a sister."

"Yep. You'll meet her. She's a lot younger than me."

"How far are we from the house? Are we almost there yet?"

"Not too far now."

They had turned onto a narrow hard top road with fields on both side and not a house in sight.

"No houses out here," Jeananne shook her head and held her train case tightly in her lap.

"Don't be scared. Out here there is a lot of land and big houses."

"I'm not scared."

"That's one of the houses." Edo pointed toward a thicket of tall bushes and trees.

"I don't see it."

"It's back there. Your home is coming up."

Edo turned onto a gravel road running along an open fence. Suddenly the house appeared. It stood out in the landscape, gray in color against the green lawn. The front porch was the size of Jeananne's trailer home. On either side of the tall pillared front doors were tall dark windows. The pillars were so big around that Jeananne wondered how many people with outstretched arms would be needed to surround just one column.

"What do you think?" Edo asked.

Jeananne's eyes grew wide and she started to cry.

Chapter 6

A woman of indeterminate age wearing wide-legged cuffed blue jeans and a sleeveless silk fitted blouse emerged from the house. Jeananne thought she was attractive, in an older woman sort of way, not like the vavavoom movie stars that her father said were sinful, more like Olivia de Havilland in *Gone with the Wind.* She looked delicate, even wearing denim.

Jeananne had not seen many movies. She and her mother had gone into Fayetteville to see the Civil War epic that everyone was talking about. When her father found out that they had gone, disobeying his general admonishment about the "pictures," he was angry. A few months later he took them to see *Sergeant York.*

"A movie about a war hero from Kentucky is worth seeing for the history," he told them. "He could shoot a rattlesnake at forty yards."

When Miss Martha spoke, Jeananne's fantasy about her similarity to Melanie disappeared. The voice had a twang and a firm decisiveness and a hint of happiness. It was a soft voice but not as soft as Melanie's. Jeananne was drawn to her. Jeananne could fall asleep listening to Melanie but Miss Martha's voice had an authority that would keep a person on her toes.

"You are, of course, Jeananne Cameron. I'm so glad to meet you. I am Martha Wilkins, but then you know that." She smiled broadly. "Welcome to my Italianate Tara. The designer didn't know if he was Southern or Italian."

Jeananne didn't have a clue what that meant. She didn't see any resemblance to Tara, no majestic columns, no oak trees lining the road. The house wasn't even painted white. It was gray and the outside walls were just plain and straight up and down with windows so big she could walk through them.

She ignored Mrs. Wilkins's comment. Instead, she walked toward her hostess/employer with her head down and halting about three feet in front of her, Jeananne presented herself.

"Yes ma'am," was all she could eke out.

"Come on in. We are going to be great friends. Edo will put your suitcase inside the door. We'll see to it later. Do you have enough energy after that long bus ride to sit down and have iced tea or do you need a sandwich, or both?"

Jeananne couldn't think of anything to say. From the entry hall she looked down a long corridor with rooms to either side. To her left was the room with the large windows she had seen from outside. The room was mostly blue. The floors were shiny and looked cool. She had never been in a room so elegant and sumptuous.

"We don't go in there often," said Miss Martha. "I can imagine seeing a place like this is confusing. Follow me. We'll go to the back of the house. The kitchen's back there. Marva will rustle up a sandwich for you."

"I need to wash my hands."

"Of course you do." Miss Martha opened a door and indicated that Jeananne should enter. "Why don't you splash some water on your face and when you come out, we'll show you the way to the kitchen."

Jeananne was grateful for the chance to refresh herself and grateful for a bathroom that smelled like perfume. She looked at herself in the mirror and was shocked to see how tired she looked. When she emerged, a small Mexican girl in a uniform was waiting for her.

"I'm Marva. You met my brother Edo. Miss Martha says you are to join her in the kitchen. She doesn't usually eat in the kitchen. I think she wants to be with you. She has been looking forward to your arrival."

"I'm not sure what I am going to be doing here."

"Miss Martha always has her reasons for her decisions."

Jeananne followed Marva into the kitchen. She joined Ms. Martha at a round table positioned in front of a bay window.

"How was your trip? My sister Faye says you were brave about leaving Fayetteville. You know you are here because of Faye. She says wonderful things about you. I know we are going to get along. I want you to be happy in Houston. I never had any children and now I am alone. You will be great company for me and you will love Houston. People are friendly in Texas. Of course, they are probably friendly in Arkansas, too."

Jeananne beamed. "I love Aunt Faye. She is a special person. It was nice of her to say good things about me. What will I be doing here? You said I would have a job typing."

"We have plenty of time to talk about work. You don't have to worry about work. Finish your sandwich and I will show you to your room. I hope you like it. We're just girls here now." She nodded to Marva.

Marva smiled.

"Why don't you show Jeananne her room and help her settle in." Martha's firm voice was an instruction, not a question. "Take some iced tea with you."

Jeananne rose, then sat again. "Are you coming with us?"

"No. I am very happy right now sitting by this window. I am very happy that you are finally here with me."

"This house is big. There are a lot of rooms." Jeananne followed Marva down a corridor lined with paintings.

"Yes, ma'am. I've lived here for two years. At first, I was scared but now I like it here, especially since I only have to keep up with Miss Martha. No one goes up to the second floor anymore so Miss Martha closed it off. It was more work when her husband was alive."

Jeananne noticed that Marva had called her ma'am. She had never been called ma'am before and found it confusing. She was taught that ma'am was a title of respect used to address or respond to an older woman. She doubted she was older than Marva.

Jeananne wanted to know Marva's age but was too shy to ask a personal question. Instead, she asked, "Do you live here?"

"Yes. I do the cooking and the everyday housekeeping. I mean I will be doing all the cooking and housekeeping. My mama taught me everything. She's leaving tonight to go back to Mexico. You come and she goes. Like I said, most of the rooms are closed off. You'll like your room, I think." She opened the door for Jeananne. "She could have given you a suite upstairs but she said it would be better if you were on the ground floor so you wouldn't have to go up and down stairs all the time." Marva entered an alcove off the hallway and opened the door. She stood back to let Jeananne go first into the room.

"This is mine? It's beautiful." Jeananne tried to take in every detail while her heart pounded in excitement.

"Miss Martha thought you would like yellow. She said it is cheerful."

"Like it? I love it." Jeananne sat on the double bed, ran her hand over the smooth golden bedspread. "I love it," she repeated.

Martha opened another door. "You have your own bathroom too, and here are your closets. She pointed to two sets of louvered doors on the opposite side of the room. "Do you want help putting your clothes away?"

"No, I'll do it. Did you say this is my room?" Jeananne found it difficult to focus her eyes on any single part of the room. One moment she was drawn to the windows with the long gold drapes that matched the bedspread. Another moment she realized the chest had five drawers, more room than she would need. The base of the lamp by the bed was a figure of a woman in a ball gown.

"Miss Martha must be rich, very rich."

"She isn't poor," said Marva. "I'll bring you a tray later with a snack in case you get hungry in the night."

Unpacking took Jeananne about fifteen minutes. She filled two drawers of the chest with her folded clothes and had two dresses to hang in one of the closets. She emptied her train case, placing her toothbrush by the bathroom sink and her hair brush and comb in the drawer of the vanity. She opened the linen closet inside the bathroom and saw that she had several towels neatly folded, large ones separated from medium ones and wash cloths all alone occupying a single shelf. Grabbing one of the larger towels, she undressed, turned on the tub tap and filled the tub with warm water. She soaked and scrubbed all the travel dust from her body, dried with the thick yellow terry towel that was large enough to wrap one and a half times around her body, slipped on a T-shirt and crawled under the soft yellow sheets. She saw the tray that Marva had promised but she wasn't hungry.

She was so tired that she forgot her prayers.

She was awakened the next morning by Marva who suggested she dress and join Miss Martha for breakfast.

"I am living a dream," Jeananne told herself. She opened "The Upper Room" devotions on the bedside table and read the day's Bible verse and homily.

"Trust in the Lord with all thine heart, and lean not unto thine own understanding. In all thy ways acknowledge him, and he will make straight thy paths." Proverbs 3:5–6

Chapter 7

Marva studied her mother's face. Her complexion was smooth, light brown like Marva's. She had large eyes, almost black and hair that waved over her forehead but in the back was pulled off her neck and tucked up into a snood. The dinner dishes were washed, dried and put away into the various cabinets in the kitchen. Marva's mother was wiping down the counter surface.

"You're looking at me. We aren't finished. Did you get the tray from Miss Jeananne's room? You must pay attention to details."

"Oops. I'll get it now."

"Go quickly and don't disturb Miss Martha."

"I think Miss Martha is asleep." Marva said.

"Hurry. No one will want you in the house if you are too slow or too loud or if your work is sloppy." Marva's mother, Juanita, scowled, turned her head away.

When Marva returned with the tray, she emptied the leftovers into the trashcan, and rinsed the plates, glass, and utensils in the sink.

"Done," she announced and joined her mother at the table where her mother was drinking a cup of coffee and lighting a cigarette.

"I want to talk to you before I go home. Edo will be here shortly to pick me up. You are going to be here on your own and I want to be sure you are ready. What do you think of the new girl?"

"Miss Jeananne? She's beautiful."

"So are you. Before I go, I want to make sure you remember everything I taught you. And I want you to know you are a beautiful young lady and I am proud of you."

"Oh, Mama, you always say that. But Miss Jeananne is really beautiful. She has red hair and amazing eyes, not brown like mine."

"Listen to me, Marva. This is important. You're going to have two people to take care of. Tomorrow would have been my day off so you would have been on your own anyway. You won't even miss me. When I was your age, I already was married and had Edo on my hip."

"Mama, I can do everything. You said yourself that I am a good maid. I'm as good as Rosa. She may be older than I am, but I can do as much as she can."

"At least you don't have any children to look after. Rosa and her mother will be over at Miss Miriam's house if you have any questions, they will help you. If the work is too heavy for you, just tell Miss Miriam. She'll listen. Or tell Carmen and she will help you."

"Do you have to go back to Monterrey? Absolutely have to go back?" Marva stuck out her lower lip in a pout.

"Yes, I have to go back. You know why. We've been over that."

"Grandma needs you in Monterrey." Marva said the words in a matter-of-fact way, sadness in her eyes. "You don't think Grandma will die, do you?"

"Mio dio. We don't know these things. We don't know the future. But it is our way. La familia primero (family first). Edo will always be with Sam Wilkins and you can count on Rosa and her mother to help you."

"Do you really think I am ready to take care of Miss Martha by myself?" Marva dropped her head and closed her eyes as she inhaled deeply.

"Hold your head up, Marva. Always hold your head up. Remember all that I've taught you." She stubbed her cigarette out and took the last sip of her coffee. "I hear the car. That will be Edo. Let him come in."

Marva opened the back door and stepped aside to let her older brother enter.

"No kiss for your big brother?" He leaned down and Marva kissed him on the cheek. "How'd it go with the new miss?"

"You picked her up at the bus station, Edo. What did you think of her?" Juanita asked.

"Pretty little thing. Doesn't know anything. I don't think she had ever seen a big city. Wouldn't know Mexico from Texas," Edo said.

"A lot of people can't tell the difference," Juanita said.

"She'll have to learn how to live with rich people. I don't think she has ever had any money. Comes from a trailer park in Arkansas."

"How old do you think she is?" Marva asked.

"Couple years older than you. Eighteen is what I hear," Edo replied.

"Miss Martha will take care of her." Juanita lit another cigarette and handed it to Edo who dragged on it and gave it back to his mother. "She'll take care of you, Marva, as long as you do the work."

"Isn't that new girl supposed to take care of Miss Martha?" asked Marva.

"Who knows?" said Juanita. "I don't know why Miss Martha is taking her in. She's not an orphan and she isn't any relation. But, Marva, she isn't a maid."

"Sam says Martha is lonely and wants a companion," Edo said.

"Rich people do whatever they want to do. Marva, don't ask any questions, just do what Miss Martha says. That's my best advice to you."

"Don't worry, Mother, Miss Martha and Miss Miriam tell each other everything and Sam tells me what they say. I'll keep my ears open. If there is any problem, I'll be able to take care of it."

"Edo, I always count on you. You can get word to me in Monterey if there's any problem."

"Mother, you don't need to tell me what I already know. There is always someone from Houston going down or coming back. What kind of problem would you be able to solve? You'll be in Monterrey. You ready to go?"

"Don't be like that, Edo. Have respect for your mother. Let me think I could help out if something went wrong."

"Like if what went wrong, Mother, and how would you help?" Edo persisted.

"Edo, don't talk to your mother that way. You know I am always your Mama and you will always be my son. You think you're the big man now and maybe you are."

"That's right, Mama. I'm the man of the family. I won't let anyone disrespect me or Marva. Are you ready to go?"

"Just let me say good-bye to Marva. Don't cry, Marva."

"Mama, how can I let you go? I'll be so lonesome without you."

"I'll be lonesome without you."

"You'll have Grandma to talk to. Who will I talk to?"

"Rosa and Carmen. Edo will help you meet some nice young people, won't you, Edo? You'll meet some nice Mexican boy. Stay away from the gringos. Don't give me any grandchildren any time soon. You need to grow up first. Pray to Our Lady like I taught you. Get my suitcase, Edo, and these bags. I've prepared some food for the trip so we don't have to stop too often."

Edo obeyed his mother and hearing his sister's sobs, he also began to cry. He opened the back door and stepped outside. "Come on, Mother."

Marva clung to her mother and the two women sobbed together.

"When will I see you again, Mother?"

"Marva, just be a good girl and remember all that I taught you."

Chapter 8

The alarm sounded, awakening Marva to her first day as the only maid in Martha Wilkins's household. The room seemed bare because her mother had packed all her belongings and had left the night before with Edo. It was the first time Marva had a room to herself and she wasn't sure how she felt about the emptiness.

Her mother had left toiletries in the bathroom, a bar of Camay soap, a jar of face cream, a hairbrush. Marva lifted the brush and ran it through her hair. She looked at herself in the mirror and was surprised that she looked the same today as she had looked yesterday. After all, life was now different. She was the sole person in charge of the kitchen, in charge of the house.

Marva showered and dressed in her maid's uniform. She made up her bed by rearranging the blanket and she tucked her cotton nightgown under her pillow. She glanced over at the twin bed that had been her mother's. She smoothed the spread on that bed and noted the time on the bedside clock. It was half-past six. She had been awake for half an hour and she had begun her routine.

Closing the door to her room, Marva entered the servant's hallway. Turning right, she walked a few steps and entered the laundry room. The linen that had washed during the night now needed drying. She removed each item carefully and hung the sheets and pillow cases on the indoor line, filling the room. She turned on the space heater and placed it on the far side of the room.

Marva next went into the kitchen and began organizing for breakfast. Miss Martha had not instructed her about where she would have her breakfast. Sometimes Marva served breakfast to Miss Martha in bed, at other times Miss Martha ate in the informal dining room or on the patio. Usually, Marva received her instructions the night before but last night she had received none.

She didn't know if the new Jeananne would eat with Miss Martha or by herself. Because both women would need breakfast, Marva removed two trays from the cupboard and placed them on the counter. She would be prepared to serve the meals wherever she was told.

She made a pot of coffee and poured a mug for herself which she drank as she took the eggs and bacon from the refrigerator. As she was starting to measure the grits, Miss Martha appeared in the kitchen in her dressing gown. She did not yet have her make-up on.

"It occurs to me that I forgot to tell you last night that Jeananne will eat with me. Have you looked outside yet this morning? What is the weather like?"

"I don't know, ma'am. I haven't been outside."

"Did you get the newspaper from the front porch?"

"No, ma'am, not yet. Do you want me to bring it to your room?"

"No, just put it in the den."

Martha opened the back door and stepped out onto the patio.

"It looks nice enough. I think we'll have breakfast outside. Move the table under the tree."

"Should I prepare eggs and bacon for Miss Jeananne?"

"Yes, and grits but no biscuits. We have to watch our figures. Eight o´clock as usual. You don't need to wake her up. I'll do it."

Twirling around, Martha left the kitchen. Marva checked the clock on the stove. It was 7:15. She poured a small glass of orange juice for herself and fried an egg which she covered with chopped tomato and Tabasco sauce. She ate standing up, put water in a pan and placed it on the stove. She then ran outside to clean off and move the patio table under the tree.

Once again in the kitchen, she stirred the grits in boiling water. Twenty minutes for the grits to cook. She would need to stir the pot every few minutes.

She quickly made another trip outside to set the table.

At five minutes after eight o'clock, Martha peeked into the kitchen and told Marva that she and Jeananne were headed outside and to serve their breakfast as soon as possible.

While Martha and Jeananne were eating, Marva stripped the sheets from Martha's bed and remade the bed with fresh linen. She entered Jeananne's room and made up her bed and straightened the towels and gently wiped off the surfaces. Her bed linen was fresh and didn't need changing.

After placing the dirty linen in the laundry room, she took the pot of coffee outside to refill the cups and she cleared the table for the two women who were involved in conversation. Mosquitoes were swarming so she found a citronella candle near the kitchen door and lit it near the table where the ladies were sitting.

Back in the house, Marva returned to Martha's suite, and cleaned the bathroom. She picked up dirty clothing from the floor and put out fresh towels. She took a cloth from her pocket and ran it lightly across the tops of the dresser, chest of drawers and bedside tables. Today being Monday was a laundry day. She would do the dusting and vacuuming on Tuesdays and Fridays. Always keep to your schedule, her mother had instructed.

Satisfied that both bedrooms and bathrooms were clean and fresh, Marva entered the laundry room and placed the sheets in a tub with bleach. She stirred the sheets with a wooden stick that had once been a broom handle and left the sheets to soak.

The air in the laundry room was damp and with the heater on, she began sweating. She turned the heater off and decided to take the hanging laundry outside to dry as soon as the ladies finished breakfast. She went to a storage cupboard in the room and retrieved dust cloths and furniture polish placing them in a basket that she carried with her right hand. In her left hand, she held a carpet sweeper. Dusting and vacuuming were usually a Tuesday activity but she thought she should be prepared for light touch-ups.

Marva walked down the servant's hallway, passing the door to the kitchen and the door to her room. She emerged in the informal dining room and from there was in what her mother had called the private part of the house. Her eyes swept the room and realizing that it hadn't been used in the past twenty-four hours, she kept walking to the room that was called the den, or sometimes Martha's study. This was the room most used in the house now that Mr. Wilkins was gone.

Marva removed the cleaning items from her basket and replaced them with dirty dishes and glassware and a full ashtray. The room was strewn with papers that Marva knew not to disturb. She managed to square the stacks without messing up their order. She went over the carpet with her sweeper and plumped the pillows on the sofa and overstuffed chairs. After dusting the furniture, she used a dry cloth to clean the screen on the new television set.

Remembering the newspaper, she ran through the hallway to the front door, opened it and saw the newspaper on the broad porch. She picked it up and ran back through the house to the den.

Hearing female chatter in the house, she continued her tasks in the den as Martha and Jeananne went into Mr. Wilkins', now Mrs. Wilkins', office. Next on her list was laundry. She reversed her steps from the den back to the laundry room, where she removed the bleached sheets from the tub and placed them in the washing machine.

Marva went outside and cleared the table of the breakfast dishes. She noted that it was just breezy enough to dry the sheets that she had hung earlier in the laundry room. The outside clothes line was some distance from the house but she liked the smell of the sheets when they were dried outdoors.

She placed the tray with the dirty dishes in the kitchen, retrieved the hanging sheets from the laundry room and pegged them onto the outdoor clothesline.

It was now eleven o'clock and she sat down in the kitchen and drank another glass of orange juice and ate a cookie. She noticed a piece of paper on the kitchen table and read instructions for lunch and dinner. She was to prepare a light fruit salad for a late luncheon and the ladies would have sandwiches (and chips for Jeananne) served on trays in the den at dinner time. Ice cream for dessert would suffice.

Stay on schedule, her mother had told her. Marva could hear her mother's voice and wondered if her mother had yet crossed the border into Mexico.

It was almost noon and Marva had more work to do.

Chapter 9

While Marva was cooking, serving, and cleaning, Jeananne and Miss Martha were spending their morning getting to know each other.

"Miss Martha, I am confused. I didn't expect such a beautiful room. I can't pay for all this." Jeananne gestured broadly with both arms. "It is beautiful and more than I imagined."

Martha Wilkins laughed. The two were sitting outside under a live oak tree. Even in summer the tree was filled with life. It spread its fullness over the near backyard. Farther out was a garden and farther still fruit trees.

"You aren't paying for anything. Faye, my sister Miriam, and I were never poor but we weren't rich when we grew up. We were blessed with family love. Money wasn't exactly a problem. Miriam and I met the Wilkins's boys after the first war. Their father and our father did business together. It was natural we would meet. Miriam married Sam and I married Wendell. I was Mrs. Wendell Wilkins and proud of it."

"And Aunt Faye didn't marry and Miriam became Mrs. Sam Wilkins."

"Right. We moved down here to Texas. Faye stayed in Arkansas with Dad. How to put it? The Wilkins brothers found oil. That's the best way to say it. They bought land that just kept pumping out oil. We still pump out oil. It has made us who we are today. We have every blessing. Except we never had children and my Wendell died last year. I am left alone in this big house."

"You have Marva and you have your sister."

"Thank God. Marva is kind and good and very young and Miriam and I are very close, and close to Faye even though we don't get to see her often."

"What about Miriam? Does she live like you?" Jeananne looked at the top of the table, speaking downward, avoiding Martha's eyes.

"Dear, look at me when you speak. No need to look down all the time." Her tone was instructional, clearly authoritative.

44

"Yes, ma'am, I will try. What about Miriam? Aunt Faye said you live near each other." This time Jeananne held her head up.

"She and Sam live a few properties over, just a little further down the road you came in on." Jeananne furrowed her brow wondering how far was a "few properties down the road."

"They have a son who is in the Army. The war is a great personal worry for them. This war is a great worry for all of us. We must all do our part. Our oil is important to the war effort. Have you ever heard of Wilkins Enterprises?"

"No, ma'am."

"No matter. There is no reason you would know it."

A slight breeze rustled the leaves of the huge tree. Jeananne turned her face to feel the cool of it. It passed quickly.

"We can't stay out long. The mosquitoes or the heat will get us. I do want to hear about you. Tell me about your schooling. Faye said you graduated high school. Did you enjoy school? Did you have activities outside school? What about friends? Let's walk inside as we talk."

Before Jeananne could respond, Martha rose and started walking toward the house.

Jeananne began stacking the dirty plates. "We need a tray," she said.

"Leave it. That's Marva's job. Come along with me."

They moved from the yard into the kitchen, past rooms that Martha said were "Marva's domain." They passed through a dark hallway.

"This house is a maze. Are you confused about where you are? We're headed for a room where we do business. It might be cooler."

Martha led the way into a dark, paneled room with leather chairs across from an enormous desk. Martha turned on a metal rotating fan setting atop the desk.

"Feels better, doesn't it?"

"This was Wendell's at-home office. I need to redecorate, make it into a feminine work space." Miss Martha withdrew into her own thoughts, then said, "Forgive me, Jeananne."

"Of course, but for what?"

"I seem to have these moments where I fade into my grief for Wendell. He was a wonderful man, not perfect, mind you, but a wonderful husband."

The two sat quietly. A faint smell of cigar and after-shave could still be detected in the room.

"This was a bad choice. Let's go into the den." Martha turned off the fan.

Off they went once again to settle themselves for conversation.

"You're getting to see a little of the house," Miss Martha laughed. "By the way, Jeananne, please call me Martha, just Martha. Or you can call me Aunt Martha, like Aunt Faye.

"Okay, if that is what you want. You don't want me to call you Mrs. Wilkins?"

"No. People would not know if you meant me or Miriam. Where were we? Your schooling, your life. I think I'll call it your life before Houston."

"I don't know where to start. I did graduate from high school. We didn't have a big ceremony because of the war. Most of the boys were enlisting."

"If you had stayed home, what would you be doing?"

"Working at the munitions plant. That's what my dad said."

"You didn't want to do that kind of work?"

"It wasn't the work of my dreams. The people who do it are heroes though, aren't they? To be honest, I didn't want to live…" her voice trailed off into silence.

"You didn't want to live in the trailer park with your parents?" Martha spoke the statement of fact that Jeananne could not utter.

Jeananne sighed audibly. "Yes. I mean no, I didn't want to live with my parents."

"You agreed to come here even though you couldn't have known what life would be like, what I would be like, what your work would entail. I think you are a brave young woman, brave and smart."

Jeananne automatically rejected the compliment by waving her right hand in front of her face as though pushing the words away. As she breathed out, she lowered her head and examined her shoes. She was wearing saddle shoes and white socks, the standard for all girls in her school. She wondered if they were the right shoes to wear in the house. In Arkansas she usually went barefoot in the trailer except in winter when she wore her socks all the time, sliding around on the slippery cold floors.

Martha gave her a warm smile that she didn't see. "Don't worry about anything, Jeananne. I am not your parent. I gave you a compliment. Just say 'thank you'."

"Yes, ma'am. Thank you."

"I think we should spend the next few days introducing you to Houston. How does that sound? And I would love, love, love to introduce you to shopping."

It was difficult to determine who seemed more excited.

Eyes wide, Jeananne said, "Oh, yes. What will we shop for? Are my shoes wrong for Houston?"

"You and your shoes are just right for Houston. It just so happens that I love to shop."

Martha told Jeananne about the Wilkins Enterprises office located in a high-rise building downtown. She said Jeananne had probably passed the building on her trip home from the bus station. She said the building was six stories high and that the offices of Wilkins Enterprises were on the top floor. She said Jeananne would be able to see the Gulf of Mexico from some of the offices.

It was arranged for Jeananne to meet with the Office Manager in the Administrative Division. Martha had set the date of the meeting for ten days in the future, to give Jeananne time to acclimate to Houston. This was code to Martha (unknown to Jeananne) for "time to buy a suitable wardrobe."

Other facts unknown to Jeananne included the company's registration as a partnership between the two Wilkins brothers. With Wendell's death, Martha occupied her deceased husband's position. What Jeananne may have viewed as a job interview, Martha considered pro forma. Jeananne would be given a tour of the office, would take a typing test. She would be officially hired and placed on the payroll. She would be hired to work four days a week under the job title Assistant Clerk.

Martha's private thoughts were many. She imagined Jeananne becoming a confident young woman who would inhabit her home, add depth to her life and become the person she had always wanted in a daughter.

Jeananne had her own secret thoughts. She dreamed of glamour (without pride) and her own money and freedom and a life of her own.

Part 2
1947

Chapter 10

"Come over here. We're going to have lunch soon."

Miriam and Martha were seated on poolside recliners near the pool deep in conversation. The women wore large straw hats, sunglasses and sarongs over their swimsuits. Neither had been in the water. Sitting side by side, their resemblance was striking. Martha was two years older but both women had porcelain complexions that they hid from the sun and similar round faces. Miriam's hair was dyed blonde and Martha kept hers brown, dulled by strands of gray. Martha was slimmer despite her healthy appetite. The added weight made Miriam appear softer.

The person calling them to lunch was Sam Wilkins. Unlike the ladies, he welcomed the sun and welcomed the opportunity to throw steaks on a grill. On a nearby table Carmen and her daughter Rosa set out Cole slaw, devilled eggs, green bean salad, potato salad and various types of bread. On a separate table were all the accoutrements for an outdoor meal, plates, napkins, pickles and the like a well as large bottles of steak sauce, Tabasco, and ketchup. Edo set out a round tin tub filled with ice in which cola, Dr. Pepper, and beer were cooling.

"I'm hungry. Make mine rare." Geoff Wilkins called out to his father from the pool as he splashed a cascade of water on a squealing beautiful redhead whose body was bouncing up and down.

"Take that," she answered with retaliatory offence of her own, sliding the palm of her hand across the surface of the pool to deliver a targeted spray to her assailant.

"Leave him alone," said the brunette sitting on the side of the pool, her legs dangling in the water. "I need some lotion on my back, Geoff." Her voice was sultry, heavily accented revealing her French roots.

Geoff made a face at the woman with red hair, the universal ugh of a bored husband. Embarrassed by this intimacy, she said, "I'm getting out now. Sam's calling us."

Quietly to Geoff, she said, "Your wife needs you."

"Always," he replied.

Saturdays in July and August were pool and family days at the Wilkins's house. Citronella candles were strewn around the perimeter of the patio far enough away from people to avoid adding to the hot weather, yet close enough to ward off blood-thirsty mosquitoes. The gardener had sprayed the lawn beyond with chemicals guaranteed to kill insects and discourage other marauders who might threaten family tranquility. Marauders of the human type were the bailiwick of Edo whose job included the detection and disposition of any unwanted intruders.

These family Saturdays followed a general pattern.

Miriam woke up, usually alone, completed her morning toilette, donned a summery dressing gown and ate half a slice of grapefruit and buttered toast at the formal dining room table, served by Carmen. At ten a.m. her sister Martha arrived and joined her for coffee. Sometimes the ladies indulged in sweet rolls baked and served hot by Rosa.

Sam made an appearance around eleven a.m., greeting the ladies with a subdued smile daring them to enquire about how or where he had slept the night before. He directed his attention to unfolding and gingerly opening the daily newspaper and placing it so that he could both read and shield himself from the eyes of his wife and sister-in-law. Rosa brought in his coffee, black and strong, in a utilitarian mug. She asked if he wanted his regular breakfast to which he replied yes. His order never deviated. He always wanted a fried egg, grits in red-eye-gravy, sage sausage, and two slices of toasted white bread smothered in butter and slathered with homemade plum jam.

Miriam and Martha removed themselves from the table to continue their conversation in Miriam's sitting room, adjacent to her bedroom. At noon, after two hours of deep discussion, sharing of thoughts, feelings and news, the two ladies changed into swimsuits or sun suits covered with lightweight terry robes, caftans or sarongs, depending on whim and mood.

Through the glass doors in the sitting room, they walked directly out onto the patio and claimed their cushioned recliner chairs. Sam had already begun poking around the grill, measuring out charcoal, giving orders to Edo, Carmen and Rosa who were hustling in and out of the house in search of Mr. Wilkins's cigarettes or lighter or to prepare a special steak rub or to find another towel to enable him to wipe sweat from his brow.

The arrival of Jeananne and of Geoff and his French wife occurred between 12:30 and 1 p.m. Jeananne had farther to travel, approximately 2.2 miles from her home with Martha while Geoff and Lulu merely had to walk from the guest cottage at the back of the property.

Sam dominated the day in his role of chef and senior man of the house. His cigar smoke permeated the outdoor space creating a screen around his immediate territory, assuring that all those who dwelled therein knew who was in charge.

The gatherings ended around four o'clock when the three older members were ready for naps leaving the three younger members to go their own ways.

During today's Saturday luncheon, Geoff sat close to his father, the two speaking quietly about matters unknown to the women. Jeananne sat near Martha and Miriam. Lulu sat alone half-way between the women and the men.

Jeananne was no longer the unsophisticated teen-ager from northwest Arkansas, Martha's protégé. She was a worldly young woman of twenty-three years. She had honed her secretarial skills in the main office of Wilkins Enterprises. She had travelled to Europe with Martha and had a wardrobe that was the envy of every woman she encountered.

Martha was also a changed person. Always practical, she would say she had simply grown older. In private she complained that she had become harder, less trusting since she had taken on increased responsibilities in the company co-founded by her husband. She had to learn to become the business equal of Sam Wilkins and that was no small feat, she admitted to her sisters.

Often the only woman in a man's milieu, she had various tricks to help smooth the differences in their points of view and tactics. She occasionally read the sports page of the newspaper to provide material for casual moments. She copiously read business magazines and everyday checked the movement of the stock market.

Most of all, she had learned to observe and listen and today, poolside, she noticed the tete-a-tete between Geoff and Sam.

Jeananne, less wary of men's private conversations, was more interested in Lulu.

"That lipstick she wears is *Cherries in the Snow,* by Revlon," Jeananne contributed. "I think it makes a bold statement with her dark hair."

"Bold, huh?" Martha made a volcanic noise in the back of her throat.

"Ignoring the unladylike sound, Jeananne said, "Crimson lips are all the rage in *Vogue.* "

"She is French, bless her heart," said Miriam, emphasizing "is" as though that explained her choice of lipstick.

Miriam raised her left eyebrow.

"How do you do that, Aunt Miriam? How do you raise one eyebrow? I've tried but can't do it."

"It's a matter of finding the muscle. Look in the mirror and practice."

"Were you born able to do it?"

"She was," interjected Martha.

"What do you think they're talking about?" Jeananne tilted her head toward Sam and Geoff.

Miriam responded, "Some scheme, no doubt. Sam wouldn't have lived if Geoff had not come back from the war. Look at them. They look like conspiring devils. Sam thinks the sun rises and sets on Geoff. He's our son and we have spoiled him rotten."

In low tones, Martha spoke to Jeananne while Miriam sipped her iced tonic. "We don't know what they are talking about. Keep your ears open. Something's up."

Not wanting to be left out, Miriam said, "Last week they were talking about the Texas City explosion. Sam said Houston was lucky but then the Houston port doesn't allow ships to load up with fertilizers. I can't understand why they have different rules in Texas City. Sam said it is all about business but I said you have to think of the risk to people's lives."

"Those poor people and those poor families," said Jeananne. "First Galveston gets a hurricane, and then Texas City gets an explosion. Is God trying to tell us something?"

Not wanting to express an opinion involving theology, Miriam rose and announced, "I'm going inside, ladies." She directed her comments to Martha and Jeananne, ignoring Lulu who made it a point to look away from the women. "I've had enough sun." She picked up her unused beach towel, draped it over her shoulder and blew kisses at her close companions. "Come in when you're ready."

In Miriam's absence, Martha leaned forward and in a low voice said to Jeananne, "Look at them, still deep in plotting and maneuvering. Geoff's doing a lot of talking. You asked me earlier what they are talking about. What do you think they are talking about?"

"I have no clue," responded Jeananne.

"Geoff is probably asking Sam for more money."

"Doesn't Geoff have enough money of his own?" asked Jeananne, now more engaged. If she thought about Geoff, she would have assumed he had barrels of money.

"Sam controls every penny. As long as he is alive, he'll dole out money very carefully to Geoff."

Their low tones were overwhelmed by a high-pitched plaintive voice.

"Geoff, I want to go," Lulu's heavily accented voice made her wishes known to all present.

"In a minute," he replied.

"Now," she insisted, her lower lip slowly inching forward.

Geoff looked across the pool at his aunt, and shook his head. Martha shrugged her shoulders in a gesture meaning, "There's no accounting for some people's behavior."

"I'm on my way," Geoff told her, irritation in his voice.

Lulu sat, expecting Geoff to be a gentleman, to help her from her seat. She was disappointed. He stood behind her, spoke over her head to Jeananne. "About tonight. There will be six of us. My old Army buddy Harold and his latest honey from the office, he said her name is Liz, are meeting us in Galveston. Harold's brother is in town. He's a nice guy. I'm sure you'll have a good time. Lulu and I will pick you up at 7 p.m."

Lulu stood slowly, ignoring Geoff, and walked to the other side of the pool. Her dissatisfaction trailing her, Lulu spoke in the general direction of the heavens, "Do we have to go so early?"

"Seven o'clock," Geoff said as he ran to catch up with Lulu.

"He is like a puppy dog on a leash," Martha said to Jeananne, "and she knows how to pull the chain."

Chapter 11

Marva walked out onto the patio pulling the screen door shut behind her but leaving the back door ajar. Although it was only mid-morning, the temperature was already hot and Marva wished she had chosen a loose dress instead of the new tight pedal-pushers that she hoped would impress Rosa's cousin. Poor Rosa and her mother had to work today as they did most Saturdays and Sundays during the summer but Marva was pleased that she had the day off. Let Rosa take care of Miss Martha.

Marva admonished herself for being catty. She didn't want to think bad thoughts about Rosa because she didn't want to jinx her date with Rosa's cousin from Monterrey. His name was Ricky and Rosa said he was good-looking and earned good money as a car mechanic.

Ricky was supposed to arrive a little after ten o'clock. He was late and Marva didn't want to seem eager so she went back into the house and poured herself a glass of water and thought about changing clothes.

At ten-thirty Ricky parked his car at the side of Miss Martha's house and knocked on the kitchen door and called out Marva's name.

"Are you there? Marva?" His voice was soft but Marva heard him.

"You're late," she said, and took a moment to look at him. He was neatly dressed in chino slacks and a plaid shirt. His hair was dark and his eyes were light brown. She saw it all in one glaring look. She decided in an instant that he would do. She would not be ashamed to take him home to Monterrey to meet her mother.

"I'm sorry but Edo asked me to run an errand for him and I..." he apologized.

"You saw Edo this morning? You know Edo?"

"Yes, I had to pick up some chipped ice for the pool party. When I'm in town I work for Edo." Marva noticed that as Ricky spoke, his voice got quieter and quieter. By the time he finished speaking, Marva could barely hear his words.

She decided it was better not to ask for more details, especially where Edo was concerned. Men have secrets, she told herself, and it is better not to know what they are involved in. She was surprised to learn that Ricky was working with Edo and no one had introduced them before.

"So, Edo is working this morning? Silly question, isn't it? He is always working. He gets along very well with Sam Wilkins. Do you know the Wilkins?"

"You don't understand. I work for Sam Wilkins, just like Edo."

"Why haven't we met before?"

"I spend a lot of time down in Mexico, working for Sam."

"Where in Mexico?"

"Monterrey. Where Sam and Miriam have a ranch. Where your mother is. I don't want to be impatient, but it's your day off. You don't want to stay here in the kitchen listening to me talk about work, do you? I would like to take you some place."

"That's nice. Where did you want to go? It's your car."

"Let's take a drive. Edo told me about a good place for empanadas."

"Rosa didn't tell me you worked for Sam Wilkins," Marva said once they were inside Ricky's car and driving away from Wilkins's property. Ricky ignored the comment and concentrated on his driving.

As they drove through the wealthy neighborhood, Ricky said, "These are big houses, aren't they? Not like the house where I came from and from what Edo said, not like the house where you are from. I lived in Monterrey for a while when I was a boy. Then we lived in a small town where my father's family lived. Now I am back in Monterrey."

"No, now you are in Houston," Marva corrected him. "Do you know that my mother and her mother are living in Monterrey? Does your family know my family? I can't quite figure out who you are."

"I know who your mother is and I obviously know Edo."

"Edo said you're Rosa's cousin. Why haven't we met before?"

"I don't know, but we can make up for lost time," Ricky smiled at Marva and she giggled.

"What kind of work do you do for Sam Wilkins?"

"I work on cars and motors, that sort of thing, boring for you, I guess."

"Do you work on the ranch? I don't usually go to the ranch. Well, you probably know that since you know so much more than I do."

Rick grinned and kept his eyes on the road.

Marva continued, "You're awfully quiet. Not like Rosa who likes to talk. I don't know anything about cars and motors, but you probably don't know anything about wine glasses and table linen."

"You got me there. I don't even drink wine and table linen is not something I know anything about."

"If you're going to have a fine house, you need to know about table linen."

"How do you know I want to live in one of those big houses?"

"Because you look like a boy, I mean, a man, who belongs in a big house."

"And I think you are a flirt. Your brother told me to be careful with you. No one crosses Edo." Ricky winked at Marva. "Let's see. How old are you? I heard you were sixteen."

"Almost seventeen and old enough to work by myself for Martha Wilkins. What do you mean, that you're supposed to be careful with me?"

"Edo just acts like your big brother, that's all."

Conversation between Marva and Ricky continued along the same lines: friendly, flirtatious, each contributing a little personal information. After their drive around town and through the Mexican barrio in southwest Houston, they enjoyed empanadas and a short walk before returning to Miss Martha's home.

"How come you aren't married?" Marva asked Ricky as they sat in the car watching the sun go down. Marva didn't see Miss Martha's car and assumed she wasn't home yet.

"How come you aren't married?" Ricky asked Marva.

"I have no chance. I work all the time. Besides, I'm too young. At least that's what my mother says."

"The same is true for me. I mean I'm not too young but I work all the time."

"Do you dream about being on your own?" Marva asked.

"What do you mean?"

"I mean dream about having a life of your own, not living the life of someone else."

"You'll have to talk plainer for me to understand you. You lead your own life?" Ricky said.

"No, I lead Miss Martha's life or Jeananne's life, not my own. By the way, have you seen that French woman over at Sam and Miriam's house? Rosa told me about her, that she's some sort of bad woman. Rosa says she has an evil face."

"I don't like to gossip, Marva, but she's not like you. She wears this dark lipstick and clothes that you wouldn't wear, clothes your mother wouldn't let you wear. You ask Rosa."

"Wow, that's what I like about you. You talk to me. I talk to Rosa when I can but we are both very busy. Most of the time I don't have anyone to talk to. Of course Miss Martha talks to me but it is usually to tell me what she wants me to do."

"When can you talk to me again, Marva? Would you go out with me next Sunday afternoon? Edo says that your boss gives you Sunday afternoons off."

"Since you already know it's my day off, you are ahead of me. Where would we go next Sunday?"

"Let's drive down to Galveston. We could walk on the beach."

"Okay. I look forward to it." Remembering a phrase she had heard from Jeananne, Marva added, "I'll put it in my calendar."

Ricky laughed and got out of the car, walked around to the passenger side, opened the car door for Marva, ushered her to the kitchen door, mumbled words that sounded like "good-night" and left.

Chapter 12

"Put the top up," Lulu yelled at Geoff who was driving the 1947 Cadillac convertible at hair-mussing speeds. "Put the top up or let me out."

"You want out. I'll let you out. You can walk back from Galveston."

Lulu shot Geoff an evil look that could stop a long-horned steer in its tracks. Her upper lip curled to reveal an ability to shred raw meat.

"Okay, I get it. You're pissed, but look, we're already in Galveston." Geoff slowed the car and turned onto a narrow road leading to the seawall that was built after the devastating and deadly 1900 storm. "Do you want out now? I'll pull in here at the Hotel Galvez. You could probably find someone who would pay your way home."

Geoff and Lulu spoke as though they were alone in the car. They were not. Jeananne sat in the back seat.

"Look, you two. I'm no peacemaker. If you don't cut it out, I'm the one who is getting out of the car, even if I have to walk back to Houston."

"Sorry about my so-called wife's behavior," said Geoff turning around to apologize to Jeananne.

"Eyes on the road, bub," replied Jeananne.

The bickering stopped when Geoff pulled the car under the canopy of the Island Casino, a popular hot spot for illegal gambling just an hour's drive south of Houston. Houston had its own hotspots but the drive and the lure of the Gulf, fabulous big band music and star acts drew the crowd to the casino on the bay. Its illegality was another enticement for souls looking for adventure tinged with danger.

One of these souls was Geoff. He had never been in the casino during a raid. Part of him, the less sane part, wanted to experience the excitement of police sirens and whistles in the distance growing louder as they neared the entrance. He wanted to see the rapid conversion of the gaming tables to ordinary if glamorous dining tables. He wanted to see the slot machines and roulette wheels covered so cleverly that their identity and presence were undetectable. Yes, Geoff knew about the possibility of a raid and found himself attracted to the risks just as he was attracted to the risks of gambling. He loved the craps table, the feel of the dice, and the momentary breathlessness of watching them fly through the air when his fate was on the line. Although Geoff, golden son of Sam Wilkins, heir to the fabulous Wilkins Enterprises, seemed to lose more than he won, he was an enthusiastic and persistent gambler.

Geoff helped the women out of the car, Lulu patting her hair into place, and Jeananne holding her purse close to her body, her hair falling into her face. Geoff threw the keys to the young valet whose glance was directed first to the fancy lady in lavender then to the convertible.

"How's my boy Wilkins?" The male voice was gravelly. For a moment the speaker's dark eyes narrowed as he intently watched the smoke he exhaled. Geoff laughed and proffered his right hand. The two shook hands heartily.

"Welcome to my humble house," said the tuxedoed Eddie Barga. "Good to see you again."

Eddie "The Touch" Barga was a personality known to all in the Galveston-Houston area as the public face of vice. His brother and partner, Emilio, kept the books and stayed in seclusion. If there were other Barga brothers, they were unknown, living under the cover of respectability in the "end of the line" island with only one road in and one road out.

Rumors about the brothers were rife in the area. They were said to have a growing business in Las Vegas, planning to move their interests in prostitution and gambling westward.

Eddie earned his sobriquet when he assumed the role of host in the two casinos owned and run by the Bargas. He admitted his touch was golden. People said he could fall into the proverbial barrel and come out smelling like a rose.

Customers frequently asked him to touch them, to bring luck. He always complied with a smile, often adding that he would rather touch the accompanying women. This always brought a laugh among the men and now and then a woman made it clear she preferred Eddie's touch to that of her husband or escort. That was the case with Lulu who eyed him salaciously, slowly and expertly dropping one of the thin straps barely holding up her lavender figure-hugging gown. Eddie played his part.

"Who's this gorgeous gal, Geoff? You've upgraded." Eddie ran his hand over Lulu's back in a gesture of assistance, demonstrating one justification for his nickname. "Need me to fix that strap?" He winked at Lulu.

"Want her?" Geoff asked and walked further into the depths of the casino following a path to the cashier's window.

Jeananne, left alone, was glad to rid herself of the conflict that had engulfed her during the past hour. She smiled at Eddie, avoiding his touch. She peered from the entry hall into the main dining room and saw Harold Carter, Geoff's friend, waving at her.

She walked in his direction. She assumed the other two people at the table were Harold's date and brother from out of town. Three additional seats at the table were empty. She guessed that Harold had planned seating for Geoff and Lulu.

"Hi, Jeananne. You look gorgeous. Where are Geoff and that French woman he picked up in Grenoble?"

They exchanged kisses. Jeananne acknowledged Harold's date and the spare man at the tale.

"I'd like you to meet my date, Liz, and my brother Paul. She's more gorgeous than me and he's more handsome."

Paul stood, nodded toward Jeananne. "Join us?" he asked. "You are worth the wait. Harold told me a little about you. You are one of the Wilkins family, right?"

"Not exactly," Jeananne replied. The orchestra had returned from break and the music hindered conversation. They were able to order dinner and drinks, and made polite efforts to communicate. Jeananne, aware of Paul's presence at her elbow, and on the dance floor had to admit she was attracted by his masculine presence.

The two extra seats at the table remained empty. After about two hours, Jeananne began to worry about Geoff, whether he knew where she was sitting, or whether he had left and forgotten that she depended on him to drive her home. She asked Harold to look for him.

Geoff was enjoying free bourbons. He never counted bourbons. If they had not been free, he would not have cared. As long as the brown liquid was Jack Daniels, he was satisfied.

The three highballs he imbibed during the first half hour of the night served to supplement the two he had drunk in Houston before he stepped into the

Caddy for the night's journey to Galveston. He did not count the beer he drank Saturday afternoon. He reasoned that beer didn't really count as alcohol.

The dice failed Geoff during the initial half hour. As he watched his chips dwindle, he knew he needed to keep playing to make up for his losses. After an hour, he needed more chips.

Eddie came over to the table and put his arm around Geoff. "Let's have a drink at the bar."

Eddie waltzed Geoff away from the craps table. Smiling, Eddie said, "You are already into me for $30,000. What's that car worth?"

"Let it ride. I've owed you more before."

"Last time, this time. You're going to owe me more after tonight."

"Do you know who I am? I'm Wilkins Enterprises." Geoff's anger was building.

"I know who you are. Why do you think we've let you run up such a large tab?" Eddie was calm, a demeanor that escaped Geoff's notice.

"I'm going back to the table, Touch." Geoff sneered.

"Under warning," said Eddie.

"Meaning what?"

"I think you know what I mean. Tonight's the last of it."

"I have friends in Houston," said a defiant Geoff.

"So do I," said Eddie, "and I'm sure mine are bigger than yours."

Harold approached the craps table where an inebriated Geoff was trembling as he tried to lift a cigarette to his mouth.

"Come on home, buddy," said Harold, "night's over."

Geoff responded by shoving Harold away.

Harold continued in his effort to get Geoff to stop but after several futile attempts, he gave in to the inevitable. He knew if he waited long enough, Geoff would lose his ability to stand.

Harold's brother insisted they leave. He argued that Geoff was an adult who should be responsible for himself.

"Think of Liz. She's ready to go home," Paul Carter said.

Harold, who had seen his Army buddy in trouble before, was hesitant. His first obligation, he thought, was to his date, Liz. Reluctantly Harold left, kissing Jeananne on her cheek.

"Sorry," he said, "but we have to go. Geoff will pass out. I've seen this happen before. Don't worry about him. Eddie will have one of his men drive Geoff back to Houston. Take care of yourself."

Jeananne wasn't sure what this meant. She assumed it meant she would have to drive back to Houston by herself, unless she could find Lulu.

She scanned the restaurant and walked further into the casino looking for Geoff's wife. She tried to get Geoff's attention but he was engrossed in dice and several people were crowded around him. He was drunk and Lulu was not to be found. Uneasily Jeananne drove Geoff's new car home, hoping Lulu, wherever she was, was safe.

When she pulled the car into the driveway of Sam and Martha's home, Edo, sitting at the entrance to the garage and hearing the sounds of tires on gravel, roused himself. He drove Jeananne home and, after he completed his task, he assumed position at the gate to the Wilkins's property, waiting for Geoff's arrival.

Chapter 13

Geoff awakened with an expanded, throbbing head. He was alone in the cottage bedroom. The windows were closed and he could feel sweat dripping down his brow. The taste in his mouth reminded him of the battlefield. He kicked the sheet off and tried to stand up. After three attempts, he managed to walk to the bathroom where he stepped gingerly into the shower and doused his body with cold then hot water.

Slowly the events of the night before returned as film, one frame at a time. The last frame captured him falling in the casino somewhere between the craps table and the men's room.

Thirsty, Geoff reached into the nightstand drawer for the bottle of Jack Daniels and gulped down a swig. "Hair of the dog" he told himself and felt less foggy. The world was coming into focus. He congratulated himself for surviving the night and thought himself ready to challenge the world.

The two-story cottage, charmingly decorated by his mother, was small, spacious for one person, snug for two. It took only a brief look round for Geoff to confirm the Lulu's absence.

"She's probably gone to church," he smiled at the picture of her kneeling for Communion dressed in the outfit she wore last night. He found the thought slightly arousing but in his current state, he shivered and headed outside.

Desperately needing coffee, Geoff walked across the back lawn to the main house. En route he nodded to Edo who was sitting outside the garage drinking from a Thermos.

"Catch you later," Geoff hollered to Edo, "after my coffee."

He strolled past the pool, squinting in the sunshine, suppressing the unsettled feeling in his stomach, and entered the kitchen.

"Carmen, I'm dying for coffee, dark and strong." The long-time maid of the Wilkins recognized the signs of a hangover. She said nothing but dutifully placed orange juice and an aspirin on the table and set about preparing percolated coffee.

"Have I told you that you are a jewel, Carmen?" Geoff flashed a toothy grin in Carmen's direction.

"You never change, Geoff," she said.

"Is anyone in the house?" he inquired.

"No. Your mother is over at her sister's. I'm not sure where your dad is, but he isn't in the house unless he came in directly from the pool through your mother's sitting room."

Geoff ate the breakfast Carmen placed before him. After he finished his second mug of coffee, he wandered through the house to his father's office. Finding the room unoccupied, he returned to the kitchen, asked Carmen about lunch, then headed to the garage.

As he was walking, he saw Lulu, dressed in the clothing she wore the night before. The straps on her gown were hanging down in the back. She was holding onto the trunk of a live oak tree near the driveway. He was tempted to yell out an obscenity to her but did not when he realized she was throwing up. Instead, he continued to the garage where he encountered Edo polishing the broad hood of the Cadillac.

"Lulu's a mess, disgusting," he said. "She's out by the driveway, sick."

Edo threw the polishing cloth on a workbench and headed out the door. Geoff walked over to his car and gazed lovingly over the hood that Edo had just dusted. He took his hand and slowly patted the shiny surface.

Edo, concerned that Lulu could be seen from inside the house, rescued her from the tree and walked her toward the garage where she threw up again. Guiding her hands to the corner of the building where he hoped she would stand and wait, he went inside and warned Ricky to stay inside. After a few attempts caused by Lulu's precarious lack of balance, Edo was able to walk Lulu up the stairs to the apartment she shared with Geoff.

Joining Geoff, Edo said "Mission complete. She's passed out on the sofa." He and Geoff moved two lawn chairs to the patch of grass immediately outside the garage. "Ricky was asleep in the back but with all the noise, he woke up. I told him to stay inside. No need to get him involved in problems he can't solve."

Geoff and Edo sat, each lost in thought. Edo did not say, "What kind of wife stays out all night and comes home drunk?" Geoff did not say anything to excuse or explain himself.

"To tell the truth," said Geoff taking a deep breath, "I don't remember much of last night. How did the car get back here? I didn't drive it, did I?"

Edo informed Geoff that Jeananne had driven the Cadillac home from Galveston the night before and that he had in turn driven Jeananne over to Martha's house before returning the Caddy to its place in the garage.

"Good man," Geoff said, "and me? How did I get home?"

"Some fellow pushed you out of a car at the gate."

"And you found me and tucked me in?" Geoff was grinning.

"Yes." Edo was taciturn.

"Do you know any of Eddie Barga's men?" Geoff asked.

"Not personally," replied Edo, "and I would like to keep it that way. Why do you ask?"

"Eddie threatened me last night, hinted he might take the car."

Neither man spoke, leaving the threat floating in the air between them.

Finally, Edo said, "Are you telling your father? He might be able to fix it for you."

Geoff corrected his slumping posture, stiffened his back. "I'm my own man, Edo."

"Barga is big trouble." This statement joined the threat, becoming the conversation's benediction.

"She'll be the death of you, son. I don't like to interfere with your love life, but surely you can see it isn't working out. She isn't exactly wifely, is she?"

"She isn't my wife, Dad."

The two men were sitting poolside. Sam was immaculately dressed in summer lightweight gabardine trousers and a white-on-white thinly striped short-sleeved shirt. He was sporting a woven straw cowboy hat and smoking a cigar. Geoff was dressed similarly but without a hat. He wore aviator sunglasses to protect his red and puffy eyes from the sun which was still bright at four in the afternoon. Aside from the clothing, the resemblance between father and son was striking.

"I thought as much. That actually makes fixing the problem easy," Sam said. "We just send her back to France. She is French, right? That part is true?"

"Yes, she's French. I met her in Grenoble. You can see the appeal."

"Like I said, that problem is solvable. The real problem is Eddie Barga."

Geoff nearly choked on his cigar. "You know about Eddie?"

Sam looked at Geoff as only a father can look at his errant son. "Of course, I know. He called me this morning. We are going to have to pay him. Do you know how much?" Sam casually flicked ash from his cigar perfectly hitting an ashtray that was placed on the table beside his chair.

"Last night he said I owed him $30,000. That's nothing to you." Geoff managed a grin to accompany the words he meant as compliment to his father.

Sam turned toward Geoff. "Do you have any idea how much you lost last night?"

"No." Geoff managed to stretch this single syllable word into three syllables.

"A lot. You lost another twenty thousand at the craps table. Eddie said he tried to stop you."

"Come on." Geoff's voice now took on a tone of supplication. "You can't believe Eddie Barga. How do you know I lost another twenty thousand? You can't believe a thug."

"Eddie said you were drinking. He said you passed out and out of kindness and respect, his men brought you home and tucked you in bed."

Geoff walked over to the drinks cart and poured himself a finger of Tennessee whiskey. He looked at the liquid and filled the glass.

Sam had more to say. "I don't like it. I don't like Eddie Barga's men on my property. I don't like any of this. We run a respectable business." Sam's soft tone had gotten harsher.

"I'll do better," said Geoff now reduced to a child's whimpering. "Sending Lulu away will take stress off me. I've been stressed ever since I got back from the war."

Sam was hearing none of Geoff's excuses. "Your mother and I have had a long talk this morning about Lulu. Your mother doesn't know about Eddie Barga. I want your word she never will. She will be happy to see Lulu gone."

"They never got along," Geoff said.

"Worse than that," said Sam. "Your mother caught Lulu in the house going through her jewelry, in your mother's own dressing room."

"What?" Geoff squirmed in his chair.

"According to your mother, whom I absolutely believe, Lulu said she came in merely to look at the jewelry. Apparently, she asked to borrow the Cartier necklace that your mother purchased before the war. At least that is what Lulu said. Your mother said Lulu was actually trying on several pieces, including those showy diamond earrings that she wears to parties. Your mother had to tell Lulu to put everything back in their boxes."

"Mother never said anything to me." Geoff's lower lip was pushed forward in a decided pout.

"No matter. Miriam told me. We've checked everything against our inventory list and all the jewelry is in the safe where it will remain until Lulu is off the premises." Sam pulled on his still lit cigar. "Everything except your Mama's ring, the one you took out of the box and gave to your French so-called wife. I can see you aren't worried about it but it's worth a damn fortune. I'll get it back or my name's not Sam Wilkins."

The bourbon was having its effect on Geoff. Unaware of the annoyed look on his father's face, Geoff leaned back in his chair and stretched his legs out in front of him. He stirred the remaining brown liquid with his index finger.

Sam stood and said to Geoff, "You will stay in the house tonight and tomorrow night but I want you to spend the day tomorrow away from the property. Go over to Martha's house. Visit with a nice girl, that is, if you can hold the attention of a nice girl like Jeananne. I will see that Lulu is packed and gone." When Sam spoke in this decisive and directive manner, no one questioned him.

"Fine by me," replied Geoff.

Chapter 14

Ricky was his own man and saw the events that took place on Wilkins's property through eyes of someone new to Houston life.

He had awakened from his dream feeling strangely elated. He was accustomed to waking up alone, usually to the sound of roosters crowing. The sounds that greeted him and ushered him into this day were unpleasant. He heard someone throwing up outside his window.

Edo popped in and said, "You're awake. Stay inside until I finish what I'm doing. I don't need any help out here. There is no problem with any of the cars. I'm dealing with people problems."

Ricky did as he was told. He didn't want to get involved in the problems of the rich gringos and if someone was throwing up, he would prefer to keep his distance.

When he was in Monterrey, Ricky looked after the ranch equipment, anything with an engine was his specialty. He lived in one of the outbuildings and rarely interacted with the family when they were in residence, except for Sam. He liked Sam, respected him. He found Sam's slow, deliberate way of doing things to fit with his own pace.

Sam knew about engines and liked to get his hands dirty but he told Ricky that his life changed when he found oil. Ricky heard Sam say, "Most peculiar thing is that before I got rich, I could get my hands dirty. Then I got rich and the women all expect me to keep my hands and my clothes clean."

Ricky liked that about Sam. He liked it that Sam would put his head under the hood of a car and fiddle around with the dirty engine. Once, as a joke, Ricky had cleaned and polished the engine of one of the cars, and when Sam joined him in the garage all ready to do some "dirty work" (as Sam called it), Ricky opened the hood and presented the sparkling, shiny engine. Ricky said the look on Sam's face was worth all the work he had done to clean that engine.

On two occasions, Ricky had driven from Monterrey to Houston, once to chauffeur Sam who wanted to move one car to Houston and another from Houston to Monterrey. The other occasion was the current one. He was called up from Monterrey because Sam wanted Ricky to work on an engine out in one of the oilfields. Ricky thought Sam had plenty of people to do that kind of work, but who was he to question Sam?

Not long after Ricky was awakened, he heard Edo talking with another man, probably Geoff Wilkins, outside his room. The room assigned to Ricky was not fancy but it suited him. It was located at the side of the garage. Ricky could access the toilet and shower without entering the part of the garage that housed the cars. This was convenient as he didn't plan to spend his entire day in his room. He planned to get up and get dressed and he hoped to talk to Sam about the job that needed doing. He also wanted to talk to his cousin about Marva.

As soon as the voices stopped, Ricky emerged from his room and from the garage to join Edo who was emptying water from a galvanized tub.

"I guess you want to know what you're supposed to be doing. I sure as hell don't know."

"Sam's okay?"

"Yes, Sam's okay but Geoff is another story. I'm going to be driving his woman to the airport later this afternoon."

"Who is she, his wife?"

"I don't ask any questions and neither should you."

Later in the day, Sam came out to the garage and told Ricky that plans had changed. He wanted Ricky to help Edo. "Do whatever Edo needs you to do. We're in a bit of a mess and we may forget about that broken-down engine I wanted you to look at. Just stick close to home."

Ricky had no reason to do otherwise. He was Sam's employee, paid to do whatever Sam wanted him to do.

"Sure, boss," he said.

"Your cousin Rosa wants to spend some time with you today. Her mother says she can be spared for a while this afternoon."

"Maybe I had better talk to Edo first, see what he needs me to do. He said he wanted me to go with him to the airport."

"Suit yourself, but I don't think he will need you until tonight."

Rosa and Ricky sat on a blanket on the grounds of the Wilkins property, drinking Dr. Pepper and munching on potato chips and beef barbecue sandwiches.

"You know how to pack a picnic, Rosa," Ricky said. "I was hungry."

"We could talk about food, but I want to know about your date with Marva. Did you like her? I don't think you've seen her since we were children in Mexico."

"Yeah."

"Yeah, what?" Rosa persisted.

"Yeah, I like her."

"Do you want to see her again? You know that she is Edo's sister."

"Sure. I met her mother once when Edo was at Las Palmas. The mother is sickly. Anyway, what's going on in the house? I'm guessing there is some problem here. I'm supposed to be on my way to one of the oil fields but here I am. Sam said the plans have changed."

"I'm not sure what is going on but I do know there are big problems with that French woman. Something is going on but we don't know everything that is happening. Geoff is hanging around the house and Miriam told Mother that he's spending the night in the house so we've made up one of the guest rooms for him."

"Edo is taking her to the airport today."

"Really? Wow, then something big is happening."

"I heard Geoff talking with Edo this morning. Sounds like he's been gambling again," Ricky told his cousin.

"Maybe the French woman is a gambler," Rosa offered.

"Who knows?"

"If I had their money, I wouldn't live like they do," Rosa said.

When Ricky saw the French woman, he was shocked. He thought she looked like a prostitute, not like someone's wife.

Ricky drove the car while Edo sat in the back seat with her. Edo gave directions and Ricky just did what he was told.

Edo was taciturn on the drive home, speaking only when he needed to tell Ricky to turn this way or that. There was no further explanation for the trip to the airport but Ricky sensed that whatever was happening was only a part of something bigger.

Despite his feeling of unease, Ricky fell asleep that night without asking questions.

He awoke to Edo's urging voice. "I need you to get up. I need you to help me. Quick, outside, follow me."

Ricky stepped into his jeans, slipped his bare feet into his boots and followed Edo.

The man on the ground behind the garage was clearly dead.

"Before the sun is up, we need to get this guy dumped in the Gulf."

Chapter 15

Late afternoon Monday Lulu was on a plane, en route to Paris, her hat box stuffed with American currency. Her hands were bare of rings.

That Monday night when Geoff slept in the main house, two of Eddie Barga's men came for the Cadillac convertible. Edo, on alert, shot and killed one of the men. The other man fled.

Eddie Barga's dead subordinate was weighed down, stuck in debris on the floor of the Gulf of Mexico.

Geoff's car was safely in the garage, parked alongside Sam's Rolls Royce.

Early Tuesday morning, Edo was on the road headed south to Monterrey, Mexico, accompanied by his sister Marva. Edo told her that she could visit their mother for a while.

Sam told Ricky to move his things into Edo's room in the garage.

Geoff and his friend Harold Carter were driving east to the Wilkins's oil patch outside Beaumont, ostensibly to survey activity, keep an eye on the roustabouts. Harold was under Sam's instruction to keep Geoff out of trouble.

Miriam's jewelry, including the diamond ring that Lulu had been wearing, was secure in the safe.

Sam Wilkins was sitting in his office at the oversized walnut desk, looking at an entry in his opened personal check book. The entry showed an expenditure of $100,000 payable to Eddie Barga.

Part 3
1950

Chapter 16

Martha Wilkins entered the room and slowly walked over to one of the six single-paned windows overlooking downtown Houston. Houston's Oil Club was not open to everyone, only to those dues paying members whose business interests involved the biggest industry in the city. While its name was unimaginative, the club frequently offered its members unusual entertainments. This afternoon's event was being sponsored by the highly successful Nieman Marcus Department Store. Both sexes were in attendance.

In a room adjacent to the ballroom, the moderator, clad in a modern Paris creation, spoke with a Texas accent, now and again telling the crowd what the "chick" woman of 1950 was wearing. No one bothered to correct her pronunciation although it was a noisy group and no one seemed hesitant to yell out comments about the wares that were being displayed.

Martha had sat through as much of the show as interested her. Now she was ready for a cocktail and a breather.

At 54 years of age, Martha looked ten years younger. A widow, she had not been eager to remarry although she frequently told her friends that being single did not mean that she had no men in her life. Dressed in Dior, she had removed her picture hat during the show to enable a better, closer view of the trays of jewels that were being presented.

Martha had been to shows like this before. Sometimes the goods were Texas-themed, diamond-studded belts, handmade snakeskin boots and the like. Often the goods were one-of-a-kind, sold as necessities to those who already had everything necessary in life.

Today's displays truly were extravagant.

When the invitation from the club arrived, Martha had paid it little attention. But that afternoon, she received a telephone call from her nephew mysteriously asking her to attend with him and his mother. Minutes later she received another call, from her sister Miriam.

"Geoff is getting ready to propose to Jeananne and he wants us to help him pick a special engagement gift for her," Miriam informed Martha. "You aren't surprised, are you? Sam is ecstatic. He thinks the world of Jeananne."

"You think he will see something at the Club show?" Martha asked. "Why not just have that fellow, what's his name from Nieman, come to the house?"

"We thought it would be fun. We'll go for lunch, then stick around for the show."

"He's not buying an engagement ring?" Martha emphasized ring because she couldn't understand why he would buy an engagement gift.

"No, he plans to give her that huge diamond ring Sam bought for me at Tiffany."

"I know the one. It's spectacular, but then Sam always has had an eye for the best." Martha suddenly in her mind saw the ring on the hand of Geoff's someone else. "I thought Geoff gave that ring to the French woman, the one he brought home after the war, the one we thought he married but didn't."

"He did let her wear it, mores the pity."

"It was your ring," Martha said matter-of-factly.

"Yes, you know I never say no to Geoff, but it turned out okay because Sam got it back from that gold-digger. I think Geoff really is in love with Jeananne. Let's support him in this. Besides, you might see something you like."

"Okay," Martha demurred, "but I am not in the mood to buy more jewelry, and I'm not sure Jeananne is thinking about marrying Geoff."

"Don't be poopy," Miriam said and both women laughed at the taunt from their childhood.

Martha gazed out the window and recalled Jeananne's arrival at her home, now eight years ago. Much had happened during those years. Jeananne had grown up. She had become a sophisticated young woman. She had held down a job with the company. She had accompanied Martha to Europe on more than one occasion. She had been the belle at a number of club dances and parties. What she hadn't been was in love.

Martha wondered if she was in love now. Miriam might think Geoff was perfect, but Martha saw flaws in her nephew's character. However, Martha told herself that she wasn't the one to make judgments.

Geoff emerged from the room where the show was ending and the noise level was increasing as people were excited about their purchases and eager to share their enthusiasms with each other. He was guiding his mother over to the window to join his Aunt Martha.

"Time now for drinks."

He waved at the waiter who took their order and they moved to a table on the edge of the spacious bar.

Geoff, to his mother and aunt always the bright but naughty little boy, grinned, revealing perfect white teeth. He asked the two women their opinions about his selection.

"Did I do her up proud, or what?" He placed the velvet box on the table and opened it slowly. "What do you think? What girl doesn't like diamonds?" Inside was a gold bracelet adorned by several clear white diamonds encircling a larger emerald-cut yellow diamond.

After both women gasped, and at Geoff's urging, each tried it on, Miriam spoke.

"You haven't given it to her yet, Geoff," his mother reminded him. "She hasn't yet said she would marry you."

"True," said Geoff, attempting to look serious. "But, I ask, who could turn me down? I mean, look at me. I'm a catch."

"And full of yourself," admonished his mother.

"What do you think, Aunt Martha? You must know how Jeananne feels about me. She still lives with you. How many years? Yeah, eight. How many fellas has she turned down?"

"Do you think I would reveal that to you? Besides, I'm not sure I know. I was hoping she would marry your pal Harold's brother, Paul," Martha said looking Geoff straight in the eye. "He is such a steady fellow."

Geoff waved at the waiter again. "We've changed our minds. Champagne cocktails, please. We're celebrating." No one objected.

"Harold's brother?" Geoff was incredulous, his voice rising as he spoke. "Harold's a nice guy and a great business partner, but his brother is not my idea of a suitor for Jeananne. Did she say she wanted to marry him?"

"She dated him a long time. I always thought he would be the one," Martha winked at Miriam.

"She's teasing you, Geoff," Miriam told her son.

"And then there was that fellow she met when we were shopping in Paris last year. I had dinner alone a few nights while she stepped out with him,"

Martha couldn't seem to stop herself. "He was so continental, good-looking and suave, unlike some men I know."

"Aunt Martha, you are shameless. You know I want to marry Jeananne. We've known each other a long time and we have always been close, ever since she came to live with you."

"It's not like you have a totally clean and consistent record to stand on, Geoff."

"Aunt Martha, I admit nothing. I have been featured in *Texas Monthly* as one of Texas' most desirable bachelors. They know what's what."

"Is a divorced man a bachelor?" Martha asked.

"Aunt Martha, you know I never married that woman. Do you expect me to prove to you that I am worthy?" Geoff's tone was playfully indignant.

"You will have to take your chances. Maybe Jeananne sees you as a desirable bachelor, maybe not. I do know this. She is ready to have a house of her own."

"She will be plenty motivated to accept my proposal. If that's what it takes, I'll offer her a house that she'll fall in love with," Geoff said as the cocktails arrived. "She couldn't turn down a handsome guy like me. It may not be romantic to say, but she is 26 years old. That's a pretty decent age for a girl to get married. I mean, some guys would consider her over the hill."

"Geoff, hush with talk about age. Are you forgetting how old you are? We won't talk about your history," said Martha. "I remember the day you were born, just as the first war was breaking out in Europe. I told Sam, you and war came at the same time. That was an omen."

The reminiscing ceased when one of the black attired young blondes from Neiman Marcus approached the table and told Geoff that he was needed in the other room. "We need your signature on the invoice, Mr. Wilkins," she said, and Geoff excused himself from the company of his mother and aunt.

"Don't wait for me," he told them. "I will telephone Edo to bring the Rolls for you. I can find my own way home later."

Martha looked the salesgirl up and down, picked up her cocktail and drank all that remained in the glass. To Miriam she said, "I guess we are dismissed. He's found something better."

Not one to let Martha have the last word about Geoff, Miriam said, "You know he doesn't go looking. Women just seem to find him."

Chapter 17

Jeananne returned the telephone receiver to its cradle. She checked her watch to note she had been on the phone for half an hour. She smiled and left the hallway in search of Martha.

August was the warmest month of summer in Houston. The newly installed air-cooling system was taking some of the stickiness out of the air and making Jeananne happy to remain indoors.

She was dressed in a sleeveless blouse and pedal pushers, advertised as the "new look for a new decade." Her legs were long, her calf muscles just visible below the hem of the three-quarter length pants.

Martha was working in the office. The room that once served as her husband Wendell's retreat was now clearly feminine. The dark paneling had been replaced by light green grass cloth. The desk was French, almond brown, gleaming with its rich patina, adorned by gold ornamental brackets. The pastel pink and green floral drapes generously covered the windows, counterpoint to the pink geometric fabric upholstering the overstuffed chairs. Martha told her friends she adored the spacious room once English and now "Louis XIV meets 1950."

Martha confessed to her sister that she now had no excuse to avoid work. She could no longer blame the suffocating feeling of dark and heavy masculine furniture. She could no long blame the recollection of her husband's presence.

It was Wilkins Enterprises work that caused her to be in the now feminine office. Busy examining papers scattered atop the desk, Martha looked up when she heard Jeananne's tap.

"I'm interrupting," said Jeananne, standing in the frame of the open doorway, stating the obvious. Her quizzical expression indicated she was hoping for a sign of forgiveness.

"I'm actually happy to be interrupted. It's your day off. Don't get dragged into my work today."

"Still organizing the report for the board meeting?"

"Yes. I'll have it ready for you to type on Monday."

Jeananne strolled casually into the room and sat in one of the comfy chairs facing Martha across the desk. The two women moved easily from talk about business to personal pleasantries. An outsider would have thought they were mother and daughter or best friends, or both.

"Paul called. He's in town and wants to go out tonight. We're going out to dinner."

"Be sure to tell Marva," Martha instructed. "It's been an on-again/off-again affair with him, hasn't it, dear?"

Jeananne winced at the word "affair." If "affair" meant having sex, she assumed it was a private matter, nothing she intended to talk about with Martha. "The relationship is difficult when one half of it lives out of town. I thought he would move here when Harold and Geoff established their business, but he chose to look after his mother's property."

"You can't fault him for that." Martha rolled her chair back from the desk. She wished she had a footstool but the decorator had not anticipated that need.

"No, he is a good son." Jeananne deeply inhaled her disappointment.

"You aren't looking for a good son, are you?"

"Not really," The corners of Jeananne's mouth rose slightly though her lips were tightly pressed together. It was a mixed message, perhaps a smile, perhaps censorship. "He has great possibilities. I could love him. He is tall and straight and yummy looking. He has gorgeous eyes and wavy hair, and he dances divinely. He treats me like Ginger Rogers." Jeananne crossed her left leg over her right leg at the knee and placed them so that they were parallel. She inched the right foot slightly further to the right. She leaned her upper body to the left placing her right hand over her left. The movement was instinctual, the position learned by watching models and debutantes. She thought the pose was feminine and chic.

"Are you talking yourself into love? I remember a girl that Miriam and I went to school with. Everyone thought she would move to St. Louis or Memphis and get a great job and fall in love with a handsome man. She was smart and came from a family that was well-fixed."

"What happened to her?"

"She landed a job working as a steno for an architect in Hot Springs. We were all jealous of her, but as the years passed the rest of us were getting married and some were having babies, and she was still taking dictation." Martha smiled at her choice of words.

"Maybe she liked taking dictation. Maybe she felt she'd found her place in the world."

"That's what we all said. In fact, we grew more envious of her when we became more tied to our homes." Martha reached for a pitcher of water atop a tray. Seeing only one glass, she stood and walked to the rectangular grill built into the wall near the door. The designer had insisted that all the large houses had intercoms. Every time Martha used the device, she congratulated herself for having it installed.

She pressed one of the buttons and, hearing Marva's voice, asked for coffee for herself and Jeananne. "I just turn it on and press the button. Voila, it works," Martha said.

"Did she ever meet men?" Jeananne returned Martha's attention to the story about her classmate.

"That's the interesting part of the story. She met lots of men, smart, attractive, even professional men. For some reason, unknown to us, she eventually married a man we all knew. He went to the same high school as the rest of us. She moved back to our little town and became like everyone else. She gave up all the excitement for a man none of us had ever found exciting, or even marriageable."

"Why are you thinking of her, Martha? Are you thinking about love?"

Martha moved her chair back into its place at the desk, put her elbows on the desk and leaned over toward Jeananne, shortening the distance between them. "Because I don't want you to move to some small town up north and miss out on all the excitement of the life you've started building here."

"I hear what you are saying. There are moments though when I am with Paul that I think I love him. My feelings are complicated." Jeananne recrossed her legs, this time in the opposite direction."

"Has he asked you to marry him?"

"Many times, Martha. He hints at a married life, but says he can't see me on the farm."

"Can you see yourself living with him on his mother's farm?" Martha's elbows were still on the desk. She cupped her chin in her open hands and looked directly as Jeananne.

"No. We could live here. In Houston. His brother is here. I know Harold would find a place for Paul at his office. Harold and Geoff's business is growing. Harold is probably making decent money. Paul could keep the farm as an investment property."

"And his mother?"

"I'm not so sure about her. Maybe she would want to move into town. She isn't young. Or maybe she would stay on the farm, and we could hire some people to help her and manage the farm. I believe we could make it work."

"It seems you have more of a plan to marry Paul than you have admitted to me or to yourself."

"It does seem that way, doesn't it? Saying my feelings out loud..." Jeananne left the thought unspoken.

Martha looked at the papers on her desk. Her mind was filled with a jumble of thoughts about the eternal triangle, in this case populated by Paul Carter, her nephew Geoff and Jeananne. She had been tempted to tell Jeananne about Geoff's intentions. He had after all made a declaration at the Oil Club and he had bought a significant piece of jewelry and vowed to buy a house. It also seemed that Miriam was in on Geoff's plans. But, Martha reasoned, the story was not hers. It was between Geoff and Jeananne.

Just as Marva entered the room carrying the coffee tray, Jeananne excused herself, saying she needed to figure out what to wear on her date. Her secret kept close to her heart, she detoured and walked from the office in the back of the house down first one hallway then another to reach the largest room in the house. Martha had taught her to call it a public reception room. "No one lives in this room," she said. "It is not a living room."

From the broad entry into the room, Jeananne imagined it filled with well-dressed guests, adorned with perfumed floral arrangements. She saw the minister at the far end of the room, Paul standing in front of him looking lovingly at her as she walked slowly down the aisle toward him. If her parents came from Arkansas, she would put them up in a motel, and she would need to buy her mother a new dress.

Chapter 18

Not wanting to seem too eager, Jeananne waited until Paul rang the doorbell three times before she calmly opened the oversized double-door entry to Martha's Italianate Tara. She was dressed in a slim pink silk shantung creation, sleeveless with a scooped neck. She had pulled her red hair into a French roll. In her right hand she casually held a matching bolero jacket. The saleslady had assured her that no one else in Houston had this one-of-a-kind ensemble. "You won't see yourself coming," she had told Jeananne.

Paul, standing at the threshold looking in, was agape. Jeananne reacted to his expression, which she interpreted as "blown off his feet with my gorgeousness," by doing a quick twirl and saying teasingly, "Do you think I look okay?"

"I think you look overdressed," he replied. She saw that he was wearing chinos and a plaid shirt, instead of more formal attire.

Jeananne's flirtatious pleasure turned immediately to shock. She pouted and tilted her head in an attitude of disbelief, both because of the attire and because of her dashed expectation.

"I thought you would like having a well-dressed woman on your arm," she said in a teasing voice meant to substitute for whining. "Don't you want to come in while I change, since you obviously think I should."

"No time. Harold and Liz are waiting in the car."

Jeananne began to realize she had miscalculated Paul's invitation for the evening as well as his intent. Surely if he were planning to propose, he would not do so in the presence of his brother and sister-in-law, and not in chinos.

Paul repeated, "No time for you to change. Come as you are. We're going for barbecue."

"Paul, I can't wear pink shantung for barbecue. Go to the car if you like and wait while I change." Her instruction was forceful, and Paul immediately retreated as Jeananne allowed the doors to slam at his back, perhaps a little closer to his back than she intended. She ran through the house, making an effort not to cry.

What was it that he had said on the telephone? Yes, she remembered. They were going someplace special, that he had something important to say to her. What could a girl think when a man said those words?

In her dressing room, Jeananne unzipped her dress and threw it along with the jacket across a chintz-covered boudoir chair. She couldn't bear to remove her lace underwear. It was her personal hair shirt, a reminder of desire and disappointment. It was also a statement of defiance. "You're not going to see this tonight, Paul Carter," she angrily told herself.

Jeananne emerged from her dressing room wearing loose wide-legged slacks, a plaid shirt, and straw flat shoes called huaraches. She walked slowly, sauntered, down the hallways to the center front double-door to the house.

She stopped, took a deep breath, blowing the air out very slowly to calm herself and clear her mind. "Pride goes before the fall," she heard her father say. Jeananne shook her head as though removing the echoes of Pastor Early.

The restaurant was on the southwest side of the city, an area filled with newly-arrived immigrants from Mexico. A new hotspot, word had spread among Houstonians about its amazing barbecue beef and rowdy crowd. Like many places that held an attraction to the rich of Houston, it had an air of sleaze. The multitude of parked cars in front and the enticing odor detected when windows were rolled down, spoke to its authenticity and popularity. The colorful banner and lights and music shouted its Mexican roots. The sagging wooden porch and the tin corrugated roof also told a story.

"Music is supposed to be as good as the food," said Harold who was driving. Liz sat beside him; her left hand slid under his right thigh.

Jeananne and Paul sat in the back seat, Paul fiddling with the window handle on his side. His attitude was one of disinterest in his date. Sensing rejection for the second time of the evening, Jeananne positioned herself close to the door on the passenger side of the car.

The evening proceeded with fabulous food, steaks, ribs, and tamales, spicy and plentiful, and with boisterous music and noise from the diverse crowd. Table talk was general, directed to no one in particular because no speaker could be heard clearly.

"Great food."

"Nothing like Texas beef."

"You know tamales are real when they are wrapped in corn husks."

"Yum…"

Liz and Harold got up to dance, leaving Paul and Jeananne alone at the table. Paul said he wanted to wash his hands. He noisily stood and walked away, leaving Jeananne alone staring at plates piled high with the detritus of the meal. The waitress cleared the table, and still Paul had not returned.

A man whom Jeananne had not noticed earlier asked her to dance. She demurred and began counting songs. In her world a respectable man did not leave a lady sitting alone in the middle of a restaurant.

After her count reached four, the musicians took a break. Paul returned, lagging behind the breathless couple, Harold and Liz. Jeananne bit her lip to keep herself from crying. She wasn't sure if she was hurt or angry or both.

"What is happening, Paul?" she said when he was seated.

Ignoring whatever was happening across the table, Harold called the waitress over and ordered margaritas for the four. He dropped his left shoulder and swung his body toward Liz who put her hands on his knees. They were a world unto themselves.

Paul looked toward the adjacent room where the musicians had been sitting. To get his attention, Jeananne spoke in a voice louder than her usual.

"What is going on, Paul? I thought you wanted to have an evening with me. A special evening."

Paul visibly gulped and for the first time during the evening, he looked directly into Jeananne's eyes. "I'm getting married," he said.

"What? To whom? Where? What did you say?" Jeananne was flummoxed.

"I met someone and we're getting married."

"And you asked me out to tell me that?"

"I thought we were friends." The drinks arrived. Paul licked salt from the rim of his margarita and took a generous sip.

Jeananne felt like throwing hers at him. She said, "Friends? You thought we were friends?" Her voice was becoming shrill.

"We've known each other a long time and it has never worked out between us. You know that. You never wanted to live my life. I think you are a great gal and God knows you are beautiful, but I'm getting married to someone who loves Mother and the farm." Paul's confident smile and matter-of-fact manner was no comfort to Jeananne. She didn't want to show her emotions but tears were welling up, tears that she couldn't control.

"I want to go home," she announced loudly.

"Now?" asked Harold whose attention had been diverted from his new wife, Liz.

"Now. Call a taxi," Jeananne screamed.

"Sweetie, we don't really have taxis in this part of town," yelled a voice from a near-by table. "I'll take you home."

"Don't worry. I'll get myself home." She jumped from the table and walked to the ladies' room. Rummaging in her purse, she found coins, placed one in the pay-phone slot, and dialed a familiar number.

"Martha, I have to come home. Now. Would you get Edo or Geoff to come pick me up? I'm upset. I'll explain later."

Jeananne entered the two-booth ladies room and allowed her tears to flow without restraint. When Liz came in and tried to persuade her to return to the table, she refused.

The next familiar voice she heard was Geoff's calling through the closed door of her sanctuary.

"What's going on in there, honey?" he asked her.

"I want to go home," she emerged from her retreat, whining and sounding like she was on the elementary school playground and had not been chosen to play.

"You got it," he said, putting an arm around her slender waist and gliding her past the man who had just disappointed her, out into the hot, close Houston night just as the music began again.

Chapter 19

When Jeananne didn't emerge for breakfast, Martha asked Marva to knock on her door. "Maybe she will let you take breakfast to her in her room. "Something happened last night." Martha shared the story with Marva, the desperate phone call, Jeananne's slipping into the house and shutting herself up in her room.

Marva prepared a tray and carried it to Jeananne's room. She tapped lightly on the door and heard a muted sound from within that she assumed meant it was okay to enter. She found Jeananne propped up in bed, still in her night clothes even though it was mid-day. A box of tissues sat atop the silk comforter and a number of used tissues were scattered on the floor.

Marva quietly sat the tray on the bed beside Jeananne, went into the bathroom and retrieved a wet cloth and a waste basket.

"You are a gem, Marva," Jeananne said. "I'm not ready to get up."

Martha stationed herself in a comfortable over-sized chair in the den facing the hallway Jeananne would have to walk down if she were to leave her room and head for the kitchen. She had selected a book from nearby shelves, but was only half-heartedly reading. Her mind was busily engaged in imagining what had happened the night before.

Mid-afternoon Jeananne appeared in the den, wearing a long dressing gown and carrying a box of tissues.

Martha knew better than to press Jeananne for details but it was obvious from Jeananne's red and swollen eyes that she had been crying.

"Want to sit down and talk? I'm all ears, if you want to talk about it," Martha said.

Jeananne sat on a sofa and reached for a cushion which she held close to her chest. She began by telling Martha about the dinner invitation and rapidly progressed to her expectation of a proposal and a wedding and a house and a married life.

Martha listened intently, silent and occasionally nodding or shaking her head in synchrony with the words and sentiment she was hearing.

"Betrayed. He betrayed me," Jeananne said. "Paul never told me he was dating anyone else. I thought he was mine. After all these years of knowing each other, dating and talking about the future, I was sure he wanted to marry me. Look at Harold and Liz. They knew each other a long time before they married."

"What you need, Jeananne, is a basketball team," Martha said.

"What? That's unexpected. What would I do with a basketball team?" Despite her tears, a smile spread across Jeananne's face.

"You should date five men. That's what you should do. There are five men on a basketball team. You need to date several men at a time to get your mind off Paul. Paul is forgettable, don't you think?"

"He is Harold Carter's brother and Harold is Geoff's business partner. We do see a fair amount of Sam and Miriam and Geoff. Plus, Geoff and Harold's business is a subsidiary of Wilkins Enterprises. We have the Wilkins board meeting this Friday. Am I sitting in? Yuk, I will never get away from the Carter family."

"Of course, you are sitting in. You sat in last year. I want you there." Martha, who had had her book in her lap, picked it up and placed it on the lamp table next to her chair. "Sam and Miriam, Geoff and Harold, and I alone? No, I'm not going in alone. I want you with me."

"I haven't looked at the reports yet, the one you've been working on. You said I would start typing on Monday. I'll see them then. Do you expect any issues at the meeting or is it just rubberstamping so we can submit updates to the various oversight agencies?"

"I expect the latter. Sam has the agenda but he always alerts me if there are any issues for discussion. I have my finger on the pulse, famous last words, and haven't detected any signs of a problem."

"That's good. I don't think I could stand Wilkins Enterprises problems on top of having to deal with being in the same room as Harold Carter."

"True, but Harold is a nice fellow. You can continue to like him and his wife. He won't think less of you. He will probably think his brother is a fool and let's face it, he is a fool." Martha emphasized "fool" making Jeananne laugh.

"Would you have said that if Paul had proposed?"

"My dear, you are so beautiful and so smart. You are a catch. Now that you have Paul out of your radar, you are ready to find the one." She emphasized the last two words with eyes agape and a big smile. "By the way, Geoff's been telephoning. He says he is coming over later. We missed the pool party."

"Oh my God. I can't be seen like this." Jeananne jumped up from the sofa, dropping the cushion, slipped her feet into her fuzzy shoes, and rushed into the hallway and back to her room.

Chapter 20

"I come bearing gifts," announced Geoff who strolled into the den where Martha was sitting. It was late afternoon, Sunday, and the sun was filtering in through the thin curtains that covered the windows. The heavy draperies were pulled back and secured with tasseled silk rope. The console holding the television sat in a corner. Along one of the walls hung several book shelves, filled with ceramics, magazines and books.

Martha had her feet up on a hassock. When Geoff entered the room, she carefully crossed her legs at the ankles and straightened her long dressing gown.

"Want something to drink?" she asked and gestured to a liquor trolley, fully supplied with alcohol and mixers. "Help yourself."

Geoff walked to the trolley and prepared a whiskey highball for himself. "Sherry, Aunt Martha?" he asked.

"Yes."

Drinks poured and in hand, he sat in his usual spot, the only semi-masculine chair in the room. After Wendell Wilkins died, Martha had redecorated several rooms in the house including the one she called her den. More accurately, she had had her decorator redecorate the rooms, this den and her office as well as her bedroom. Her instruction to the decorator had been to make the rooms fit her personality and since Martha came across to all as "girly," the rooms were soft and feminine with a hint of the new geometric fabrics. Martha loved pastel colors and the house was awash with light pinks, blues, yellows, and greens, mostly florals. Here and there were fabrics with angular unidentifiable repeated shapes. The public rooms had not yet been redone and Marva was hopeful that the kitchen was on the list. Martha promised herself, and Marva, that these were her next projects. Secretly she was hoping to have the front reception room updated for a wedding.

The so-called masculine chair in Martha's den was a wing chair covered in leather. Unable to reconcile the traditional brown color of Texas leather in her pastel room, Martha resigned herself to dark blue, the only color in the room that jolted the eye. The decorator had assured her that the dark blue was a better color for men than the sky blue that Martha preferred. True to the promise of the decorator, any man who made it past the public spaces into Martha's personal den, chose the dark blue leather wing chair.

"Gifts, Aunt Martha, I come bearing gifts." He handed a folder to Martha, then sat down, drink in hand. Martha immediately opened the folder and began rifling through the contents.

"I see the agenda here for Friday's meeting."

"Dad said you would want Jeananne to type it. Also in there are the figures for my outfit. The oil transport business has been good. I may have to increase our salaries!"

"You jest," said Martha.

"No, I'm serious," Geoff sat his drink on a side table and continued, "Harold and I did not take out any profits last year. We put them back into the company. I think we are entitled."

"Has your father looked over the numbers yet?" Martha pulled one sheet of paper from the folder. "I'm looking at the numbers but need to examine them a little more closely. What does your father say?"
"Aunt Martha, I am thirty-six years old. I know how to juggle figures."

"That's what I am worried about."

"No need to worry. Where's Jeananne? I brought something for her." The cocky look on Geoff's face was a signal to Martha to drop the topic of finance.

"She's in her room. Why don't you use the intercom and call her?"

Geoff walked over to the far wall and pressed a button that indicated Jeananne's quarters, and hearing static, determined that the system was on.

"Jeananne, come out, come out, wherever you are," he said.

"Where are you?" said Jeananne, recognizing the voice. The intercom system did not reveal the location of the caller.

"I'm in the den with Aunt Martha. I would like to see your beautiful face. Come join us. I'm only here for a little while. Come join us if you want to see me."

Geoff returned to his seat. He turned the chair slightly to enable a direct view of the hallway.

"There she is," he shouted, "there she is, Miss America!"

"Have you been drinking, Geoff?" Jeananne smiled. She was dressed in long fitted ankle pants and a silk brocade tunic.

"You are Miss America!" Geoff enthused. "Aunt Martha, isn't she the loveliest woman on earth?"

"Why, thank you, Geoff." Jeananne had used pancake make-up to cover the redness in her face. Afraid that the red in lipstick would undo the work of the foundation, she had gel on her lips to make them shine. Hers was a face that rarely needed improvement with cosmetics. She walked past Geoff and sat on the sofa, carefully crossing her legs to his visual advantage.

"You look better than you did last night. I've decided you could use a change of scenery and a change of company. After the board meeting Friday, I'm flying out to Las Vegas and would like you to come with me."

"Just like that?" Jeananne was embarrassed to receive a "dirty-weekend" invitation in front of Martha.

Feeling that she was an intruder in Jeananne's private life, Martha picked up her book and excused herself. "I'll leave you to your business," she murmured.

"We don't have that kind of relationship," Jeananne said loudly enough for Martha to hear as she was hurrying away.

"I always stay at the Flamingo. They love me, always have. It will be easy for me to get a room for you. We'll have a good time, see the shows, gamble a little."

"I've heard they have entertainment at those places. Big names."

"Yeah. I'll introduce you to some of them. I know them all."

"I could have my own room?" Jeananne asked meekly. "I would need to have my own room."

"Oh, sure. No problem. We fly out Friday afternoon, arrive in time for dinner."

"How long would you stay? How long would we stay, if I went?"

"For the weekend. We would return to Houston, say, next Tuesday. That would give me Saturday, Sunday and Monday…" he didn't finish the sentence. If he had, he would have said that he wanted three full days to gamble, mainly to play at the craps tables. "I'll show you how to play at the slot machines. You'll enjoy it. It's easy and you might win some money."

Jeananne did not reply. She was thinking about having a vacation in a hotel in Las Vegas. She could swim and go to the spa, surely the hotel would have a spa or a salon. She could take some of her special-occasion clothes. Harold would know that Geoff had taken her to Las Vegas and he would tell Paul. Geoff had promised her a room of her own. She assumed Geoff would pay for the airfare and the room. She had money of her own that she could use to pay for the spa and for the slot machines, if she decided to give them a go. She had not found fun in losing her money.

"Geoff, I would love to go, as long as I have my own room."

"Okay, it is decided. I'll send Edo over Friday morning to pick up your suitcase. We'll go to the airport right after the board meeting. I promise you will have a vacation like you never have had before!"

Geoff rose from the wing chair and walked across the room to the sofa. He leaned over to kiss Jeananne. She moved her head slightly and his kiss fell atop her nose. She smiled as he backed off and left, humming.

When Jeananne told Martha of her plan, she emphasized the separate rooms.

Chapter 21

Jeananne's head was spinning. She was sitting at the front of an airplane, leaving Las Vegas and headed to Houston. She couldn't focus her attention on anything for more than a few seconds. The blue sky and white puffy clouds outside her window were strong competition to the sleeping man on her left, his body snuggling hers, his head close to her shoulder. When not looking at these phenomena, she was drawn to the ring on her left hand.

"What have I done?" she asked herself. "How did this happen?"

She shook her head to bring back the memory of the past two, no four, days. She thought first of last Friday, the board meeting. There had been a row. Usually the annual meetings of the family were tame and all participants were agreeable but not last Friday. Nothing was out of the ordinary until the subject of annual draw-downs came up on the agenda. Martha suggested they each continue as they had the year before, with the same withdrawals from profits. She argued that their enterprise had increased profits that should be reinvested in the company, used for expansion of their secondary and tertiary oilfields. Geoff had intervened, saying that he and Harold were adding to the company profits with their subsidiary business and they deserved increased salary.

In her mind, Jeananne could see Martha's searing open-eyed stare of anger and she could hear her words. "You mean you want more money, Geoff. Your current salary, let's see, I believe it is at least quadruple the average salary for a family in America. A family, Geoff. You can't manage to live on it?"

Geoff had replied, "Aunt Martha, I love you, but this is business. My company can handle paying me more, and paying Harold more." Geoff at this point, produced several documents that Martha had not seen prior to the meeting.

"These are the figures I am looking at. You can see how much our subsidiary is contributing to the overall business."

Indeed, Jeananne thought, when she saw a copy of the figures produced by Geoff and Harold, she was impressed. She did not bother to look at any numbers but those at the bottom of the third page. Geoff was calling attention to that number as support to his argument.

Sam spoke up at that point and it was agreed by all that Geoff and Harold were due more salary. The meeting ended soon after that. Geoff and Aunt Martha had hugged, Geoff saying he hated for her to be wrong and for him to be right, but business was business.

Jeananne had felt uneasy, especially since she and Geoff were leaving after the meeting. She wanted Martha to feel good about her trip. All the plans had been made by Geoff. While the family usually celebrated the close of the board meeting with a catered luncheon, Geoff had informed them that he and Jeananne would not be participating as they had to make it to the airport for the chartered flight.

Before leaving, Jeananne hugged Martha and said, "I'm sorry."

"About what?" Martha responded. "This is the way meetings go when you have a family business and ours is complicated. Thank goodness, we have such good fortune. Go and enjoy yourself. You know you don't need my blessing."

They exchanged air kisses and Jeananne collected her purse and walked out of the room to join Geoff who pushed the elevator button as soon as he saw her approach.

Jeananne felt Geoff's head drop to her shoulder. It was heavy and he was making a slight whistling noise as he slept. She could hear it over the airplane's engine noises. The past two nights, when she had shared a bed with Geoff, she hadn't noticed his making noises in his sleep.

She grinned and repositioned herself in the spacious seat. They hadn't slept much the first night. That night followed their trip to the Little Church of the West where she saw photos of celebrity weddings: Betty Grable and Harry James, Zsa Zsa Gabor and George Sanders. After exchanging vows, they posed for their own picture. She had a copy in her purse to remind her that they really did get married and she supposed another copy would be posted in the chapel along with the myriad others who married on the spur of the moment in Las Vegas.

She reconstructed the day in her mind. She joined Geoff for breakfast in the casino restaurant. He needed a shave. He said he had been up late, most of the night, in fact, and was going to his suite to shower and nap after breakfast.

While they ate, they planned their day. Geoff, in fact, planned Jeananne's day, suggesting since she had had a good night's sleep, she might want to spend the morning at the pool and maybe the afternoon at the spa.

Jeananne agreed. Geoff accompanied her to the concierge's desk where Jeananne scheduled her afternoon.

They agreed to meet for drinks at four o'clock that afternoon.

Jeananne recalled those details. What followed was a mixture of alcohol, gambling, the high ringing and clanging of slot machines, the thrill of winning with coins falling into the tray, the lights, and Geoff touching her, hugging her, kissing her hair, her neck, nuzzling her ears. Somehow it all ended up with Geoff telling her how beautiful she was, how sexy, how he had fallen in love with her, how he wanted to marry her.

What Jeananne remembered most clearly was the ring. He magically pulled the ring, encased in a turquoise velvet box, from his jacket pocket. It was a spectacular round diamond. He pressed it onto Jeananne's ring finger. She remembered being dazzled.

Her next recollection was the limousine, the courthouse, the chapel. She remembered being deliriously happy.

They returned to the Flamingo and Jeananne heard their names booming over a microphone in the bar, drinks all round, champagne toasts. Then came the sex.

That first night was a night of fumbles, as far as Jeananne could remember. She was eager to please but unsure of herself. Geoff kept telling her what to do and she felt she was busy following instruction.

Day number two, in Jeananne's mind was better. They sat side by side at the lunch table. Word had spread that they were newlyweds. Strangers came over and congratulated them. Geoff seemed very pleased to show off his beautiful bride.

Sex that afternoon was better for Jeananne. She asked Geoff if he was happy. He replied that he was.

In the plane, Jeananne looked at her husband, Geoff Wilkins. She spoke softly, "I am very fond of you, Geoff. And, I will grow to be a good wife."

Chapter 22

The parquet floor of the Oil Club ballroom gleamed, in competition with the candles on every table edging the dance floor, the light from the crystal chandeliers multiplying in the mirrored walls, and the mesmerizing color-changing reflections and refractions of the jewels adorning the guests.

"Are you happy?" whispered Geoff Wilkins into the ear of his new wife.

"Delirious," she replied.

"This is all for you," he said.

She could feel his warm breath on her ear. She shivered.

"Are you cold?" he asked.

"No."

Geoff moved his chair closer to her and put his arm around her. She could feel his fingers slowly massaging her left shoulder.

From across the table, Sam said, "We always hoped you two would get married. Jeananne, you keep him in line. Geoff, you let that sensible girl keep you in line."

"Sure, Dad," Geoff raised his champagne glass to his father, winking. "You know it! Just like you listen to Mother."

Both Miriam and Martha laughed. The two looked like twins, both dressed in shades of purple, one in lavender and the other violet.

"Did you two mean to wear the same dress?" Geoff teased.

"We aren't wearing the same dress," Martha chided. "You just don't have any sense about color. They are different colors and different styles."

"You are sisters. I never thought about how alike you look. I wish Aunt Faye could have been here," Geoff said. "You would probably look like triplets."

"She's not well enough these days. Let's drink to her. After all she is the one who brought Jeananne to us. Thank you, Faye," said Geoff's mother.

They paused to pick up their glasses.

As he was indulging in his drink, Harold and Liz approached the table. "We can't believe you managed to catch her. She's too good for you, Geoff," said Harold loudly enough for guests at several near-by tables to hear him. "Too good for you. We both got beauties, didn't we?" Harold gazed upon his wife, Liz, who rolled her eyes.

"Congratulations, both of you. I guess we'll be seeing more of you both now," Liz said.

"Lucky you," replied Geoff.

To Jeananne, Liz said, "We've always enjoyed Geoff's company. Well, almost always. Now we'll enjoy the company of Geoff and Jeananne, two for the price of one."

Jeananne looked puzzled but said nothing. She wasn't sure what Liz was saying.

Liz tried again. "He's been single and I have had the pleasure of two men. No, that's not quite what I mean."

Miriam, uncertain about Liz's intent, interrupted, saying, "They make a beautiful couple, don't they?"

"Sure," said Liz.

Saying nothing, Harold grabbed Liz by the elbow and steered her away from the head table.

"Strange, that one," said Martha. "Changing the subject, I think I did a pretty good job of organizing this "do," especially on such short notice." She emphasized the word "short." What do you think? It's not like you two gave us any warning about getting married in Las Vegas."

Picking up on the theme, Miriam said, "Yes, I wanted to be at your wedding."

"And I was going to have my front reception room redecorated for you to have your wedding in Houston. Now it will never get redecorated." Martha stuck out her lower lip in a pout.

"Sorry to disappoint you two, but the time was right. Speaking of right times, I have something for my bride." Geoff reached into an inner pocket of his tuxedo jacket and produced a gift wrapped beautifully in gold and silver paper. He handed it to Jeananne with a look of love.

Jeananne opened the box while holding her breath. "What a beautiful bracelet. More diamonds. The diamond is yellow! I'm thrilled."

"What you are is married to the man who was the hottest bachelor in Texas. He can't be seen with a wife who has no diamonds. Put it on," Geoff bragged. He helped her with the tricky latch. "It has a special lobster latch on it so that it won't fall off. Martha and Mother were with me when I bought it."

Martha interjected, "Before you went to Las Vegas. He was sure of himself. I thought it was going to be an engagement present, but you two didn't have an engagement."

"Were you sure of yourself?" Jeananne was calculating when she had been more or less jilted by Paul.

"I am always sure of myself," said Geoff. Seeing Jeananne's questioning expression, he added, "and hopeful."

"The bracelet is beautiful. I love it. Thank you all," Jeananne said, admiring the gleaming jewel on her wrist. "And I love my ring. Thank you, Miriam, for letting us have your beautiful diamond ring. Thank you, Sam." Sam had been busy talking with various acquaintances, men mostly, who wanted "a word."

Miriam nudged him. "You're being thanked, Sam."

"Oh, that ring. I bought that for Miriam, didn't I?"

"Yes, Sam, but we've given it to Geoff for his bride," Miriam spoke as though it were a reminder but it was the first time Sam had learned of his and Miriam's gift. He recovered quickly, "What is mine is yours, son. And, Jeananne, that includes you."

Miriam smiled at him, proud that he had generously recognized that the ring now belonged on Jeananne's finger.

"You two have some decisions to make. You haven't said where you are going to live. Are you going on a honeymoon? Your father and I were planning to go to the ranch for Thanksgiving. Jeananne, maybe you and Geoff would want to come to Monterrey for the holiday. You've never been to Las Palmas. Have you told her about the ranch, Geoff?"

"Jeananne's going to move in with me for a while. My house is too small for us to keep for long. We haven't talked about it yet, Mother. I'm guessing we will build a place of our own. We've received enough checks to pay for a nice piece of property. Our friends are a generous bunch."

Jeananne said, "Like Geoff said, we haven't really talked about a honeymoon. Everything is happening so fast that we have a lot of decisions, like you said. I like the idea of designing our own house."

The discussion continued between Geoff and his father regarding residential construction, possible locations, contractors.

Jeananne turned her attention to Martha and Miriam. "I want to see the ranch. I've never been in Mexico. I've been to Europe." She smiled at Martha, a smile of recollection of past trips.

"You could go down for your honeymoon," Miriam said. "We have a housekeeper there year-round. Edo goes back and forth with us. It's rustic. The house is comfortable but the place is a ranch. The hands are never in the house. You would have the place to yourselves. I imagine Geoff would love to show it to you. He has always enjoyed our trips to Monterrey."

"Yes, Geoff, feel free to take Jeananne down to the ranch. Your mother and I will be there late November. Go down whenever you want and we'll join you for the holiday. Show her the mountains and the cattle. I'm sure she would want to see the cattle! Can you ride a horse, daughter-in-law?"

"I haven't ridden in a long time but I think I would remember how," Jeananne said.

The noise level in the room increased as the band returned.

"Aunt Martha, I don't know how you managed to book Bob Wills and the Texas Playboys with so little notice but I am most impressed."

"Can't give away all my secrets, but where we grew up wasn't that far from Tulsa where Bob has family. He's great, isn't he? I think the dance floor is empty, waiting for you and your bride." Martha tapped her finger in time to the music.

Geoff and Jeananne rose to enjoy a two-step promenade around the dance floor. As they made their way around, their guests jumped to their feet and yelled out whoops that would have been fitting for any ranch.

The band began playing *San Antonio Rose* and someone shouted out, "How about Houston?" Geoff signaled to the crowd to join them and soon the floor was filled with enthusiastic couples.

Geoff whispered to his bride, "Do you want to go to the ranch for your honeymoon?"

"I'll be happy anywhere as long as we are together," she said and placed her head on his shoulder.

Part 4
1957

Chapter 23

Everything happened quickly. I was in the police station in Monterrey one second, and the next I was standing in front of the orange door at the entrance to our home in Houston. I reached into my purse for the keys. I always kept the keys inside my purse, in an inner pocket easy to find with my fingers. The keys were there, where they should be, even though we've been in Mexico these past two or three months. I can't remember how long. When did we go to Mexico? I don't remember at this moment where I was two days ago. My memory is just shot. It has escaped me.

Nothing seems real, except Harold who is standing too close, behind me, engulfing me with his body. I can feel his sour breath on my neck. I place the key in the lock and as I move a stench arises from my own body. My knees buckle. Harold holds me upright. My feet aren't touching the ground, but I am moving through the opened door. The first thing I see is the painting Geoff and I bought, our first purchase together, a splurge during our honeymoon. Tears fill my eyes.

Chapter 24

The house was familiar to Harold. He and Geoff went into business together in 1945, right after the war. Five years later, flush with success, newly married with oil money bestowed on them by his father, Geoff and Jeananne bought a lot in Oakside, hired an architect, and their house on Duchamp Road was born. Long, low, glass everywhere ("hurricane bait," Geoff called it), where the Wilkins's house was the ultimate in modern, the Carter's home was traditional Georgian. If a home was a reflection of lifestyle, the two couples led very different lives. Harold had suggested the Carters lived in a work of art. Liz insisted that while one house was art the other was artistic. This was a debate among at least three of the parties. Jeananne had no opinion on the matter.

Today Harold was revising his opinion. He still thought the house was "artsy," but when he delivered Jeananne to that orange door he had the same warm and welcoming feeling he had when he entered his mother's farmhouse.

Harold was a big man, large enough and strong enough to hold Jeananne upright when her knees were failing her.

"Don't faint on me now. Let's find Rosa." He slowly guided Jeananne through the entrance. He knew it was better to keep moving, to get her safely inside, into the care of Rosa. He wouldn't feel he had completed his mission until then.

"Give me something to do," he had told Geoff the night before. "I can't bear doing nothing." Geoff had relieved Harold's misery by giving him an important task, one he himself could in no way complete.

With effort Jeananne said, "I can manage from here, Harold. Geoff will thank you for helping me. I don't know when he will come home. Do you know? Did he give you any details?"

After saying all these words, expressing herself with more words than she had uttered in several hours, Jeananne stood inert, her eyes blank, her shoulders fallen, pressed down with fatigue.

Harold still had his arm under her elbow and he gently guided her to a sofa and helped her sit down. When he looked up, Rosa had joined them. He was surprised at the feeling of relief that surged through his body. He accepted responsibility readily, but having his business partner's wife in his care was at the upper limit of his reach.

Rosa looked at Harold with kindness. It was a look that said many things. *Good job, Mr. Carter. Thank you for bringing Jeananne back to me. I will take good care of her. Your task is done.*

Jeananne seemed to relax somewhat in the presence of Rosa. Harold couldn't identify why he felt Jeananne's burden was lighter but he knew that he wasn't needed. He began to lean over to kiss his friend's wife but instinctively stopped himself. Instead, he backed away.

Feeling exhaustion setting in, Harold said, "I'm going home now, Jeananne. I think Geoff will probably telephone you as soon as he is able to leave the police station."

To Rosa, "You have my number. Call if you need me."

Harold left with a feeling of satisfaction that he had fulfilled his duty. He had promised Geoff that he would get Jeananne out of Monterrey and back to the safety of Houston. Harold and Geoff had always been straight with each other, committing only to what was possible. In their business an exaggeration of truth or a downright lie could cost millions. In this personal matter, Harold had offered, accepted a responsibility and now he felt the concomitant feeling of satisfaction that was reward enough.

But the satisfaction was rapidly replaced by concern.

Harold had left Liz to pack up and get herself back to Houston. He had left Geoff to the Monterrey police. He had been grateful for the job Geoff had given him but now he felt uneasy, uncertain. Harold didn't like the situation Geoff was in. He was aware of a boiling in his belly, a surging of overwhelming anger.

Chapter 25

Harold opened his eyes and blinked, trying to focus on the Seth Thomas clock on the bedside table. While his vision was not yet clear he could just make out that both the big and little hands were on twelve.

Not good, he thought. *Early to bed, early to rise, makes a man healthy, wealthy, and wise.* And if that wasn't enough proverbial wisdom, he immediately remembered another: *The early bird gets the worm.*

I am not a worm. I am not wealthy, maybe not wise but I am healthy.

Enough of this, he thought, but he was not moving from his comfortable bed.

I wonder about Jeananne, if she is okay. I should be thinking about Liz. Hmm, let that thought go.

His mind went blank again and he stared at various items of furniture and decoration in the room. Everything reminded him of Liz. That chair is where Liz sits when she puts on her stockings. The drawers in that chest have all been filled with Liz's things. The curtains that he now realized were a match to the bedspread, they were chosen by Liz.

I need to get out of here. I am living in a woman's room. With that realization, he got out of bed, hurried into the bathroom where he showered and dressed to go into the office.

The Carters' home sat on an acre of land, proudly facing a private street about two streets over from the artsy house built by Geoff and Jeananne. Two stories, it was made of red brick. Harold was proud of the house but even prouder of the garage. The decision to buy the house had been made based on the triple garage with room for some of Harold's toys.

He grew up on a farm near New Harmony, Indiana, where Harold had been fascinated by tractors and farm equipment. He had a way with all things mechanical. The family farmed corn and lived with the temperamental behavior of the Wabash River. During the Depression they had managed to survive by growing and canning garden crops, selling eggs, and by stretching every penny as though it were their last.

Deeply religious, Harold's parents believed in self-improvement, in using the gifts granted by the Lord to the betterment of the world. They taught Harold to value learning and had hopes for his becoming the first Carter to go to college.

Harold did not disappoint them. He earned a scholarship to a land-grant college nearby, lived at home and worked the farm with his father while he studied late into the night. He never slept until both the big and little hands were on twelve.

At the age of twenty-two, a college degree in hand, but with no jobs in southern Indiana, he said good-bye to the farm and made his way to Texas to work in the oil fields.

Then he met Geoff Wilkins. Geoff had the good looks, smooth charm and athleticism of Douglas Fairbanks but he was blonde and didn't mind getting down and dirty with the other roustabouts. Shortly after they met one of the men filled Harold in on Geoff's pedigree.

"You may think he is just one of us, but he isn't. His folks own this outfit. All of it. He is stinking rich and doesn't belong down here. He's taking a job from some decent fellow who could use the money to buy food for his family. You didn't hear it from me."

Harold was living on-site in a trailer along with other men on the crew. He sent money home to his parents and lived modestly.

After a month on the job, Harold got a reputation as a "goodie-two-shoes" who didn't booze, go after women, or gamble. He was a pariah among the men and his roommates poked fun at him, suggesting he was still living under Prohibition, didn't know it was over. Another tried to set him up with a local woman, but Harold thought she was too old and had on too much make-up.

The harshness and teasing were tempered in front of Harold as the men respected his size and strength. He was after all born and bred on a farm where he had grown to over six feet in height and in the oil patch, he could work pumps and carry steel poles using the muscles he had developed while carrying huge baskets of corn, oiling and greasing tractors and before that plowing fields with a horse. He was a strong man.

Harold continued to keep his head down, to do his job, and he became known as Steady Harold. Steady and reliable Harold.

Geoff was a contrast to Harold. He gambled, went to beer joints with the other men, and was known to womanize. He showed up at work on Monday's stinking of booze and sex but no one said anything to him even in jest because he was the Wilkins son of Wilkins Enterprises.

It was a surprise to Harold when Geoff approached him two days before Christmas in 1937 and asked what Harold was doing for the holidays.

"Staying here. My family are in southern Indiana," Harold said.

"The guys call you Steady Harold. Would you like to spend Christmas in Houston? My folks have a big house and there's room for you."

"Why me?"

"To be honest, my folks think I'm not mature. They treat me like a child. I want them to see that I have a steady friend."

"You want me to impress your parents?" Harold was flabbergasted.

"Yeah. Could you do that for me?" Geoff said with sincerity that Harold had not expected. "I could use a friend," he added.

"Houston it is, but I don't want to lose my job," Harold said.

"You won't lose your job," Geoff promised. "My folks will be thrilled to meet you. They don't always like my friends but they will like you, Steady Harold."

Geoff, with his blonde unkempt hair, his boy-like shifting from one leg to another as he talked, his promises, and his seeming sincerity were convincing.

Chapter 26

Geoff studied the brightly colored picture hanging on the wall behind the commandant's uncluttered desk. Dressed in blue blazer and white trousers, he diverted his attention to a small spot of red wine, near his left knee, an unwelcome reminder of the party where he and Jeananne had shared their last moments together.

All had gone to plan. He knew he could count on Steady Harold. He had telephoned Harold before he called the police. Before Diego and his men arrived at Las Palmas, Harold had picked up a shaky Jeananne and taken her to the airport. No need, thought Geoff, for her to be questioned. Who knows what she might say? Geoff had his story clear in his mind. He just wanted the tricky part to be over.

It had been a party like all the other parties in Monterrey, American expats, all on first name basis. The men were executives, engineers, entrepreneurs in established or developing businesses associated with the oil industry. A few were from Canada or other parts of the U.S., but mostly they lived within a ten-mile radius of each other in Houston and belonged to the same clubs, enjoyed the same music, had their names on the rosters of the same churches, and donated to the same charitable causes. In Monterrey they pretended to escape the "rat race" of Houston, on occasion deals were discussed at their parties and Mexican-themed celebrations. Banal conversation went something like: "Hi, John. How's the golf game? Heard you just arrived from Dallas, or Oklahoma City or Shreveport. How's that son of yours? He's at University of Texas, or Texas A and M or LSU or Georgia Tech? Did you just close a deal with Texaco or Esso or Murphy, you son of a gun?" John's wife would be with him. She would be a dazzler, probably blonde, maybe a red-head, dressed in the latest moderne look, re-imagined with Mexican flair to express her playful side. A diamond or two would fit right in on his hand as well as hers.

111

Women were extensions of their husbands, rarely having opinions in variance with their partners, and capable both of retaining secrets when necessary and sharing gossip with their husbands when it could help further his business interests. Primarily, they knew the cardinal rule. They had to give to get. The giving took several forms such as giving time, giving attention, giving parties, giving their bodies, giving forth children, giving homage, even giving love and honest affection.

Liz and Harold were the party hosts. Liz was beautiful and Harold was charming. The guests were friends and the conversation lively. Booze was plentiful and the weather was cooperative. Altogether it was a perfect Monterrey evening.

When they walked to the car after the party, Jeananne had noticed the stain on Geoff's trousers and had commented on the hope that club soda would take it out. At least, she had never noticed his watch. He told himself if she had, she probably wouldn't have noticed that he was not wearing his Rolex. Would she have known the difference between his Rolex, the one he never travelled without, and the cheap Timex he wore now? He decided she wasn't that attentive to him and what he wore.

In the commandant's office, Geoff looked at his right hand, fingers automatically covering the wine spot. He noted his missing onyx ring, the one his parents gave him for his fortieth birthday.

He reached for his monogrammed pocket handkerchief and daubed at sweat on his brow. He took a deep breath and looked again at the comandante. He wasn't accustomed to revealing an appearance of discomfort. Geoff was normally the man in charge, decisive, even aggressive, commanding respect. Doing necessary business in this cramped office, Mexican office of the State Police, was no pleasure.

In the manner of thoughts, Geoff's passed through his mind quickly. "What is the difference between need and want? I don't want to be here. I need to be here to legitimize the theft. I need to be believable. I want the insurance money. Hell, I need the insurance money."

Comandante Diego Gonzalez was speaking to Geoff in Spanish. Geoff considered his Spanish language skills good enough. He could order a meal and pay the bill (plus generous tip). He could discuss money matters with his Mexican banker. He could read road signs and if necessary, he could instruct the gardener or the local gas attendant.

Hola amigos. This he said to his Houston business associates when he joined them in the board room or at the club. Hello, friends. And they gaily replied with an Hola of their own, many of them as much a devotee of Mexico as was Geoff. More often than not, in Monterrey, his favorite expression was "la cuenta, por favor," asking for the dinner bill as he made the universal hand motions to the waiter.

Paying the dinner bill was easy for Geoff. He had always had money. Born rich. Not technically, but close enough. Born near-rich, but rich soon enough to fudge the truth. Born to a mother who drove her Rolls Royce for fun, who excused the chauffeur when she wanted the joy of driving the large cumbersome machine.

Geoff knew by heart the story of his father's journey to success. It was the story his father told not only to Geoff but to all who were eager to share in the glamour of Sam's wealth. Geoff knew he was born to a father who had bought Texas land and Texas oil as a lucky gamble. Sam said a salesman knocked on his door when he was living in Oklahoma, offered acres of undeveloped East Texas land for sale, land promised to be good for cattle. And, Geoff's father, then young and reckless and hopeful, said I'll have some of that and reached into his pockets and found enough dollars to buy forty acres. Forty acres, all his. Not one to hide his light behind a lamp, Sam often embellished the story by saying, "And then I bought more and more until I owned a spread bigger than anyone else in the state."

When the Texas oil boom hit, boom went Geoff's father's bank account, boom went his life, boom went his future. Geoff's mother, blonde and beautiful, had attracted him when the two were teenagers. She refused his first and second confident proposals but with an expectation of a glamorous adventure, and with a father who knew potential when he saw it, said yes. They said their vows in the minister's parlor. A year later, hundreds of gallons of oil later, along came the baby boy destined for a golden bassinet and a platinum future.

Geoff's parents Samuel and Miriam (who came from zealously religious families) thanked the lord for good fortune. They believed that wealth was God's gift to deserving people, that they were rewarded for their devotion and piety.

Reincarnated as East Texas royalty, Samuel and Miriam purchased a two-story brick house large enough for their new-born son and for future babies who did not materialize. The house was property befitting a man of means, and was comprised of substantial house and outbuildings and grounds. It had a garage with an apartment upstairs and room downstairs for a yard man, a gated entrance and a grove of fruit trees out back. The only thing it didn't have was a swimming pool, but Sam and Miriam wanted the luxury of dipping their feet into cool water in the summers and within a year of owning the house, they hired a designer and contractor and had their pool built.

With new-found oil money, Miriam hired a maid and began accumulating a wardrobe. By the end of Geoff's toddler years, Samuel had a truck and a Rolls Royce, a founding membership in the Oakside Country Club, a seat on the board of the Better Business Bureau, and Miriam had a yen for jewelry.

When Geoff was school age, past the age of succumbing to summer complaint that killed young children living in reclaimed swamp land, Samuel and Miriam purchased a second home, a hacienda on the southwest edge of Monterrey, Mexico. The home was an investment, they said. It sat adjacent to the original forty acres plot that Sam had purchased years earlier. While America was in a heated argument with Mexico over government acquisition of foreign-owned property, Sam was adding to his estate by lining pockets with oil money, contributing to the local growing Institute of Technology (in exchange for his name on the building to house a Department of Geology), hiring local indigent peasants, and publicly stating his alliances with those in power including the Municipal President and members of the City Council. When asked how he, as a foreigner, was able to own private land in Mexico, he usually smiled and said his property was owned by the local bank to which he paid huge amounts of interest that benefitted the economy of Monterrey. To some he said he was practically Mexican himself.

The locals didn't question Sam Wilkins's right to do whatever he wanted. He didn't interfere with local life and most of the time he wasn't even in Mexico. They were more accustomed to Edo who was from Monterrey. His mother and grandmother were part of the local community and that made Sam more acceptable. They reasoned, "If Edo says Sam Wilkins is an okay hombre, then he is."

Geoff, now sitting in the Monterrey commandant's office, said wearily, "Gonzalez, I've told you the entire story. You say you want to hear it again?"

"One more time, amigo. Just the two of us."

Chapter 27

Comandante Diego Gonzalez was a short man, solidly built with a belly that hung over his silver belt buckle. He was dark-haired and sported a black moustache that contrasted with teeth as sallow as his skin. His looks and his concrete-block office suited one another, and when he spoke it was obvious that he expected attention and obedience.

The comandante knew most of the expats in his town. He was determined to give every benefit of doubt to Geoff Wilkins whose family was a part of Monterrey's history. Gonzalez had a personal connection with the family. His father had been on the Wilkins's payroll back in the wild days when Sam and Miriam Wilkins were the only white people to own land in the state of Nuevo Leon.

A young Diego Gonzalez had introduced a fearless Geoff Wilkins to the art of skinning snakes, a childish thrill that enticed young boys but horrified the gringo mother. When the boys grew older, they explored local cafes and Geoff had his first view of naked women in the company of Diego. Their friendship had endured good times and bad for Diego, times when his pockets were empty, times when he came close to siding with men whose aims were less than honorable, times when the cerveza and whiskey ruled him. For Geoff, the golden boy, money always flowed freely and when money could solve problems, he did not hesitate to use it to help his friend.

Now in Diego's small office, one sat on one side of the desk as comandante and the other sat as victim. They were alone in the room.

A ray of the moon lent an eerie light across Geoff's face. He adjusted his chair and began his story.

Geoff spoke freely. "Maybe someday this town will expand and wise fathers will decide to put lights on the highway but as you know there are no lights now on the road to the hacienda. No lights. It is dark as the ace of spades.

I was driving the Oldsmobile, new '57 model. Of course, Jeananne was with me. We'd been to a party in Old Town, home of Harold and Liz Carter. Lots of expats were there, just the usual crew. We left about ten-thirty. I'm not sure exactly as I didn't check my watch."

In an automatic gesture, Geoff looked at his left wrist to check the time. When he realized the watch wasn't there, he drew his hand up to his face covering his lips as though to appear thoughtful or perhaps to censor himself. During the party he had checked his watch several times and had each time been astonished at the differences between his usual Rolex and the substitute Timex he was wearing. They didn't even feel the same on the wrist. He bit his finger, a gesture that brought him back to the present task. He congratulated himself for having given away the Timex.

"I pulled off the highway onto our drive. It was bumpy. No rain lately. I was annoyed because I didn't want to throw the suspension out on the Olds. The metal gate was closed. I had closed it when we left. I parked the car, left the lights on and got out to open the gate. If I had known those sons of bitches were waiting for us, I would have said to hell with the car and driven right through the gate."

"That probably wouldn't have helped you," volunteered the comandante. "Go on."

"Without warning, three men with guns appeared out of nowhere."

"Could you describe them?"

"Hell, no. They were all Mexicans. They were wearing masks. I've been around guns all my life. You would think I would have noticed details about the men but all I saw were the guns. One had a handgun and two of them had shotguns. What flashed through my mind was my body being blown to smithereens. One of them said to hand him the keys. Like a fool, I had to ask if he meant the car keys." Geoff shook his head in disgust with himself.

"In English? Did he ask for the keys in English?" Diego asked.

"Yes, he asked in English. I mean how difficult is it to say *keys*? I would have known though if he had used the Spanish word, *llaves*. We use the Spanish word so maybe he said *llaves*. I'm not sure."

"Where were the car keys? In your hand?" The comandante glanced at a large ring of keys on his desk as if to prompt Geoff into focusing on keys.

Geoff followed Diego's lead and settled his gaze on the keys.

"They were in the ignition. Then I thought about Jeananne. She was in the car. As I stepped back toward the open car door on the driver's side, my side, to reach for the keys, I saw Jeananne's terrified look. I wanted to say something to her, but the fellow with the hand gun, a long barrel hand gun, he opened her door and told her to get out. That is when I knew I had to do something."

"What were his exact words?"

"I'm not sure. Who the heck cares? Next thing he had Jeananne in front of him, her back pulled toward his filthy body. I don't know what he did with the gun. He had a knife in his right hand at her neck." A small bead of sweat trickled down Geoff's forehead, most unusual for him.

"Would you like some water?" The comandante rolled his chair toward a file cabinet, opened a drawer and pulled out a bottle of beer, which he placed in front of Geoff. "A little liquid helps," he offered. Water, beer, it was all the same to him.

Geoff took a long swig of the cerveza and continued.

"One of the thugs with a shotgun told me to hand him the keys. I said nothing and threw them into the bushes."

"That could have gotten you killed. What were you thinking?" Diego's eyes were barely open. He had his hands palms down on his desk and he leaned forward in his chair.

"I wasn't thinking. It was just an instinct. It didn't work. Son of a bitch made me walk through the bushes to find them. I found them and handed them over. Jeananne was crying. She was bleeding. Blood was dripping slowly onto her shoulder, but she was still standing and didn't look like she was in pain."

"You don't seem to be too worried about Jeananne." Diego sat back and spoke in a matter-of-fact tone, trying to sound non-judgmental.

"No, like I said, she wasn't in pain and I figured if the guy was going to hurt her, he would have done it already." Geoff sipped the last of his cerveza. He wanted another.

"We can be grateful they didn't do more harm to her. I'm surprised they let you get away with the key business. Throwing the keys into the bushes wasn't the smartest thing I have ever known you to do. What about the thugs? Did they just get into the car and drive away?" He reached for another beer and handed it to Geoff.

"No. The fellow with the knife used it to point at Jeananne's jewelry. Oh my God, she was wearing Mother's diamond ring, a 2 ½ carats first grade diamond and other jewelry. You've seen it."

"You know I am going to need more details about the jewelry, at least a list. If I could have the appraisals, it would help. You do have appraisals or receipts for what was stolen, right?"

"Gonzalez, don't for a minute think we've just lost a ring or two. We have a rule about leaving all the jewelry at the hacienda. When we go out, the jewelry goes in a long flat case that can be hidden under the back seat floor mats. Usually, I throw a blanket over it all."

"All the jewelry?"

"What isn't being worn."

"How much are we talking about?"

In a very clear voice, Geoff replied, "A few hundred thousand US dollars. I have all the appraisals. Everything is insured. I want to be certain you have descriptions of each piece. I'll have to inform the insurer immediately and they will require assurance of a police report."

"I am absolutely shocked. I've known you for a long time, Geoff, but I have never known you to be careless or stupid. Except I have to admit, you have always been free with your money, at least when you were around me. Why did you bring all that jewelry to Monterrey? Driving a new flashy car. You were asking for it."

"Don't ream me out. This one is on Jeananne. I told her to pack the paste but she insisted on bringing the good stuff. She always says the jewelry is less safe in the hacienda. She feels no one is likely to steal out of the car. Besides we parked the car behind a locked gate at our friend's house."

"Jeananne wanted to bring all that jewelry down here? Any idea why?"

"Something about thefts in Oakside, where we live in Houston. So, she left the paste in our safe at home. Yeah, the fakes will be safe." Geoff hesitated, took a deep breath and continued; I don't think Jeananne really loves the jewelry. I guess it is a good thing since it is gone. Jeananne is the kind of woman who loves money. She isn't all that excited about jewels."

Diego was silent, looking up toward the high window, the one through which the moon was still visible.

"My attitude is different. I'm telling myself, we got out of this drama with our lives. To hell with the car and the jewelry. You have to enjoy yourself,

Diego. You can't just lock up all the perks and never enjoy them. Besides everything is insured. Don't get me wrong. Not all jewelry can be made into paste. My Rolex is real. It's gone. Even if we had brought fake stuff, some of our jewelry would have been real."

"I don't like it, Geoff." The comandante looked directly at his friend not indicating the "it" that he didn't like. For a moment neither man spoke. The one trickle of sweat on Geoff's forehead became two trickles. Diego picked up the keys and began toying with them. The jingling was the only noise in the room. Each waited for the other as though they were playing the familiar game of "chicken" with each other. First one to speak is…a rotten egg.

Geoff spoke first. "We'll have to take your car out to the hacienda. Remember, I don't have a car right now."

Chapter 28

Half an hour after Harold's departure from the "artsy" house, Rosa headed into Jeananne's bedroom carrying a tray. She sat it atop the mirrored dresser and turned to leave to allow Jeananne to undress in privacy.

Before she had passed through the door into the hallway, she heard Jeananne's plaintive voice.

"Would you get a dressing gown out of my closet, please? Any one will do."

Rosa did as she was asked, crossing the wide bedroom, opening the door to the walk-in closet, selecting a quilted long silk robe. She draped it on the bed and again began to leave the room. Once again, she was given a directive, this time in the form of a gesture. Jeananne waved toward a chintz-upholstered wing chair indicating she wanted Rosa to sit.

"I want company. I've been through a terrible ordeal. Tell me about the house. Did anything happen here while I was gone? Has your father's health improved? Distract me. Please, Rosa."

"There were no problems. I kept the house clean and spent most nights here. I stayed one or two nights with my father. He is feeling okay. My sister takes him to the doctor and her husband is running the store. The news here is good. Everything about the house is good. Your news is more important. I don't know what happened to you in Monterrey. Mr. Carter said you had been robbed. Are you okay?"

Rosa was a beauty. Even in her maid's uniform, she was elegant, her legs long and slender, her body shapely and her dark eyes deep-set, belying secrets and inviting confidence. She was born in southwest Houston, Texas, to immigrant parents, twenty-five years ago, during the Depression that left many families bereft and destitute. Her father, a trained physician in Mexico could not get certification to practice in the United States. Grateful to be in a land he thought offered opportunities, he managed to open a small confectionary in their neighborhood, to all appearances a Mexican barrio.

The family remained together, Mr. and Mrs. Gomez and their two daughters of which Rosa was the younger. The confectionary business survived the Depression and the War. To supplement the family's income, Rosa's mother, Carmen, did "day work," a euphemism for being a maid. She started working days for Geoff's mother and eventually dropped all her other clients working only for Miriam Wilkins.

During summers and on weekends as Rosa a became a teenager, Mrs. Gomez often took her daughter with her, at first to keep an eye on her then to teach her a trade. Meticulous and skilled in her job, she taught Rosa the finer points not just of cleaning but of housekeeping. She also taught her how to be interested, kind and concerned while being an employee.

"Remember," Carmen Gomez told her daughter, "You can be proud about being a maid. You're a good maid. Be kind to these people but remember that you are their employee. We work and they pay us. They are not our friends."

Rosa was able to complete high school and with good references from her teachers and priest, and more importantly from Geoff's mother, got a maid's job working for Jeananne and Geoff Wilkins. Initially she worked only three days a week but advanced to a full-time live-in position.

Rosa did take pride in her work, but she wanted her own home, a loving husband, and children. On Duchamp Road, she had her own quarters, a bedroom and bathroom near the laundry room and kitchen. She had privacy and no complaints about her pay or her time off but she wanted more out of life. She hoped her subservience was temporary but she had no plan for immediate change.

Geoff Wilkins left household matters to his wife. While he noticed Rosa's beauty, he did not interfere with her. "You should see what I've got at home," he said to his buddies in the oil patch, and he gleefully hinted at sexual intrigue and intimacy both with his young wife and the lovely Mexican housemaid.

Rosa rebuffed all his efforts at familiarity and given her access both to his wife and his mother, he kept physical distance, enjoying instead a rich fantasy life.

After ten years of marriage, home life for Geoff lacked excitement. He was enthusiastic about his work, the thrill of wildcatting, of an oil well coming in, of being informed about production and of the myriad hours spent considering deals with refineries and resellers.

Now, after experiencing life and death situations during the war, he preferred indoor safety. He preferred deal-making, negotiations. He didn't mind being in the board room. He didn't want the "down and dirty" work. He was satisfied with good tailored clothes, a name-brand watch, a luxury car, and excited about deals made over martinis and whiskey.

If asked, Rosa might have admitted to the same truth, that her life was filled with routine. But for her excitement was more elusive. Long past was the thrill of a clean refrigerator. She enjoyed the smell of freshly washed towels and loved preparing tamales in the Mexican way she learned from her mother.

She cared deeply for Jeananne and liked doing what she could to make her happy. Clearly Jeananne was her boss but at moments they were more like sisters or best friends, perhaps due to Jeananne's limited social circle. Rosa remembered her mother's advice but she thought there were exceptions to the rule.

Jeananne busied herself with charity work. She volunteered at the church library two hours every other week. Occasionally she attended lectures at the art museum. Primarily, she told Rosa, her job was being Mrs. Geoff Wilkins. He owned oil wells. He was the son of oil money. He had his own subsidiary in the business of transporting oil to and from the refinery. His oil and his name were as good as gold, no, better than gold, in Houston.

Jeananne explained the concept of expectations to Rosa.

"I am expected to maintain my figure. I am expected to accompany Geoff to events at the Oil Club. I am expected to host an event for the Heart Association or the Cancer Society at least once a year. I am expected to dress the part. If I make Houston's annual Ten Best Dressed Ladies list, I can expect a new bauble from Tiffany's or now from the Nieman Marcus that just opened downtown. Geoff won't have to go all the way to Dallas anymore to buy although I think he enjoyed those trips. Do I really need more jewelry, Rosa?"

Rosa felt sorry for her employer because the expectations and the pay for service rendered did not seem to make Jeananne happy.

Back now in Jeananne's bedroom three-quarters of an hour after her arrival home from Mexico, the story began to unfold.

"I have lived a nightmare," Jeananne said as she climbed into her bed and adjusted her pillows to enable her to sit up and talk. "I honestly thought they would kill me. One of the men put a knife to my throat. I can't bear to think of it. Geoff tried to save us but what can you do against three armed men? They took my jewelry but most of what they got was stowed away in the back seat of the car under a blanket. All of that was paste. It has a value but not like the real jewels. You know how much I loved my beautiful engagement diamond ring? They didn't get it because at the last minute before we left the Houston house, I switched it for the fake one. Even that ring was beautiful and looked like the real one and truly it was made of gold but the diamond wasn't real. It looked real but it wasn't. I knew it wasn't real but I thought maybe it was best not to take something so valuable, in case of theft. I must have had a premonition."

"Thank God you took the fake jewelry." Rosa knew enough about jewelry in general to know that it fell into two categories, real and not real. The only real jewelry she ever saw were the rings and necklaces that Jeananne wore most often.

She was under the impression that everything of value was kept in the safe which was tucked away in a closet in the bedroom. Rosa had no idea what was in the safe considering matters such as valuables to be out of her realm of interest. She never even approached the safe except to clean the exterior with a feather duster when she did her spring cleaning.

"Yes. I never haul all my jewelry around with me when we travel." When Jeananne said this, Rosa tried to imagine hauling jewelry but couldn't quite picture it.

Jeananne continued, "Geoff is still in Monterrey finishing up with the police. He's lost the car. I don't know whether he will want to go back to Monterrey ever again. I certainly do not plan to return. I'll never go back there."

"So, Mr. Wilkins will be home soon?"

"I don't know. He might want to stay down there to sell the hacienda. He has to deal with the police. I have tried not to think about it, but maybe he will have to look at pictures of suspects, that sort of thing. Liz Carter, you know her, Harold's wife, is still down there. She'll look after him. Good night, Rosa."

She sank into her bed and closed her eyes. Rosa walked over and looked at her benevolently. She effortlessly turned off the lamp on the bedside table, gently tucked in the almost-asleep figure in her care, and tiptoed out of the room.

Chapter 29

Liz Carter parked her car in the only vacant space on the street in front of her villa. She reached for her purse and for the string shopping bag containing a bottle of tequila and a sack of limes. With her belongings in tow, she opened the car door and passed through being careful not to compromise her newly polished fingernails.

She walked along the stone lane to her home in Monterrey's Barrio Antiguo and silently congratulated herself for her recent decision. She had, the night before, encouraged her husband Harold to accompany the distraught Jeananne home to Houston.

Poor Jeananne. No one deserved to be robbed at gunpoint. No one deserved to have all her jewelry stolen. In an eye blink, all gone. No one deserved to have a knife at one's throat. That was unthinkable.

Poor whimpering Jeananne. She had no strength, no survival ability. She was a dependent sniveler. Liz had no patience with fools and snivelers.

Liz was certain Jeananne had no idea about her affair with Geoff. She wouldn't suspect anything because Liz and Geoff were cautious, discreet. Maybe not always discreet, she admitted to herself. There was that one time in the coat closet at the Oil Club. Better to forget how close to discovery they were, but that was part of the fun of it.

Liz Carter did not have Jeananne's physical beauty. She had a round face, untamed thick brown hair and a snub nose. Even in Monterrey heat she wore sandals with little heels to give her a boost in height. She had one, no two, assets: a very large bust and a quick, analytic intelligence. She was accepted in men's circles where she was admired and rejected by women who didn't trust her.

Liz's young life was spent in Mississippi and like Elvis Presley and his parents, Liz and her family moved to Memphis for a better life. Liz's brains got her through high school. Wanting to do something with her life, she applied for and was awarded a scholarship to Miss Smithson's Secretarial College.

The college had a reputation for producing the highest quality graduates. If you had a certificate from Miss Smithson's, you could type, take shorthand, organize, problem-solve, time-manage and dress appropriately.

Liz learned to wear shoes that matched her purse, white shorty gloves with long sleeved jackets (and three or six button gloves when suit sleeves were three-quarter in length). She learned not to wear shoes that were brighter or lighter than the hem of her skirt. She improved her balance and posture by walking around at home with a dictionary atop her head. The latter was a challenge as she frequently broke out in laughter when she saw herself in her bedroom mirror.

Liz also learned the fundamentals of typing and shorthand. During the introductory course on bookkeeping, Liz learned that she had an innate facility with numbers. She could do calculations in her head. She liked balancing debits and credits. She liked recording financial transactions.

When Liz completed her courses at Miss Smithson's, graduating with honors, she accepted the school's help in finding employment. The war had just ended and the U.S. economy was booming. Lots of men were coming home looking for jobs but they weren't looking to become secretaries.

Liz wanted to leave Memphis, to start her new life in a new city. New York would have suited her dreams but she was afraid of "the North" which she thought had too much hustle and bustle, too many taxis, subways, and noise.

When the school's placement advisor directed her toward a job in a Houston company just starting up and owned by two soldiers just home from service abroad, Liz thought she had a chance at success and she grabbed it. She packed one suitcase. It was a graduation gift from her parents and luxuriously had her initials on the handle.

Her father told her that Houston was a cow town, built on swamps, but instead of discouraging Liz, he gave her enough money to last for a couple of weeks until she received her first pay check. In her suit, hat, matching purse and heels, carrying her one suitcase, she boarded a train for Houston.

When she arrived in Houston, Liz settled herself into a room in the downtown YWCA where she felt safe and could conserve her funds.

Within two years, she had established herself as an essential employee of, Wilcarco: "Wil" for Wilkins, "Car" for Carter, and the obvious "co" for company. She was managing the books in the growing firm and she was married to one of her bosses.

Walking now through the crystal beaded curtain into her Monterrey home, Liz was focused on what lay ahead. Geoff, as far as she knew, was still at the police station, but surely would soon be finished. Harold and Jeananne would have arrived already in Houston. She was on her own. She was deliciously on her own.

Setting her purse and sack down in the kitchen, pulling her loose dress over her head, she stood wearing only her bright red bra and panties. She looked around the room and said out loud, "What I need is a long soak in the tub, a margarita, and Geoff."

Chapter 30

One of Monterrey's attractions to Texans was its warm winter weather. In summer it was hot both in Houston and Monterrey but in winter Monterrey's temperatures were more pleasing. While Houston had gray skies, rain, and what Houstonians thought of as cold weather, Monterrey was bright and sunny.

Year after year as he was growing up, Geoff's family spent Thanksgiving at the hacienda. They could expect friends to do the same making for an enjoyable holiday party. It was a tradition that was a part of Geoff's life. When he was very young, he played with other children on the estate, children of the cook or the housemaids. When he grew into his teen years, he had the pleasure of running wild with Diego Gonzalez, the son of a gardener who had come to work on the hacienda in the days when Geoff's parents were renovating the grounds. Occasionally Geoff brought Diego into the main house but more frequently the two boys stayed in a bunkhouse usually inhabited by men who wrangled the cattle. They were keen listeners of cowboy tales and discovered secrets of being men.

Now in November, 1957, Geoff's plans for Thanksgiving would have to be scuttled. Robbery trumped holiday celebrations.

Riding shotgun in Diego's Jeep, travelling from the police station in town along the hardtop road south and east, Geoff felt the breeze against his face. If the breeze on Geoff's face had been cool, it would have been welcome but the warm dry air and tendrils of dust that whirled about him imbedded in the pores of his face. He positioned his right arm on the door frame and leaned back viewing large cumulus clouds in the bright blue sky simultaneously waving his hand in front of his nose to free his breathing.

Blue-gray mountains rose in the distance surrounding them. The most dominant was the Cerro de la Silla, Saddle Mountain. Geoff fixed his gaze on its familiar outline. When his parents purchased the Monterrey property, their one requirement was a view of Saddle Mountain.

Geoff corrected his posture, sitting upright in the Jeep, his feet flat, his knees spread and turned his head toward Diego, speaking loudly to be heard. "It's such a kick to see mountains every day. You people who spend your lives in Monterrey don't know how special it is to look out your window and see amazing mountains."

Diego, who had been quiet during most of the trip, grinned. "I appreciate Monterrey. You don't give me enough credit. I know these hills. Yes, I know the trails, the roads, the people."

"I'm not putting you down, Diego. I am admiring these mountains. You've got canyons and deserts, and forests, and real mountains, not just hills. You should see Houston."

Diego cocked his head toward his passenger. "Never seen Houston. You're right. I know what I know and I know what I don't know."

Geoff laughed. "Houston is flat, not a hill in sight. Definitely no mountains. But we have our share of good things. We've got mosquitoes. We've got hurricanes. We've got plenty of water. We've got oil. Oil, brother Diego."

"Brag on, man. We all know you're rich."

Geoff smirked. "Loud and proud, that's me."

"Since you were a kid," replied Diego as he turned off the main road onto Geoff's property. After a few minutes on the bumpy dirt road, dust in his throat, Diego braked, the swinging metal gate in view ahead.

Both men got out of the Jeep. Diego walked forward and leaned on the hood. He pulled a cigarette from a pack in his shirt pocket, lit it and inhaled.

"Have anything more to tell me?" he asked.

Geoff walked slowly toward the metal gate scanning all within range. "Not a thing I haven't already told you."

"So, show me where the gunmen were standing."

Geoff pointed toward the Jeep. "You parked about where I parked. The robbers stood here, here and here." He pointed to each location, none more than a few feet apart. "I threw the car keys into the bushes over there. You can see where those I brushed against those bushes."

Diego blew smoke rings. He was not interested in the bushes where Geoff said he had thrown the car keys.

"Si, into the bushes. Can you describe these Mexicans?" He emphasized the last word, Mexicans.

Geoff said earnestly, "I wish I could. It was dark and to be honest, they were dark. They just blended into the background."

"How about the guy with the knife?"

"Yeah. He was tall and dark and younger. I think he had a lot of hair, but he had on a hat. Hell, I think they all had on hats. Look, Diego, I'd had a few drinks at the party. I wasn't exactly at my best."

Diego didn't move. He stared at Geoff, but Geoff's eyes were cast down. For a few moments, neither spoke. Geoff broke the silence.

"Look, I would like to get up to the house, take a shower and get out of these stinking clothes. When have you known me to like playing in the mud?"

Geoff climbed into the Jeep, waited while Diego rubbed out his cigarette with the heel of his boot.

In silence they drove from the gate deeper into the estate. Traditionally-built in Spanish style, the hacienda buildings were enclosed by a wall. The personal life of the property occurred inside the walls. The view at entry was of a strong wall with ornately carved heavy double doors installed in center front. Colorful pottery plates surrounded the door frame adding a touch of homeliness in the midst of utilitarian strength.

The building that housed the Wilkins family was surrounded by the walls. It was two stories, u-shaped, built around a tiled courtyard. Las Palmas was its fitting name. Majestic Royal palms reigned over the front garden. Full flowering hibiscus bushes lined the walkway from the double doors of the protective wall to the colonnaded main house. This part of the property was lush, green, watered as needed by the current staff gardener.

"You don't need to come in with me. I don't need a babysitter, Diego. Like I said, I want a shower and a good sleep."

"I'll need that information about the jewelry and the papers on the car."

"I'm sure I can find paperwork. Appraisals were done for the insurance company. We probably have copies down here in the files. Hell, I just bought the car so everything you need should be on top of the desk." Geoff was opening the unlocked doors to his inner sanctuary. "I'll bring that to you tomorrow. I'd like to be able to tell the insurance company that you have all the information you need. I want to get the business finished as soon as possible and have this behind me."

"Geoff, take care of yourself. You're in Monterrey, not in Houston."

"What the hell does that mean? I know where I am, and I know what I'm doing. Hasta luego."

Diego ground the Jeep into gear and peeled off, leaving a dust trail behind him. Geoff didn't see it as he was already inside his Eden having closed the solid double doors behind him.

Instead of walking directly into the house, he passed through the hibiscus bushes and made an immediate left turn paralleling the colonnade. He walked to a corner and turned right, then lengthened his stride until he had passed the main house. Another twenty paces and he confronted an outbuilding that served as a tool shed and garage for the estate.

"Edo, Eduardo, are you in there?"

A tall, thin man about Geoff's age, maybe older, wearing rugged outdoor clothes and a straw hat, appeared at the door "Looking for me, boss?"

Chapter 31

"Where are we headed, boss?" asked Edo sitting alongside Geoff who had his right foot pressed against the gas pedal of the old Ford. They had just pulled onto the hardtop road that ran directly south from Las Palmas. The sun was climbing in the sky portending a warm day. Geoff found sunglasses tucked behind the visor and put them on.

"Maybe you don't need to know," said Geoff. "Maybe it is better if you don't know."

"Maybe it is better that I know what I'm headed into," Edo replied. "You look like you have trouble on your mind."

"Yeah, it could be trouble, but I think I have everything under control. Those shotguns on the rack, you'd best get them down and be sure they're loaded. We may need them."

Edo did as he was told. He leaned over the small backseat and one at a time, he maneuvered the two shotguns from the clips that held them in place against the back window of the truck. He reached into the glove box for ammo and rapidly loaded one of the shotguns. The other one was already loaded.

When he finished, Edo said, "It would be better if you told me what we're headed into."

"I've dealt with these guys before and they are tough. They'll be armed. We're meeting them at the roadside taqueria, that barely-standing taco place, about fifty miles south of here, just over the line from Nuevo Leon."

"Okay, so you don't want Diego Gonzalez involved? Who are we meeting?"

"Right. I don't want Diego involved. He's got no power outside Nuevo Leon." Geoff pulled off the road at a small stand where two men were sitting, their hats low over their eyes. He reached into the glove compartment for an envelope containing pesos, and then he and Edo got out of the truck.

"You got any beer? Cerveza, por favor. Dos." One of the Mexicans reached into a cooler and grabbed two bottles, exchanging them for some of Geoff's money. While Edo held onto the bottles, Geoff walked behind some low bushes and emptied his full bladder then returned to the truck where he and Edo drank in silence.

Back on the road, Geoff sped along avoiding the many soft spots on the road where the tar had melted and formed sticky, bumpy ridges on an otherwise flat surface.

"Okay, I'll tell you what's going on. I am planning on meeting with three men who've done some work for me. They've got my car and some of my belongings."

"Doesn't sound like you got the strong end of the deal," Edo commented.

"Yeah. I got the deal I wanted but these guys screwed up one thing. I told them they could keep the car and Jeananne's jewelry, but I never said they could keep my ring. They shouldn't have taken that ring. I guess they didn't hear that part of the deal. They got overexcited last night and took more than the sons-of-guns were entitled to and I intend to get my property back."

Edo knew Geoff well to envision the scene Geoff was describing, at least in outline. "I don't have to know how deep the well is to know it's wet," he reminded himself. He couldn't quite see how these men Geoff was talking about could have stolen all the jewelry but left Geoff with his ring. What Geoff expected didn't make sense but he wasn't about to question his boss. The larger question loomed. Why had Geoff allowed his car and Jeananne's jewelry to be stolen?

Edo silently turned these questions over in his mind, then said, "Geoff, I don't need to know everything. You know I've got you covered, but do these three guys have names? Maybe I know them."

"Probably. One of them worked for my family years ago, right after Dad bought the hacienda. They had some sort of dispute. I think one of them or both of them was drunk and Jorge drew a gun on my father. That did it. You know my father wouldn't allow him to stay on the property after that."

"You're talking about Jorge Manuel. I remember him and how furious your father was at the time. So, Jorge is still alive. Surprising. You caught up with him?"

"Yeah. I went looking for him and it turns out he was not that hard to find. I had this job I wanted done. I figured that anyone brave enough to draw a gun on my dad could do the job I had in mind."

"Who'd you have killed?" Edo asked.

"No one. He did the job and no one got hurt. In fact, I think my life is going to improve now that Jorge did the job, even if he did screw up and take my ring."

"What's so important about your ring?"

"It was the one I got for my birthday, from my parents. They will kill me if I don't have it."

"You're scared of your parents? For God's sake, Geoff, how old are you?"

"It's the principle of the thing. I'm drawing a line. These guys took something that was mine and I'm getting it back."

"You said they took Jeananne's jewelry."

"Doesn't count. I wanted them to take that stuff."

"Do you mind telling me what all of this is about," asked Edo as he sat with two shotguns, butted on the floor of the truck.

"Do you remember Eddie Barga?"

"Si. Bastardo."

"He's threatening me over money he says I owe him. Gambling debts. I told him I would pay but he is not a patient man," Geoff said looking over at Edo. "He's also a greedy man, always wants his money."

"You had Jorge Manuel steal Jeananne's jewelry. What's the play?" Edo asked, and then the light bulb went off, "I get it. It's about insurance. You gringos are big on insurance. Will the pay-out be big enough for Eddie?"

"Yes. Eddie's waiting for it. He knows if he hurts me or kills me, he'll have no chance of getting his money. Right now, my plan is working. I've convinced Diego. He'll write a believable report that I'll forward to the insurance company and voila, I'll get my money. It's a shame I have to turn over most of it to Eddie." Geoff laughed. "I wish we had gotten two more beers."

"We can get them at the taqueria," Edo said smiling. "Just one thing bothers me about this. Why didn't you get Sam to give you the money? You could have paid off Eddie and kept your car."

"Dad shut off the tap, said I was on my own. I tried to work on Mother but she wouldn't cross Dad. Stuck. They left me stuck. I sometimes wonder how they expect me to live."

The taqueria was a wooden building that looked as dusty and dry as the ground surrounding it. The structure sat close to the ground, its entrance just a few feet from the road. There was no parking lot to speak of, just dirt and a few handfuls of gravel. A truck was parked on the side, its front tires pointed toward the building. Its license plate was crooked and wires were hanging down below the back left tail light.

"They're here," Geoff said. "I recognize that piece-of-crap truck."

"Park right in front, up against the building. Keep the key in the ignition. There's no traffic on the road." Edo handed one of the shotguns to Geoff and kept one for himself.

Geoff followed Edo's direction. When Edo opened the passenger door, he needed only to take one small step to be inside the taqueria. Geoff followed casually carrying his shotgun. Edo was more alert.

Inside were three tables and an ersatz kitchen, a counter separating the two areas. On the counter was a sign advertising the special of the day, Conchi's burritos, homemade. The shelf attached to the back was filled with bottles of every brand of tequila, whiskey, and sweet liquors made of cactus and berries unknown outside Mexico.

A woman, presumably Conchi, stood behind the counter. She looked warily at Edo and the blonde gringo Geoff as they entered. They were not regulars and they were armed, two facts that led her to back away from the counter.

"No problemas," she said, "no trouble."

Edo positioned his body to face the three men seated at one of the tables. They were the only customers in the place. To Conchi, he said "We don't want any trouble. This fellow here has business with these three."

Jorge Manual smiled at Geoff. "We thought we would see you. You want to go back on your deal?"

"No," said Geoff, "I plan to keep my deal. You got my wife's jewelry and the car. Keep them. That's what we agreed to. You got one piece of my property that I want back, the onyx ring, my ring. You were supposed to take her jewelry, not mine."

"Man wants his ring," taunted Jorge, grinning at his two companions. "Which ring would that be?"

Jorge waved his right hand before his face, palm inward, taunting Geoff. The understated dullness of the onyx stone was like a red cape to a bull.

"You son-of-a-bitch," said Geoff. "Don't play with me. Do you know who I am?"

"Pretty ring. Expensive, I'd say." Jorge continued to grin.

"Not part of our bargain," Geoff said, his voice getting louder.

Edo placed his finger on the trigger of his shotgun, wiggling it slightly as though to prepare it for action.

"Who says I have to give you something that is mine?"

"I say," said Edo, now pointing the shotgun at Jorge.

Jorge sat unmoving but the two men with him stood and held their hands away from their bodies.

"No guns here," said one of them.

Geoff pointed his gun at Jorge also.

"You can only kill me once," laughed Jorge. "Take your fancy ring. I'd rather have one that has a little shine to it."

Jorge dropped the ring into Geoff's extended hand and Geoff put it in his pocket.

"And the other ring. The one you took off my wife's hand," demanded Geoff, feeling emboldened now that he had his own ring in his possession.

"You are going back on our deal," Jorge snarled his lip as though he had come across a dead animal on the road.

Geoff nodded to Edo and the two men slowly began raising their shotguns.

"Okay, you win. Which ring? There was more than one, but I don't have them here. Go get them," Jorge nodded his head at his two companions who together ran quickly past Edo and out the door.

"Conchi, beers while we wait," Geoff said to the woman behind the counter.

Conchi opened two bottles of beer and set them on the counter.

Edo began inching himself out the curtained door. He placed one foot outside, peered through the opening and saw two or three men coming in the direction of the taqueria. He nodded to Geoff, "Trouble outside."

Shots were fired. First man down was Jorge Manuel. Edo began firing toward the approaching men as he and Geoff ran into the truck, both sliding through the passenger door, Edo first. With heads down, Edo peeled out, tires screeching, Geoff shooting out the window.

"Thankfully this old truck still has life in it," Geoff hollered as Edo pressed the pedal for more speed. "Are they following us?"

"Not that I can see," Edo replied. "You're not hurt?"

"No, but we might have lost Jorge," Geoff said and pushed his lower lip out in a childlike pout. "So sad," he added.

"You got your ring back. Was it worth it?"

"Hell, yes. It's a family heirloom."

"I better put some men around the house tonight," Edo said.

"Probably a good idea. I'm staying at the hacienda tonight and tomorrow I'm moving into town."

"And your wife?" asked Edo.

"She's already in Houston."

Chapter 32

"Won't this truck go any faster?" Geoff shouted toward Edo who was driving. Both windows were down allowing air to blow into the cab creating a hot and dry cross-current that teased the sweat forming on Geoff's face.

When Edo didn't reply, Geoff again shouted, "Faster, Edo, can't you go any faster?"

Edo kept his eyes on the road, breaking his concentration only to check his rear-view mirror.

Geoff leaned toward the driver, preening his neck to get a view of the speedometer.

"What are you doing?" Edo frowned as he pushed Geoff aside.

"Trying to figure out how fast we are going."

"As fast as we can. My foot is on the floor. No one's behind us which isn't to say we're home free."

"I just wish we had brought those two beers with us," Geoff said and grinned at Edo.

It was late afternoon when Edo turned off the road onto Wilkins's property. He was sure that they had not been followed. As he was driving, he was working out his plan. He was sure the taqueria woman would telephone police. He and Geoff had not hidden their faces. She would probably be too scared to describe them accurately. She would be scared of Jorge's men too. Yes, she would claim ignorance. She would know nothing.

But Jorge was not alone. He didn't operate alone. His men would want revenge. They would come after Geoff, and Edo. They wouldn't stop until they got even. Someone would have to die for Jorge. As best as Edo could understand, Jorge's men had Geoff's fancy new car and they had jewelry to sell. Maybe the car was already broken down into parts or sold and the jewelry out of their hands. None of that mattered because Geoff didn't want the car or Jeananne's jewelry. He did want his ring enough to kill a guy. Crazy gringo,

Edo thought. They get rich and then they want more. It's not my business. My job is to keep myself and Geoff alive.

These thoughts were filling Edo's brains during the travel from the taqueria to the hacienda. Now was the time to put his plans into action. He nudged Geoff who had been sleeping while he taunted and teased the truck to improve its performance.

Noticing Geoff's drooping shoulders and squinting eyes, he suggested Geoff might want to shut himself inside the hacienda, and go down for more sleep.

"Aside from this snooze in the truck, how long has it been since you slept?" he asked Geoff.

"I've lost track," said the already half-asleep Geoff. "I think maybe two days."

"We need you alert in case trouble comes. It will come. Before you slip into that bed, you need to round-up whatever weapons are in the house. I'll take care of extra talent for outside. Go while it is quiet. You may need your energy later."

After dropping Geoff off at the front gate, he pulled the truck around to the side of hacienda where it would not be visible to anyone entering from the main driveway.

Geoff obeyed, shuffling into the house, locking the door behind him, confident that Edo would take care of lining up men to patrol the property. He fell on the first sofa he saw and within minutes was sleeping as though he were a fully clothed, booted dead man.

When he woke up, it was dark and Edo was standing nearby with two holstered guns and a shotgun crooked over his right elbow.

"What's the story, Edo?" Geoff didn't move from his prone position on the sofa. He was lying on his back, his legs strangely buckled at the knees to enable his tall frame to fit his makeshift bed. As he waited for Edo's response, he shifted his weight and sat up shaking his head to clear the cobwebs. Looking at Edo's shadowed silhouette, his first thought was that he was glad Edo was on his side.

"You're ready for a fight? How many guys do we have?" Geoff said.

"We had twenty men shacking up in the bunkhouses, another ten with the cattle. The twenty are working in shifts outside the wall. Two men are walking the house."

"Everyone is armed?"

Geoff couldn't see Edo's frowning face in the darkness. "Is Mexico hot in the summer?"

"While you're doing your thing, I've got business to take care of." Geoff rose from the sofa and stiffly walked toward the back of the house. He had no difficulty finding his room in the dark. His mother had assigned a new, larger room for him when he married but she sentimentally retained his childhood bedroom intact. It was in the boy's room that Geoff now sought refuge. He looked longingly at the bed but thought better of lying down for fear that he would immediately fall asleep.

Realizing that his clothes and adult personal belongings were upstairs, he backed out of the room with its cowboy-themed wallpaper and reorienting himself sought out the bedroom on the upper floor where he stripped his clothes off, throwing to the floor the white trousers with the stain from the party that seemed to have occurred years ago. He showered quickly, reviving himself in the cold water. Toweled at the waist, he reached across the bed to the telephone and dialed a familiar number.

"Oh my God! It's you! Finally! I've been so worried about you. Are you okay? How did it go with the sheriff? What's happening?" Liz's voice was clear and insistent. Geoff imagined that she was propped up in bed by pillows, the phone beside her. He also imagined her wearing her turquoise dressing gown, sheer except for a ribbon that tied at her neck.

"Geoff, are you there? Talk to me."

"I'm okay. I've had a bit of trouble. You know about the robbery? Have you heard from Harold?"

"Yes, Harold telephoned and said he and Jeananne are in Houston. He turned Jeananne over to the maid. All is well on that front. When will I see you?"

"Maybe not tonight. We may be under siege."

"From Eddie? Surely he isn't in Monterrey." She corrected herself, "No, I guess he wouldn't come. He would send his men."

"No, not from Eddie. I'm taking care of that problem. He won't bother me. At least not yet. The problem at the moment is some Mexicans." Geoff was trying to figure out how much to tell Liz. He decided not to say more about his current difficulties. "Don't worry about me. I don't want you getting frown lines worrying about me." Geoff could sense Liz pouting on the other end of the line. "Don't fret over me. I have to come into town tomorrow to do business with Diego. Why don't I come over to your place afterwards?" It was more of a statement than a question.

"Oh, sweetheart. I won't see you until tomorrow? I guess I had better get a good night's sleep tonight so I'll be ready for you."

"Keep talking like that and I'll come right now."

"Bye for now, you sexy man," Liz blew kisses into the phone.

Liz's Mississippi accent ringing in his ears, Geoff went into his bathroom and splashed water on his face. He hadn't shaved in two days and wasn't sure he liked the stubble rapidly covering his cheeks and chin. What was the sense of shaving now? He looked at himself again in the mirror and decided he looked good. As he stood there studying the shape of his nose, the fullness of his lips, his sandy blonde hair parted on one side and swooped over his forehead in a wave, he decided for a fellow past forty, he could pass for thirty-five.

Chapter 33

The staccato sharp and loud pop awakened Geoff to sunlight pouring into his hacienda bedroom through an undraped window near the ceiling. He lay completely still, his body tensed by the sound of the single gunshot, his heart rate rapid as he abruptly realized it was daytime and he was in danger. Events of the last two days embodied in places and people's faces flooded his memory in no particular order, the taqueria, the ring, Liz, the expat party, Diego, Edo. Edo, reliable and capable, fearless even, would have everything under control. That thought allowed Geoff to relax slightly.

He slid his hand under the pillow on the right side of the bed and grasped the loaded gun that had been his sleep mate. Lifting his body from its prone position, planting his feet on the floor, the gun firmly in his grasp, he stood and briefly held his breath, listening for sounds of intruders, hoping to hear Edo's voice of reassurance.

There were no sounds.

Geoff quietly closed and locked the heavy bedroom door sequestering himself in his upstairs refuge. He tiptoed across the room and sat in a chair facing the door, ready to shoot whoever managed to get it open.

In the quiet, Geoff heard the crowing of a rooster. He glanced at a clock and saw that it was mid-morning. He realized he had slept for twelve hours during which apparently there was no siege, unless the gunshot that awakened him was the beginning of an attack. But there had only been one pop. Trying to form a scenario to explain the noiseless night and the abrupt awakening, Geoff decided he possibly was not at risk, at least not at risk at that moment.

He rose, opened the door and stepped cautiously out into the upper hallway. Sunshine was beaming through a skylight illuminating the stairway. Looking up Geoff could see large cumulus clouds overhead. A sense of normality overcame him and he casually released the tension in his right hand.

"Edo, are you there?" he yelled into the stairwell.

"Eating breakfast," was the reply. "You're awake. Come down. I'll fix you some eggs."

Geoff returned to his bedroom, placed the gun on the bed and walked into his bathroom where he slowly completed his morning toilette, shaving the stubble that he had examined the night before, and dressing in clean slacks and blue cotton shirt. Looking for boots, he remembered they were downstairs where he had crashed on the sofa. Grabbing his gun, he descended the stairs and after booting up, he joined Edo in the kitchen.

"Where's the cook?" Geoff asked noting her absence.

"We sent all the house servants home," Edo informed him. "Too dangerous. I don't want the men spending their time guarding the cook or the housemaids."

"I can't believe how hungry I am. Give me some of those eggs," said Geoff, satisfied with Edo's explanation. "I guess I can live without a cook. I can get some food in town. Smells pretty good in here now."

Edo scooped scrambled eggs from a skillet and shoved the plate toward Geoff. He stood at the stove, his double holster around his narrow waist. He seemed intent on his task.

"I'm not the best cook, but I can scramble an egg. If you looked in the closet, you'd see plenty of provisions. I don't think you'll go hungry. Have you got the stomach for jalapeños in the eggs? I like mine hot."

"No peppers in mine. As long as I have Tabasco, I'm fine."

Between bites of soft buttery eggs that Geoff had generously dotted with red Tabasco pepper sauce, fork in hand Geoff asked Edo about the gunshot that had awakened him.

"You heard it, huh? It was one of the boys killing a snake. We patrolled all night and no one tried to get onto the property. Most of the guys are in the bunkhouse now. I don't expect them to surprise us in daylight."

"That's a relief. Maybe Jorge's guys are satisfied with their haul." Geoff reached for the coffee pot boiling on the back burner of the stove and poured himself a mug of the strong, dark brew. "I need this," he said and handed the pot to Edo who poured a mug for himself.

Since neither man had more to say about the lack of an attack, they drank coffee in silence, each lost in thought. Neither said anything about the probability that Jorge Manuel was dead. Neither said anything about the probability that his men would seek revenge.

Geoff was the first to speak. "I don't think we should let up on the patrol, especially at night. You'll keep that going tonight?"

Edo nodded in consent.

"I have to go into town on business."

"Need me to come along?"

"No. I'll need one of the trucks though. Maybe you can find one that is a little snazzier than the one we used yesterday." Geoff stood, smiling at Edo.

"Sure, boss, how about the one your dad drives when he's down here? Will that do? Your decision." Edo looked blankly at Geoff, a look that said he wasn't empowered to make decisions that involved Sam's property.

"That'll work. Bring it around to the front in about half an hour." Geoff removed himself from the kitchen, leaving his plate and mug for Edo to clean. He walked into the den and began searching a file cabinet for copies of jewelry purchase receipts and appraisals. Congratulating himself for having those copies made and for bringing them from Houston to Monterrey, he began humming a song he had heard on the radio of his now-stolen convertible. He did a little hip-swivel and thinking he looked pretty sexy, told himself he would show Liz his new talent. If Elvis can do it, so can Geoff Wilkins.

Then he remembered he needed the ownership documents for the car. Those were easy to find because the car was a recent purchase and the papers were still on the desk, unfiled.

Placing the all the collected papers in the zippered pouch that contained the manual for the car, he did another hip-swivel while strumming an air guitar.

"I just wanna be your teddy bear," he sang.

Chapter 34

The telephone rang as Geoff was starting to walk through the door. In an automatic gesture, he turned to answer it.

"We just heard what happened to you. Glad you and Jeananne weren't harmed. You both are okay, right?" The voice was recognizable to Geoff, one of his oil business buddies, Mike Cavanaugh, the owner of a successful oil-drilling company also based in Houston.

"We're okay. Harold took Jeananne back to Houston. Has the word gotten around?"

"Yes. We want to help. I already called the Sheriff's office and spoke to Diego Gonzalez just to let him know how much it means to the expat community and to the Monterrey economy to have us Americans protected. I also talked with the mayor. We have to make our voices heard. Hell, I'll call our senator if I have to because we have to be able to be assured of safety for ourselves and families if they expect our money down here. Your name is on that building at the University. No one should mess with you."

"Mike, it was probably just some punk Mexican kids who wanted a new car."

"They got that new car and I heard they got some of Jeananne's jewelry, probably worth more than a hill of beans. You're insured of course, through someone in Houston?"

"Yes, in Houston. I'm on my way now to Diego's office to pick up the crime report. I thought I would send it up to my man along with the rest of the paperwork. Do you happen to know if anyone is flying up to Houston today or tomorrow? Who's got their plane down here?"

"Geoff, my plane is here. If it can wait until tomorrow, I'm sending one of my men up north. We've got some equipment in Port Arthur that needs attention and no one seems to know what to do about it. They'll fly into Houston Hobby Airport, pick up one of the mechanical fellows, and then head over to the installation that is mucked up. If you give me the name of the agent, I'll have the envelope couriered to your agent from Hobby. He'll have your claim tomorrow."

"Mike, I owe you. I'll leave the papers with Diego. Had any experience filing claims? I don't want the money to get hung up in some bureaucratic red tape. It's my money after all."

"It's better if your insurance is all with one outfit. That way they would lose the premiums for your business insurance if they failed to pay out satisfactorily on your personal insurance. At least, that's how I've always seen the matter."

"Good. My father set it up and I'm sure he did it that way. Dad's always been able to get what he wanted out of those insurance guys."

"I don't think you should give it a second thought. They'll take good care of you and I'll help you out, too. We'll pick up the papers tomorrow and get them to Houston for you. Just write the information on an envelope so we know where to have the courier take them. There's more than one way to skin a cat." The two men laughed congratulating themselves for their ability to face a problem and to solve it quickly and efficiently. "Hopefully you won't be out of pocket for long. Are you staying down here or are you going back to Houston any time soon?"

"I'm not sure but at the moment I'm thinking I might stay in Mexico for a while, maybe not in Monterrey. I feel like I want a bit of a break from the office and the scene in Houston. Harold is holding down the fort. He'll take care of the easy matters, that is, if we ever have anything easy to deal with, and the tough stuff will wait until I return. Besides, the police might need me."

"Good thinking. Don't worry about the delivery of your claim. I'll see to it for you. Won't keep you any longer. Love to Jeananne." With that Mike Cavanaugh solved a problem for Geoff and without knowing, helped Geoff determine his next move.

Geoff examined the Rolodex on the desk, found the entry for his Houston insurance agent. He stuffed all his collected documents into a large envelope and carefully wrote the address on the outside. Thinking perhaps he should contact the agent personally, he picked up the phone and dialed the international operator, sat and waited until the call to Houston was completed.

His Las Palmas tasks completed, Geoff strode out of the house and crossed the lawn to find his father's truck parked outside the wall surrounding the estate. He slid into the driver's seat, removing the handgun from his waistband and placing it on the seat beside him. When he drove through the property, he noted two of his men patrolling the perimeter. One tipped his hat as Geoff drove past.

Once on the main road into town, Geoff realized he was alone, that Edo was not backing him up. Anxiously, Geoff drove, scanning the mirrors, aware of parked vehicles along the route, aware of groups of men sitting in front of the occasional cafe, aware of cars and trucks passing him on the road or trailing behind him.

As he approached the city, traffic increased. Donkeys vied for space with motorcycles, trucks, and cars. Mostly older men were tending the donkey carts, a reminder of early Mexico, pre-Revolution Mexico, and pre-World War II agrarianism. Roads recently paved were making way for the progress that Monterrey anticipated with its growing attraction to North American business.

Geoff weaved his way through the traffic, passing construction sites and outdoor markets. His destination was the small concrete block building that housed the State Police and the office of his childhood friend now Comandante Gonzalez. Geoff parked and entered the empty lobby. He had been in this very space twenty-four hours earlier, but had not noticed how spare it was. He had not seen the cactus plants in the one aluminum-framed window. He had not seen the framed drawings of the new office, now being built adjacent to the Municipal Courts.

When, after a few seconds of reorienting himself, no one appeared to acknowledge his presence, he lost patience, and walked down a hallway to the room he knew to be Diego's office.

"Hola. I didn't expect to see you here today. Get some sleep?" Diego looked up from the report that he had been examining.

"No one was out front," Geoff explained.

"No, everyone is busy today."

"I want to get a copy of the police report to send up to Houston. Is it ready?"

"Yes, I'll get it for you," Diego rummaged through the various loose sheets of paper until he found the right one.

Geoff took the copy that was his and placed it in the envelope he had brought with him. He explained that Mike Cavanaugh or one of his employees would be picking it up later that day or the next.

Expecting that information was the completion of their business, Diego indicated their conversation was over but Geoff continued to stand shifting his weight from one leg to the other.

"Was there something else, Geoff?" asked Diego.

"Yes. I wondered if you had any leads on the robbery. Did you want to fill me in? Anything new in the barrio?"

"I don't have anything to report. One of our suspects was killed yesterday over in Tamaulipas. I got a call about it this morning. Sit down. Know anything about it?" Diego opened the desk drawer and tossed his pen into it. Placing his elbows against the rim of the desk, he lay his hands palm down in front of him as though to keep the papers from blowing or flying away. He looked directly at Geoff.

"Don't know anything about Tamaulipas," Geoff said, mispronouncing the name of the coastal state adjacent to Nuevo Leon. He tried to appear disinterested but could not stop himself from asking for more details. "Who got killed?" he asked.

"A fellow named Jorge Manuel."

"I guess you don't have any witnesses. That would make your job too easy. In Mexico, there are never any witnesses."

"You're right about that," responded Diego. "By the way, what's your plan? Are you going back to Houston?"

"I don't have a plan yet but Edo will be at Las Palmas and he can always get hold of me."

The two men nodded to each other and Geoff, having killed the proverbial two birds, left feeling unburdened by the law. His greatest conundrum was whether to go directly to Liz's home or to stop on the way for coffee.

Chapter 35

Geoff parked in front of Liz's house in Barrio Antiguo just as the bells from the neighborhood church were ringing, reminding him that it was midday and he was hungry. He parted the beaded curtain that served as a warm-weather door and stepped into the dark interior. Liz had several plants scattered around the room mostly displayed in colorful pots. On the floor were rag rugs in reds and yellows and a rich blue that matched bottles sitting on a windowsill. Geoff struggled to recall how many hours it had been since he was in this space.

Hearing Geoff, Liz called out from the back of the house inviting Geoff to join her.

"I'm having a snack. Come on back," she said.

"A way to a man's heart," laughed Geoff wrapping his arms around her as she nibbled on sliced carrots.

"My mouth's full," Liz mumbled, managing to pout.

"You call this food? We're in Mexico where we have great food and you're eating carrots?"

"I was hoping you would take me out to lunch," Liz lowered her head slightly, opened her eyes wide, and looked flirtatiously at Geoff.

"Sure, lunch can be on the menu, I mean, on the schedule. Hell, I don't know what I mean." He began caressing her hair, leaned down and kissed her.

"Okay," she said laughing, "I get the message. I'll see your kiss and raise you…hmmm, I never was a poker player."

"I know what I'll raise," Geoff said playfully.

Liz broke free and ran to the bedroom with Geoff following in chase. They made it to the bed, throwing off clothes and making love as though it were a game.

"I see robbery hasn't slowed you down," Liz teased. She sat up in bed and pulled her knees up to her chin.

"You are gorgeous," Geoff said, pushing the odd shoe off the bed onto the floor. "You are gorgeous and I am hungry. I wish I could move. Wouldn't it be wonderful if sex left us feeling energetic instead of making us feel sleepy?"

"I'm not sleepy," said Liz.

"Watch out, here I come."

Geoff reached for her and within minutes they were both asleep.

Later, over lunch at a cafe around the corner from Liz's home, Geoff told Liz that he wanted to leave town and he wanted her to go with him. He told her that he wanted to put the robbery behind him. With Jeananne in Houston and Harold looking after Wilcarco, now was the time for the two of them to escape, to have some time to themselves without anyone intruding.

"What about Eddie Barga and what about the Mexican trouble you mentioned?" Liz asked.

"There is nothing I can do about Eddie until I get the money from the insurance claim. "Geoff explained about Mike Cavanaugh's offer of help delivering the claim to the Houston insurer.

"That was gracious of him," offered Liz and asked again about the Mexican trouble.

"Edo will take care of it. Let's get out of town, go somewhere. Edo can call me when the insurance money arrives. I asked for the check to be sent to me in Monterrey."

"Why did you do that?"

"Because I don't know how long I will want to stay here and I want that money in my hands."

Liz let the matter pass. "Where shall we go?"

"Where do you want to go? I want to go where there is action and a lot of people. We can get lost in the crowds."

"Let's go to Mexico City," Liz suggested. "What do you think? When do you want to go?"

"I like the idea of Mexico City. Let's go today. We can catch a flight easily enough. I have to take the truck back to Las Palmas and pack a few things. Can you lock up your house and leave early this evening?"

"I think I can. I like this spontaneity. It's exciting. I'll telephone Harold and give him some explanation. Any ideas what I should say?"

"No, darlin', you're better at dealing with Harold than I am when it comes to personal matters, but ask him to tell Jeananne I'm staying in Mexico until the robbery business is sorted out. As highly as he thinks of Jeananne, I doubt that would be a problem for him. There's nothing else she needs to know. She'll just spend her time sitting around the pool or gossiping with Martha or my mother. She won't even know I'm gone."

Liz knew better than to engage in conversation with her lover about his wife. She guessed that Jeananne would figure it out. She would have suspicions about his behavior, particularly when she learned that Liz was also staying in Mexico. Let the chips fall where they may, thought Liz.

"I'll meet you at the airport," Liz said.

They agreed on a time, finished their lunch, and walked back to Liz's house in Old Town.

By ten o'clock that night, they were checked into a hotel in Mexico City. Having enjoyed dinner and a sufficient number of bourbon highballs during the flight from Monterrey, they were both too tired to unpack.

Over nine hundred miles away, Jeananne hung up her telephone. She told herself, in another life, at another time, I would cry and feel sorry for myself, then I would feel guilty, that bad things happening were my fault, but not tonight. I'm a sophisticated adult now. (Jeananne laughed to herself when this thought passed through her mind.) I've grown up living among wealthy, generous people. I've truly grown up. I'm not the little girl from Northwest Arkansas that I was all those years ago. I have a brain. I have a house. I have people around me who love me. What I don't have is a faithful husband. What am I going to do about it?

Jeananne was tempted to telephone Martha, her mentor and confidante and friend, but she realized that it was late and she wanted to have time to absorb what she had learned from Harold. He had not said outright that Liz and Geoff were having an affair, but what would you expect from Harold? He would think the best of his wife and his business partner, but even so Jeananne had detected the uncertainty and a touch of sadness in Harold's voice. Harold didn't deserve a wife who cheated.

Jeananne turned on her television and let herself be distracted by a new late night TV host, Jack Paar. She wasn't sure if she liked him, but for a few minutes she was able to forget about her problems.

Chapter 36

"Rosa, if you weren't working as a housekeeper, what would you be doing? No, that's not the question I want to ask. I'll rephrase it. What do you want to do with your life? What are your dreams?"

Jeananne was at her desk writing checks, paying for mundane household expenses. Long ago in her marriage she had realized that money management was not Geoff's strong point. Fearing overdrafts and unpaid bills, she told Geoff that she liked dealing with money matters and would remove the burden of daily affairs from his plate of responsibilities. With agreement from Sam and Martha, who were the controlling interests in Wilkins Enterprises, of which Geoff's business was a subsidiary, Jeananne arranged for Geoff's salary to be paid monthly directly into a household account. Both their names were on the account but Geoff rarely interfered with Jeananne's decisions about their day-to-day expenditures.

Jeananne assumed that Geoff had additional access to money through the subsidiary although she understood that Harold Carter kept a close watch on the finances for that company, and rightly so, as he co-owned the company with Geoff. It was common knowledge among the family members that Geoff was the beloved of his parents who had been ever eager to indulge him. Geoff never complained to her about money and she kept her eyes closed and never asked about the source of funds for his extravagances. She told herself that Geoff probably got his "walking around money" from her and his "other" money from Sam.

Rosa entered the office smiling. "I thought you might want some coffee. Shall I bring some to you? I just took galletas out of the oven."

"Wedding cookies? Yum, my favorites. No, don't bring food in here. I'll come into the kitchen. Just give me a minute to write the last of the checks."

Rosa left and Jeananne quickly finished her bill-paying, stamping then stacking the envelopes on the desk, ready for posting. She had been home from

Monterrey for a week and had not heard about Geoff except through Harold who had talked with Liz directly after the robbery.

She felt conflict about what she should do about her current marital situation. She knew in her deepest soul that Geoff was lost to her, that he was lost at least for now. If she were honest with herself, she had known for some time that her marriage was not, and here she struggled for a word, heavenly, perfect, working. Jeananne wasn't sure her marriage had ever been "heavenly" or "perfect," but then she was sure she had never seen a perfect marriage, certainly not her parent's marriage. Maybe Miriam and Sam had a perfect marriage but Jeananne didn't see herself as being submissive like Miriam. She knew Miriam was loved and had everything she wanted in the way of house and clothes and jewelry. She thought Miriam was happy even, but she simply wasn't like Miriam. And Geoff wasn't Sam.

Jeananne had never met Martha's husband, Wendell. He had already passed away by the time Jeananne met Martha and became part of the family. Martha spoke lovingly of him, but Jeananne had not seen them first-hand as a couple.

When Jeananne thought of Geoff in Mexico with Liz, she could not imagine how they spent their days. She could imagine how they spent their nights, but when those images came to mind, she tried to suppress them. She remembered some of the teachings of her father about forgiveness and she decided that a good wife should support and forgive her husband's transgressions. But these recollections were clouded by her feelings of pain and dissatisfaction and by her nagging feelings of inadequacy and guilt that she had done something to cause her husband to stray.

She wandered into the kitchen, pulled along by the aromas of Rosa's cooking and she allowed herself to swallow her confused feelings.

Rosa seemed pleased to have Jeananne with her in the kitchen. The two women had a sense of comfort with each other. Jeananne had no secrets from Rosa who had witnessed Jeananne's awkward early years of living with the Wilkins family. Rosa herself spent her adolescent years being molded into a useful servant to the family. In every sense both women belonged to the family and both were in subservient roles.

"You know just what I want!" exclaimed Jeananne. "Pour both of us some coffee and sit with me. Bring a tray of those cookies. I don't care about the calories!"

Rosa laughed as she piled a stack of cookies on a plate, poured two cups of coffee, gathered napkins, cream and sugar, coffee spoons, and delivered all to the table while Jeananne watched, impressed by Rosa's efficiency.

"You can do it all, Rosa," Jeananne mused. "Just for the heck of it, tell me, if you could do anything with your future, what would you do?"

"I have a job. I need to work," Rosa said.

"I mean, if you didn't have to work, to do housework, the cooking and cleaning and taking care of us, what would you do? What do you dream about?"

Rosa didn't answer. She remembered her mother teaching her that she was an employee, not an equal.

Jeananne persisted. "Come on, I know you work for me, but if you didn't have to work for me, which I know you love to do, what would you do that you dream about doing? For instance, I dream about running Wilkins Enterprise. Don't tell anyone I said that, but I do. I dream about being important, making decisions that would make an impact on the world. Tell me, what do you dream about?"

"I would like to have my own panaderia, my own bakery. I like to cook for people, especially I like to bake dulces, sweet things, pastries. I would like to be my own boss." Rosa pushed the plate of cookies toward Jeananne who bit into one, cupping her hand under the cookie in an effort to catch the confectioner's sugar that cascaded to the table.

"Sorry about the mess. Don't get up. We can clean it up later," Jeananne said, using the side of her hand to brush the sugar off the side of the table onto a napkin.

"I'll clean it up," Rosa scooted her chair away from the table.

"Not yet. Stay with me. I want to know more about the bakery you dream about. I am really interested."

Jeananne lost herself in Rosa's dream.

"My father ran the confectionary for years. It was a good business, a lot of work, but a good business. That's what I would like, a good business where I am my own boss."

"There isn't a Mexican bakery anywhere near Oakside, is there?" asked Jeananne.

"No, but many Mexicans live in Oakside, in the big houses. They plan the food and do the shopping and the people who own the houses keep hiring them so they must like the food. I don't think the big house people always eat Southern fried chicken. I think they eat a lot of Mexican food."

"Your logic is wonderful. Since the cook is Mexican, the gringos eat Mexican food so why not open a Mexican bakery because you would have plenty of customers." Both women laughed at their simplicity. "Give me another cookie, please. I'll exercise later."

Chapter 37

Jeananne returned from dinner with Harold Carter, "two bachelors," he had called themselves cheerfully. Harold's good spirits were his second greatest asset, second only to his steady reliability. He had conversed positively throughout dinner about how smoothly the business was running, how he expected a profitable quarter because weather had been good with no hurricane disruptions and only one tropical storm to slow traffic. Wilcarco had not suffered due to Geoff's absence, he related, and Sam had checked in with him several times, the two men confidently had discussed the pros and cons of various crucial operational decisions which in all honesty, Harold said, he could have managed single-handedly.

Harold was perhaps the "perfect" man, Jeananne mused, curled up on a soft deeply cushioned chaise in her sitting room, a glass of French Chardonnay glistening in her left hand. She held it up to lamp light and swirled the wine enjoying its sparkle and beautiful pale color. He is kind and polite and capable.

Competing with thoughts of Harold's perfection and the glow of the wine, were comments that were made at dinner about Liz.

"She telephoned me from Mexico City last night," Harold revealed.

"I thought she was staying in Monterrey," said Jeananne whose curiosity forced her to pursue details. "You said she decided to stay in Monterrey because of some problem with the house that she needed to attend to. What is she doing in Mexico City?"

Jeananne's mind was spinning. Maybe Liz and Geoff weren't having an affair. Geoff was in Monterrey. At least that is what she thought. If Geoff was in Monterrey and Liz was in Mexico City, maybe Jeananne had rushed to the wrong conclusion.

"Liz said she was shopping and going to museums. She sounded like she was enjoying herself."

"Did she go to Mexico City alone?" Jeananne tried to ask the question without indicating how eager she was for the "right" answer.

"I'm sure she went alone. She didn't say anything about anyone being with her." The ease with which Harold shared this information made Jeananne feel guilty that she had suspicions about Liz and Geoff.

Jeananne picked up her telephone, dialed "O" and asked for the international operator. When the connection was completed, she found herself talking to Edo.

"Sorry it's so late, Edo. Why are you answering? Is Geoff there?"

"It isn't late, ma'am. I'm just looking after the property here. Is there anything I can do for you?"

"Yes, could I speak to Geoff?"

"He's in Mexico City."

"Oh. Did he say what he was doing in Mexico City?" Jeananne wanted information and she knew Edo was not the talkative sort.

"No. You know he does what he wants to do without telling me his business."

"Of course, Edo. Did he say when he would be back in Monterrey?"

"No."

"Okay, Edo. Is everything okay at the house?"

"Yes."

Jeananne rang off, a sour feeling growing in her stomach. It did not take a genius to figure out that both Geoff and Liz were in Mexico City together.

"Poor Harold," she thought. "He hasn't a clue."

The morning after Edo's revelation, Jeananne sat at her desk and reviewed her financial assets. She owned the house and the primary household bank account jointly with Geoff. Wilcarco was jointly owned by Geoff and Harold and she had no ownership stake in Wilkins Enterprises. One of the cars was in her name and she thought all of the jewelry was rightfully hers.

She unlocked the safe and removed several cases stacking them in front of her, then opened each to remind herself of the contents. She placed the beautiful, Tiffany diamond ring that had belonged to Miriam, on her left hand. It was after all her engagement ring. As spectacular as it was, she chose not to wear it every day but now was perhaps a time to rethink that decision. It would be a major asset if she and Geoff were to split up. The fabulous yellow diamond bracelet that Geoff gave her for an engagement present was also in the safe. She was tempted to remove all the jewelry but decided against it.

Also, in the safe were deeds to properties and stock certificates, most of which were in Geoff's name. Their wills were in sealed envelopes and she debated about opening Geoff's but decided against it.

If we were to divorce, I would want the house, the car that is mine, the jewelry and a settlement of some sort because I would need money to live on. I could work. I have work experience with Wilkins Enterprise.

With thoughts of divorce, Jeananne's mind began to fog and for a moment she sat twisting the Tiffany diamond ring on her finger, twisting, twisting. The phone interrupted her perseveration.

The caller was Martha with bad news. Jeananne grabbed her purse and keys and ran toward the garage, yelling en route to Rosa to explain the urgency.

It was late September, still warm enough in Houston to enjoy summer activities. Trees had not yet begun to change color and here and there in Oakside were sounds of yard work as lawns still needed mowing.

A beautiful vase of marigolds and asters from the garden graced a round table in the entry hall of Martha Wilkins's home.

Jeananne entered the home through the formal front entrance, something she rarely did, but she felt the gravity of the situation called for formality. She found Martha and Miriam seated in the reception room that once had impressed Jeananne because of its opulence. Miriam was crying. Martha was daubing her own face with tissues.

"I am so very sorry," Jeananne said, realizing the room was so vast that neither Martha nor Miriam would hear her unless she moved in closer to them. She went first to Miriam and repeated her condolence. Hearing Miriam's sobs, she began to choke up.

"Come, sit beside me," Martha said, reaching her hand out to Jeananne who leaned over and kissed Martha on the cheek.

"When did it happen?" asked Jeananne.

"The doctor telephoned about two hours ago and said that Faye had taken ill at home and died right after the ambulance arrived at the hospital. They tried to save her."

Miriam added through her tears, "So now it is only Martha and I. Our mother and father are gone and now, Faye. Faye was such a wonderful person."

Jeananne began to cry. "Aunt Faye was... she saved me."

Over tea laced with whiskey, the three women agreed that Martha and Jeananne would fly the next day to Little Rock, rent a car and drive to Elmore to make funeral arrangements and to handle Faye's affairs. Miriam did not feel strong enough to make the trip.

Chapter 38

Despite the sadness that necessitated their journey, Jeananne and Martha enjoyed the drive along Highway 64, a two-lane, hard-top major thoroughfare for lumber trucks and local traffic between Little Rock and Northwest Arkansas. Every little town en route had one or two stop lights, slowing them enough to see small stores and the occasional gas pump. Once they passed through Clarksville, the Ozark Mountains came into view.

At the town of Alma, they turned north on Highway 71, a road that was more familiar to Jeananne because Elmore Community where she lived was too small to have its own schools, and she had to walk along the Highway 71 to nearby Winslow every school day.

Jeananne's mother always said that Winslow was the kind of town that you would miss if you blinked. Remembering these words brought tears to Jeananne. She didn't blink and noticed the familiar sign pointing out the direction to Devil's Den State Park, a place her father refused to enter.

In Winslow, population 300 said the sign, they stopped at a small store and purchased a few groceries. No one was in the store except the proprietor who asked them no questions and looked at them with suspicion.

"We may look like strangers," offered Jeananne, "but I'm from Elmore. We're back here for a funeral."

"Faye Farris," said the proprietor. "Fine lady, she was."

"Yes, we are relations." Jeananne felt the softening of the store owner's features as he mumbled words that she thought were an expression of condolence.

After Winslow, they turned onto a gravel and dirt road and drove back through the woods to Elmore. On either side of the road were majestic pine and hickory trees. Soon they came to a large rock placed there by the Civilian Conservation Corps announcing that they had arrived in Elmore and telling onlookers that the settlement was established in 1872. Jeananne stopped the car and the two ladies opened their doors to enjoy the breeze.

"October in Elmore is almost cool. I had forgotten about mountain weather. I wonder if you will find that Elmore has changed." Jeananne asked Martha.

"You'll remember I came here a few years ago when my father died. That time Miriam came with me and we stayed at the house with Faye. It was shocking to me then because Elmore had changed greatly since we lived here as children. Would you believe that Elmore was considered a resort when my parents built that big house?"

"Elmore was a resort?" Jeananne raised her eyebrows in disbelief.

"Yes. People came here in the summers from Fort Smith and Fayetteville to escape the heat. Mother and Dad loved it and decided to stay. Anyway, several of the big, old houses were built at that time."

"And the trailer park came later?" Jeananne smiled. "Much later, I expect."

"Yes, people like your parents found they could live here cheaply. There is a lot of poverty in these mountains and plateaus but some people manage to make a living from fruit trees or raising chickens." Martha sighed. "Elmore is not incorporated so there are no municipal taxes. Enough of this talk, let's head to the house. I don't imagine you will have trouble finding it in this big metropolis?"

The two laughed, returned to the car, and within minutes were parked on the roadside in front of the Farris family home.

When Martha drove to the hospital in Fayetteville to talk with Faye's physician and to make arrangements for the funeral at the Community Christian Church, Jeananne walked to the trailer park.

The "Arkansas Traveller Motor Inn and Trailer Park" sign had been painted over with white paint and on it was written in block letters "Lambs of the Lord." The one-room units that had given rise to the park's right to call itself a motor inn, now appeared to be the permanent homes of residents. Some were decorated with Arkansas state flags, one had a cross in the front and a sandstone walkway leading to an added-on porch. She saw children playing what looked like a game of Red Rover, and two older women sat nearby on metal lawn chairs watching them.

To her right were the trailers and among them was one familiar to her, the same faded awning draped over poles along its side. She walked up to the screen door and knocked, yelling out, "Mama? Dad? Are you home?"

Jeananne's mother came to the door and cried out, "Could that be you, baby doll? We've been waiting for you." The two embraced and admired each other's appearances although Jeananne thought she detected many more lines on her mother's face.

Jeananne stood waiting for her mother to invite her inside.

"There is so much to talk about," Jeananne began talking through the still-closed door. Before she could say more, her mother interrupted her.

"First, I want to talk. Come on in and sit down. Have some tea." She opened the screen door to admit her daughter but blocked Jeananne's path to the kitchen table. She pushed a glass toward Jeananne and reached into the small refrigerator for a pitcher of sweetened tea.

"Your Daddy and I are really busy preparing for a revival. I'd ask you to sit down but we are mighty busy. People are coming from all over. I've been cooking and collecting hymnals and figuring out the music. Daddy and the other men are putting up the tent. There is so much to do and we are all exhausted but your father says it is service to the Lord and we should be grateful for honest work. Maybe you could help out."

Jeananne stood listening to her mother who was absorbed in her own life. Taking advantage of her mother's need for a sip of tea, Jeananne said, "You did get my letter, right? You know why I'm here?"

"Yes. Poor Aunt Faye. She was old. I guess Martha will plan some kind of high-falutin' funeral for her. Those Farris girls always put on airs."

"Aunt Faye was wonderful to me. Without the two of you, I never would have left Elmore."

"Yes, and look at you now, living the life in Houston, Texas. Your father and I never went to Texas, not before you were born or after. Arkansas is good enough for us."

"Are you angry at me for going to Houston? You realize that was a long time ago, during the war."

"Yes, you gave up your roots. Look at you. You don't look anything like you did when you were a teen-ager."

"Mother, I am not a teen-ager. I'm thirty-three years old. I'm married." Jeananne was trying to keep herself calm but was becoming increasingly frustrated.

"I know how old you are. I was there when you were born, remember?"

"No, Mother, I don't remember but I know you gave birth to me and I am grateful."

"Wait till your father gets here. You might want to wipe some of that lipstick off your face. I can't keep you talking though because I have work to do."

Chapter 39

Pastor Cameron arrived with the banging sound of the slammed door to the trailer. Jeananne, startled, jammed the lipstick-covered tissue into her purse and stood up greeting her father with a bright smile.

"Who have we here?" her father roared. "It is the prodigal daughter!"

Jeananne continued to smile, stepped hesitantly toward her father, leaned forward and kissed him on the cheek.

"How are you, Father? Mother says you're setting up for a revival. I guess I've come at the wrong time, but you know why I'm here. Faye Farris died."

"The wrong time? What do you mean?" the pastor frowned. "I would say a revival is the right time. Revivals are always the right time."

"I meant I've come when you're busy and I am interrupting your work," Jeananne explained.

"Step aside, girl, and let me sit down. No one interrupts the work of the Lord. You have become arrogant since you left us. I could tell from your letters. 'Blessed are the meek: for they shall inherit the earth. Blessed are the pure in heart: for they shall see God.' You do remember the Sermon on the Mount, don't you?"

Jeananne did not try to redirect her father's attention away from scripture because she did not want to be disrespectful. When he stopped for breath, she said, "You are looking well, Dad, and you obviously still have energy and enthusiasm for life."

"Thank the Lord, your mother and I have our health and we have the love of this great community. You must have noticed how the trailer park is the home now of the Lambs. We're not some little group of four or five people. We fill the trailer park. I guess your old man is doing okay, in the eyes of the Lord, that is. And we have food on the table and clothes on our backs. The Lord sees our righteousness and rewards us with his Grace."

Pastor Cameron reached for Jeananne's hands. "Let us pray together, that you will find again the path of God."

Jeananne offered her right hand, changed her mind and pulled it back.

"It is kind of you to pray for me," she said. "I'm only going to be in Elmore for a short time. I was hoping to find you in good health and to learn if there is anything you need."

Jeananne's mother had a look of horror on her face because of her daughter's sass.

He said, "From your letters I have concluded that you have chosen riches and the sin of the city over living a humble Christian life. We Lambs choose to live in isolation so that we will not be tempted by those sins. As far as I am concerned, and I speak for myself and for God, you have chosen to expose yourself to sin. Clearly you are refusing redemption although I am offering it to you this very minute. Look around you. Do you see wickedness? Do you see displays of wealth? Jesus threw the moneychangers out of the temple. We are poor Lambs of the Lord. I ask: will you join us? Which will it be: heaven or hell?"

"Dad, I do not want to insult you or annoy you. I don't want to be unkind, but I cannot stay and listen to your preaching. Silly me, I thought you would ask about me and my life and that you would be happy about the person I have become." Jeananne clenched her teeth together in an effort to prevent crying.

"It's always about you, isn't it? We believe in a Higher Power."

"As do I, Dad, but my Higher Power is loving." Jeananne stood, grabbed her purse and for a moment looked intently at her parents, taking full measure of their expressions, her father's look of self-satisfaction and her mother's blank stare and pursed lips.

"Ye are the salt of the earth: but if the salt has lost his savor, wherewith shall it be salted? It is thenceforth good for nothing, but to be cast out, and to be trodden under foot of men." Pastor Cameron cleared his throat and sipped the tea.

"I have to leave. I am sorry," Jeananne said.

"If you leave, don't bother to come back," her father said.

"Good-bye," Jeananne opened the door and stepped onto the concrete blocks that served the stairway to and from the trailer. Behind her was her mother's voice, asking Pastor Cameron if he wanted more tea.

Jeananne reversed her steps through the trailer park and instead of going straight to the Farris house, she turned right. She inhaled deeply and told herself that she was exhaling the negativity of her past. "Out with you, out with all your rules and all your rejection of me and my hopes and dreams, and out with all your not caring about me."

She began walking toward a clump of trees just north of Elmore and found a path she knew from her childhood. Brushing aside overgrowth on either side of the path, she began the upward climb. Within minutes she arrived as a clearing where someone recently had built a campfire. It amused her because this was the very spot where she had built campfires. Without thinking, she kicked dirt over the embers.

She stuck to the path, climbing higher to a plateau where she had sat many times in the past when she had wanted to escape her life. She perched on a large boulder and looked out past a wide ravine to an expanse of forest, alive, she thought, with unseen animals busily preparing for winter.

Aloud, she said, "Okay, Jeananne, you are an adult, truly an adult. You have faced your father and now it is time to face the rest of your life. This beautiful part of the world was once your home, but now your home and your future are Houston."

She knew in her heart that she would never return to this glorious but flawed place.

Chapter 40

Jeananne slowly opened her eyes and, in an effort to untangle the bedding, grabbed the crumpled quilt with her right hand and pulled it over her shoulder. The temperature in the room indicated late autumn and it was still dark. Grandpa Farris's room, she still thought of it as his, was at the front of the house and the bed that Jeananne had been sleeping in these past nights was placed near a rattling window. Perfect sleeping weather, Jeananne told herself, and, hugging a feather pillow, she turned onto her side and closed her eyes.

When she awoke the room had taken on a muted gold color, and she could hear morning sounds from the kitchen. She sat up and eased herself into the long chenille dressing gown that she had found in Faye's closet.

"I'm awake," she called out.

Martha appeared at the doorway holding a steaming cup of coffee.

"Good morning, sunshine. Lots to do today." She smiled. "I've been up for an hour and finished packing. Coffee's ready. We have another couple of hours before people start arriving."

"I'm getting up," Jeananne said, unnecessarily, as she was already on her feet.

People did come: the young woman who had been helping them sort and box Faye's belongings, the men with the Goodwill and Salvation Army vans, and the antique dealer who was buying the furniture. Shortly after noon, the lawyer arrived to accept the house keys. He helped Jeananne and Martha load their suitcases into the rental car and waved them off, wishing them happy travels and promising to keep in touch regarding the sale of the house.

In Winslow, Jeananne stopped the car in front of her old school.

"I guess this is good-bye," she said, directing her comments to the building.

"The past is always with you," said Martha. "That's my view, anyway. We're Southerners. We can never escape our past."

"I'm leaving this part of my past behind, forever," insisted Jeananne.

166

"This place will always be a part of me. Faye and Miriam and I had wonderful childhoods. Growing up in this beautiful, natural, unspoiled corner of the state, corner of the world, was idyllic."

"You were very lucky," agreed Jeananne.

"We were, but sometimes you have to make your luck. I am filled with gratitude today," Martha wiped tears from her eyes with a tissue from the glove box.

"I'm grateful we're going back to Houston."

"Me, too. Work awaits me. I've been away from the office too long. Poor Sam has had to pull weight for both of us. He'll be ready for me to get back into action. A big business does not run itself. We're still recovering from Hurricane Audrey."

"That was just three months ago, but seems like a lifetime."

"Barely three months ago. When you type this year's reports, if you do, you will see how much money we have to make to cover the damages to our oil rigs. There's something to cry about," Faye said.

"I don't think I have cried in my life as much as I have cried this past week. I think I am all cried out. I cried over Faye, over my parents, over being held at knife-point in Mexico, about my marriage. I don't think I have any more tears in me. I was in Monterrey just a couple of weeks ago. So much has happened that I have lost track of the date."

"You've barely had time to get over that horrible night but you've been helping me! I can't predict the future, Jeananne, but I think you have what it takes to get through the crises. Let's go." Martha placed her closed purse in her lap and with her feet planted firmly on the passenger side floor mat, she had the appearance of willing the car forward.

The two women spent the night in a motor inn near Adams Field, Little Rock's burgeoning airport. The next morning, they returned the rental car, boarded a four-engine DC4, and found their way to the first-class section where they drank coffee from China cups and toyed with a light lunch of chicken salad.

With Edo in Monterrey, neither Martha nor Jeananne had arranged for anyone to pick them up on arrival. Instead, they made their way to a cab stand and within less than half a day after leaving Arkansas, they were in their homes in Houston.

The first thing Martha did was to telephone Sam and Miriam. The first thing Jeananne did was to telephone her husband.

Martha was able to arrange a meeting with Sam to catch up on business matters and she was able to commiserate with Miriam about the loss of their sister.

Jeananne wasn't able to accomplish anything as Edo answered the phone at Las Palmas and told her Geoff was still somewhere in Mexico City.

Chapter 41

"I'm not the damn 'phone answerer," Edo mumbled to one of the Las Palmas vaqueros. The cowboy grinned and said nothing, instead walking out of the room to allow Edo to answer the ringing phone in private.

Edo listened to the caller, his face scrunched up in concentration.

"Yes, I'll do as you say. The boss is in Mexico City. When he calls me, I'll tell him to call you in Houston. You're the insurance agent?" Edo wrote details on a notepad on the desk.

A drink in one hand and the 'phone in the other, Geoff stood in the living room of his hotel suite, intently listening to the information being provided by his man in Houston.

"Let me see if I understood you. The check is for two hundred fifty thousand US dollars, most of it the value of the jewelry from Cartier and Tiffany. What about the car? It was brand new."

The conversation continued as Liz swept into the room, wearing a large hat and sunglasses. Geoff shushed her as she was saying she was ready to go out. He mouthed that the call was important, that he was talking about insurance money.

"Courier the check down here. I'm sure you can find someone to bring it down. I'll be at my place in Monterrey tomorrow. Yes, deliver it to me in Monterrey."

He raised his glass skyward before drinking the two fingers of whiskey in one gulp. "We're home free, baby," he said to Liz. "It's back to Monterrey for us. Run down to the concierge and have him get tickets for us on the next plane out. I want to be in Monterrey tonight."

"You're trying to organize me," Geoff complained to Liz when they were seated comfortably on the airplane travelling from Mexico City to Monterrey. "I'll figure out a plan when the time comes. I'll be busy at Las Palmas."

"Meaning you won't have time for me, for us," she said.

"There's a time for everything. You've had a good time, haven't you? Now I have work to do. You'll figure it out. Why don't you look at a magazine or something?" Geoff gestured to the stewardess and busied himself ordering drinks and a "magazine for the lady."

Liz continued talking. "Of course, I'll figure it out. I'm trying to determine what you are going to do. So far, all I know is that you're going back to Las Palmas to get your insurance pay-out. Then what? What about Eddie Barga?"

"You worry too much, Liz. I am big enough to take care of my own business. I have never needed a woman to manage my business before. Maybe you need to think about returning to your husband." As soon as he said it, Geoff wished he had not.

"I don't believe it. You are telling me to go home to Harold? Dear, reliable, dull Harold. You're dropping me?" Liz's voice was shrill.

"Not at all. I didn't mean it like that. I was simply recognizing that you might not want to stay in Monterrey while I had to take care of things."

"Meaning? What things? Eddie Barga?"

"I told you, I am not worried about Eddie. I have the money to pay him off. He won't be bothering me, but I have to do it carefully so that he doesn't spread the word around that I'm an easy touch."

"That doesn't make sense," Liz said.

"I wouldn't expect this kind of business to make sense to you. That's why I said it would be better if you got out of Dodge, so to speak." Feeling that he was in control, at least with Liz, Geoff added, "Tomorrow."

"Is there something you aren't telling me?"

"No. You know everything you should know." Geoff told himself there was no reason for Liz to know about his problems with the Mexicans. Every day while in Mexico City he had spoken with Edo and so far there had been no cause for alarm, no attack from Jorge Manual's crew. In his hopeful moments Geoff told himself that the crew broke up after Jorge's death, then he pinched himself, returned to reality, and looked over his shoulder to see if anyone was following him.

Receiving her drink from the stewardess, Liz took a sip and made a face of appreciation. "Everything is better when you have good whiskey in your hand and in your mouth."

"Couldn't agree with you more. So now we're all okay, right? Can you fly back to Houston tomorrow?"

"You are in a hurry," Liz said.

"I have my reasons. Have I ever steered you wrong?"

Before leaving the airport in Monterrey, Liz had purchased her ticket back to Houston for a flight the next afternoon. Geoff dropped her off at her home in Monterrey's Barrio Antiguo, carrying her suitcase into the house and giving her a perfunctory kiss, missing her mouth and bussing her cheek. She was too tired to complain.

Her first task once alone was to telephone Harold and inform him of her plan. She told him that she had had an exhausting time in Mexico City taking in the museums and shopping. She said she was ready to return to normal. Harold asked if she had seen Geoff.

"Not for a while," she hedged. It had been about an hour since he had dropped her off and she thought that qualified as "a while."

"Should I let Jeananne know you are coming home?" Harold asked.

"I don't know why."

"She seemed worried about you," Harold said. "She's been out of town, but I think she's back now."

"Really? Extraordinary. After the shock of that robbery here in Monterrey, I'm surprised she hasn't just stayed home with her head under the covers."

"Are you being unkind, Liz? You know she isn't that meek. Give her a break. Martha's and Miriam's sister in Arkansas died and Jeananne accompanied Martha back there for the funeral. Jeananne is from the same small town. You know all that."

"That was good of Jeananne to help out," Liz said with conviction in her voice. "I'm sure she was a help to Martha. So, Miriam stayed in Houston?"

"Yes, we'll talk more about it when you get home."

"You'll pick me up at the airport?"

"I don't think so. I'll send someone. Things are crazy here in the office. The big news is that we've decided to buy out Western Transport and on top of that I'm covering for Geoff, doing all that he should do but somehow always seems to slither out of."

"We know our Geoff, such a pampered Mama's boy," Liz said to her husband.

Chapter 42

When Jeananne entered the kitchen, she found Rosa singing *Jailhouse Rock* in Spanish. The radio was tuned to a station that played to the Mexican audience in Houston.

"I didn't know that Elvis sang in Spanish," Jeananne yelled out over the music.

Rosa, startled, quickly turned off the radio and said, "You surprised me. I didn't hear you come in. In fact, I didn't know you were coming back today. How was your trip?"

"First, was that Elvis?" Jeananne was standing in the door of the kitchen. After the taxi dropped her off, she had entered the house unnoticed, walked to her bedroom and deposited her suitcase before wandering toward the kitchen.

"No, but that's his *Jailhouse Rock.* Everyone is singing it."

"Hmmm. I like it. I've never heard it in Spanish. Got anything to eat?"

"Sure. I can make something for you." Jeananne smiled broadly because she knew that Rosa could prepare something for her with no notice.

Jeananne said, "I'm glad to be home. Saying good-bye to Aunt Faye was sad and it was sad to see the old house. It was particularly difficult for Martha but she got through it and made all the decisions she had to make. She is an amazingly capable person."

"How about your parents?" Rosa asked as she reached into the refrigerator for a jar of homemade salsa and two eggs. She began making a Western omelet while carrying on her conversation. Jeananne filled a glass with water and carried it to the table and sat down.

"Better not to think about my parents. My father was his usual grumpy, judgmental self. I have come to the conclusion that I can never make them happy. I have to stop trying and live my life."

"I am sorry to hear that." Rosa grated cheese into the bowl with the eggs, milk, and cumin. She poured the mixture into a skillet. Jeananne watched her, admiring her efficiency. Placing a slice of bread in the toaster, Rosa said, "Nothing new has happened here while you were gone. I put your mail on the desk in your office."

"How about your family, Rosa?"

"I saw them over the weekend. They were managing." Rosa plated the omelet, spooned a dollop of salsa on the side, buttered the toast and served Jeananne.

While Jeananne ate, Rosa hummed *Jailhouse Rock* and cleaned the kitchen counter. The two women seemed comfortable to be in each other's space, each involved in her own activity.

Her meal finished, Jeananne said, "I had an idea while I was gone. I was sitting by myself up in the mountains. It was beautiful and peaceful and I had plenty of time to think. I've decided it is time for me to take action."

Rosa tilted her head, questioning the meaning of Jeananne's words but not voicing her thoughts.

"I wonder if you are serious, Rosa, about wanting to open a bakery?"

"It's my dream," Rosa said.

"How would you feel about my helping you? Not with the actual baking or selling or anything, but with financial backing. I can help you get started."

"Really? I don't even know what questions to ask or what to say. Where would we begin?"

"First, you need to decide that it is something you are willing to pursue seriously because if I am involved, I intend to help you start a business that will succeed. I have the money and I have been living around a super-successful international business for years so I have seen what it takes to run a business." Not entirely sure of herself, Jeananne added, "Sort of." Then, deciding that it was best to be confident, she said, "I have seen enough. I've always been on the side-lines but I watched and learned. I'm ready to fly on my own."

"Yes, yes, yes. But what if—"

"Ridiculous to think about the what ifs. I think we should start looking for a location, maybe near here to take advantage of shoppers from our neighborhood. I'll start exploring, maybe narrow down a couple of locations for you to look at. There are all sorts of things to think about, like the right kitchen equipment and supplies, but I think I'll begin by looking around the area for the right spot."

"I should begin organizing my recipes and thinking about what I could make and sell."

"I'm thinking we should take some of your baked goods, maybe some cookies and muffins, over to the church and give them away, as samples to entice people. It will also give us an opportunity to get some feedback." Jeananne added as an afterthought, "Oh yeah, let's take a couple of trays down to the office. They are all big eaters and are always willing to give their opinions."

"There are probably some other places we could take samples, like outside the grocery store, but don't you think I should have an actual space and a name for the bakery?"

"I think it should be Rosa's Bakery. That name is easy to remember and says exactly what it is, or will be. It will be Rosa's Bakery. Agreed?"

Rosa stood unmoving, eyes wide, "Agreed."

Later that day, Jeananne looked through her mail, throwing most of it into the waste basket. She had spent the better part of the last ten days with Martha and she missed her. Telling herself that she would make sure that Martha got home okay, she called. After a few assurances that all was well in both households, Jeananne said, "I've got a new project. I need to do something more with my time." She explained that she had been living too long without purpose. "Our trip to Elmore had an effect on me. I feel more adult, like I need to do more for myself."

"You've been doing some work for Wilkins Enterprises," Martha reminded her.

"Yes, and I will continue to help prepare the documents for meetings. Helping Rosa start a business will not take all my time. I intend to have plenty of time to fulfil obligations to you and to the family."

"Speaking of family, I hesitate to ask, but have you heard anything from Geoff?"

"No. He seems quite taken with Mexico. If he has communicated with Sam and Miriam, I guess they would tell me."

"Miriam says she is worried about him. She's afraid he might be in trouble. He never said anything to them about the robbery. How about you, dear? Have you gotten over the robbery?"

"I'm not sure a person ever gets over being frightened, being held at knifepoint, but I think I have done as much as possible to get it out of my mind.

Our trip to Arkansas, being busy, now my planning to help Rosa: all are a help. I just wish we would hear something more from Geoff, something…" Jeananne couldn't identify the right word. She tried again, "I just wish we would hear that he is okay. I'm not sure how he feels about me. Would a man who loves his wife want to be separate from her especially after they've gone through a trauma?"

"You said he needed to stay in Mexico to finish the insurance claim," Martha said in an effort to console Jeananne.

"Does that make sense to you? I've been wondering about that claim. We did lose the car and some of my jewelry but thank goodness, I didn't take the expensive stuff with me. It is all still in the safe. I checked before we left for Faye's funeral."

"I, for one, am very proud of you, Jeananne. You've handled yourself very well. You've been very brave. Now, Miriam, has not been so brave. She seems to be in a slump. I don't know if it is because of Geoff or because of Faye."

"I hate hearing that. I am running around some tomorrow in the car and I'll stop by to see Miriam."

Jeananne kept her word. Using the telephone book, she located the nearest bakery. It was about halfway between Oakside and downtown, a distance that required a special trip. She decided it wasn't close enough for a daily run. She would look for an available property closer to home.

Next, she collected Miriam for a drive around the neighborhood. She could look for possible commercial locations and visit with Miriam at the same time. She also hoped that including Miriam in her reconnoiter would help pull her mother-in-law out of her slump.

However, Miriam showed only a little interest in Jeananne's project. Her main concern was that her son Geoff had been robbed and she was worried about his safety. She said Sam called him several times but had only spoken twice to him.

"We're glad you are back here and safe. Now we just need to get Geoff home," Miriam said.

Chapter 43

When Comandante Diego Gonzalez entered the Barra de Juegos, one man sitting alone warming his hands around a cup of coffee looked up and nodded his head in recognition. The other customers continued eating and drinking and those who were standing at the fruit machines continued feeding the machines with coins, pulling downward on the levers, and occasionally moaning or yelling out excitedly.

Gonzalez slowly walked over to the bar and asked for very hot coffee. He scanned the room for familiar faces, noting several men whom he knew to be regulars at the games tables upstairs. Gonzalez prided himself on his knowledge of locals. He counted on their votes. He counted on their support when trouble came. He took his duty to protect seriously and felt an obligation to his oath. He grew up in Monterrey and if the remainder of his life were to be lived in Monterrey, he intended to live that life in peace.

He noticed a person who didn't fit, a chunky middle-aged man who met his gaze with a searing stare. As he began the process of recall, reviewing past experiences, trying to associate the face with someone or some event, the barman leaned forward and whispered, "Señor Manuel is in his office. He wants a word."

Gonzalez finished his coffee and walked to the stairs, climbing to the second floor where Señor Manuel kept his office.

"It looks like your business is thriving, Manuel. Plenty of customers downstairs."

"I've been wondering when you would show up. It's been days since Jorge, my son Jorge, was killed." Señor Manuel was surrounded by a cloud of cigar smoke and the room and even his person was glazed in a yellow fog. He sat behind a vast wooden desk, a small lamp illuminating a metal case filled with paper money.

"My condolences about Jorge." The Comandante stood in front of Señor Manuel's desk and avoided looking directly at the cache of money.

"What are you doing about it?"

"You know I am not in charge. The unfortunate event took place over in Tamaulipas, not my district."

Señor Manuel waved his hand toward a chair and Gonzalez sat down.

"Señor, what do you hear? Jorge's crew aren't talking, at least, not to us. Maybe they talk with you or your men?" If the Comandante had more information, he didn't want to share it. Señor Manuel looked down and appeared to be examining contents of the metal box. "We all know Jorge had a lot of irons in the fire. I expect one of those irons came back and burned him."

Comandante sat motionless, hoping that Señor Manuel would reveal something he didn't know about Jorge Manuel.

"Did you notice that gringo downstairs?" Señor Manuel asked.

"The chunky guy?"

"Si. He's looking for one of your friends. Eddie Barga sent him down from Galveston."

"That's news to me. I have a lot of friends. Who is he looking for?" The Comandante had already figured it out but wanted to verify what he thought.

"Wilkins, of course. He owes Barga a lot of cash."

"What are you to Barga?"

"You're fishing, Comandante, but I'll tell you. Barga is putting money up for the new casino we're building down here. Monterrey is growing and it's time for gaming to grow with the times. He sent his man down, Ernie G, the gringo downstairs."

"Looks like he brought you a little down-payment on the new casino."

Manual slammed the lid shut and placed the box in a desk drawer. "My money is not your concern. Your concern is who killed my son."

"So, Eddie Barga sent his man down here to pump Geoff Wilkins for money?"

"You got the picture. I don't think your friend Wilkins has the money. I heard he staged a robbery for the insurance money. Funny, isn't it, how these rich Texans seem to have no money."

"Staged it, huh? They held his wife at knifepoint."

"So?"

The room was quiet for a moment. Gonzalez reached for a handkerchief and wiped his eyes which were beginning to burn from smoke irritation.

Gonzalez said, "The thieves got a car and some jewelry. You're saying the insurance would cover the cost of his debt to Barga. I don't know how much he owes. What do you know about it?"

"Nothing. But if I did, I'd say the jewelry was probably not genuine." The old man glared at Gonzalez and repeated for emphasis, "not genuine."

"You think Geoff Wilkins was looking for a way to raise money and he hired someone," (Gonzalez stressed "someone"), "to rob him so that he could claim insurance company to pay off his debts."

"Not just any old debts…a big debt to, well, you know his name. The Touch is not known for forgiveness. And don't forget it is possible that the folks that Wilkins hired to do the robbery were actually double-crossed."

"How did Jorge end up dead?" the Comandante asked.

"Go figure. Surely there was a witness. Jorge was found dead in that taqueria run by an old woman on the road into Tamaulipas."

Realizing that Señor Manuel had already decided that Geoff Wilkins was behind the murder of his son, the Comandante began to think about Geoff's whereabouts. He still had a question about the appearance of Ernie G, Eddie Barga's man.

"I hope you will let the law handle the problem."

"This Geoff Wilkins character is in debt. He owes Barga and he owes me."

"That is pretty clear, Manuel, but I was elected to handle this sort of problem."

"You already said it isn't your job. Simple, just stand back and let justice occur."

"Justice, or revenge?" Gonzalez stood up and left the room.

On his way out, he stopped at the table of the man whose name he had learned was Ernie G. "I just want to introduce myself," the Comandante said.

"I'm Ernest Greer. Everyone calls me Ernie G."

"So I hear. Señor Manuel tells me you represent Eddie Barga."

"Yeah. He's about to go into business here in Monterrey. This is one fine games bar but I can see why the town needs a full-sized casino. It will bring in a lot of money to this town."

"We always appreciate business growth in Monterrey. What we don't appreciate is bad faith. We take care of our people and that includes Americans expatriates who expect security and safety when they spend their time and money in our city."

"Understood, Comandante. I expect you mean to protect me as well." Ernie G began to laugh.

Chapter 44

Edo grinned broadly when Geoff Wilkins bolted into the living room of Las Palmas. Geoff's speed was accompanied by the noise of the slamming door. Seeing Edo in front of him, Geoff halted abruptly as if awaiting great news. Edo didn't disappoint.

"The envelope you've been asking about arrived this morning. The delivery fellow said he was just supposed to leave it at Las Palmas for you. I signed the delivery slip like you asked me to."

"You did the right thing, Edo, just like I asked." Geoff quickly tore open the envelope and studied the contents. "It is exactly right, just what I expected." Geoff exhaled loudly as he looked a second time at the contents.

Sensing that the delivery brought change with it, Edo asked, "Boss, do you want us to keep the guard in place?"

"How many men do you have?"

"Just the same as before. We've been out on the property every night but none of the men have had anything suspicious to report."

"Better keep the men alert now that I'm back. I'm going into town." Edo knew his boss well enough to refrain from delaying him with further questions or information. "I'll need the truck."

In the manner of all obedient employees, Edo took immediate steps to meet his boss's need. Within a few minutes, the truck was parked in front of the hacienda wall, the keys in the ignition.

A man with a check in his hand large enough to pay a threatening debt is a man who can taste freedom. For weeks Geoff had attempted to avoid the anxiety that accompanied his fears by developing and executing a plan that had the opportunity of success or failure. Geoff now saw the tangible evidence that his plan had succeeded. He held the check for $250,000, a vast amount of funds sufficient to satisfy his nemesis. He believed the check to be his right. His reasoning went something like this: I paid for the insurance for the precise purpose of reimbursement of the value of my property if stolen. It is only good business now that the insurance company has fulfilled its obligation to me.

As Geoff drove the familiar route into Monterrey, his thoughts of ownership of the money represented by the piece of paper he carried, increased. Flashing before his eyes were all the efforts that went into his planning, his decided brilliance at involving his unsuspecting wife, his ability to convince the comandante of his sincerity, and the icing on the cake, the proof of his manhood to the Mexicans who had been merely his lackeys. By the time he reached his destination, he had convinced himself that he could satisfy his debt with half the amount of the check. He decided that he deserved to keep the other half for himself. Geoff did not think about his wife, or his father or his mother. He did not think about consequences of paying Eddie half the money owed. Rather he thought about what he deemed rightfully his. Eddie Barga, after all, relied on Geoff to continue to do business with him. Eddie Barga relied on Geoff's goodwill. Eddie Barga's reputation could be damaged if he treated Geoff badly. After all, Geoff was a Wilkins, and the Wilkins business was known all over Houston, all over Texas, in fact, it was known all over the world. Eddie Barga should be happy, no, grateful, to receive half of what he said Geoff owed.

Further, Geoff reasoned, who's to say how much Geoff really owed Eddie Barga. While gambling, the casino always plied Geoff with alcohol. They saw to it that Geoff was heavily in drink so that he would continue gambling. Maybe Geoff owed even less than Eddie Barga claimed.

Geoff's destination was the North American Bank of Monterrey situated on the main road through town. It was a free-standing building. Its four stories made it one of the tallest structures in town but with the university expanding and a new city hall and police central station in development, the bank's claim would soon be outdated. But for now, it was easily identified by its towering over the one- and two-story buildings nearby. The bank owed its prosperity to the increasing number of expatriates who were beginning to flood into town, riding on the waves of growing enterprise north of the border and the search for cheap labor. The university was promising an educated work force, ready for the challenges of the decade ahead.

Geoff entered the bank with confidence and expectation. He was greeted warmly and shown into the office of a Vice-President who apologized because the bank's President was on vacation. Refusing refreshment, Geoff took the direct approach, producing the insurance company's check to him for the large sum of $250,000.

Geoff had no real plan for the repayment of Eddie Barga. He assumed Eddie was in Galveston. Always in the past when Geoff owed money to Eddie, one or more of Barga's men would come to Geoff. With this in mind, Geoff decided to tell the banker that he wanted $125,000 in cash, American dollars. He knew that Eddie Barga would not accept a check. He figured Eddie or his men would find him, whether he was in Houston or in Monterrey.

The banker said he could produce the $125,000 in US capital but asked if Geoff would consent to depositing the remainder in his account. When Geoff hesitated, the banker offered another option. Would Geoff accept the remaining amount in Mexican currency? After all, the bank was located in Monterrey, Mexico, and Geoff and his family did plenty of business in Monterrey. Surely Mexican currency would be desirable and useful to Geoff.

Geoff consented to this plan and asked for the currencies to be separated. As it would take a while for the bank to accommodate Geoff's requirements, Geoff decided to walk to a nearby cafe for a kick start to his evening of celebration.

With the air of a man of means and no problems claiming attention, Geoff not only drank to himself but insisted on treating the half-dozen men in the cafe.

He returned to the bank to endorse the check and retrieve his funds.

When he left the bank, on foot, he turned to the left and walked the short distance to the Barra de Juegos. As he walked, he convinced himself that it was good to contribute to the Mexican economy. Head held high, he walked into the games bar thinking about spending a little of the Mexican currency that he now had in his possession.

Chapter 45

Zach Coleman arrived on time for his appointment with Jeananne. His appearance was enhanced by a well-sculpted moustache and an uncontrolled beard indicating either a balanced personality or one not yet fully formed. Opening the door for him, Jeananne noticed his green MG parked in the driveway. She hesitated while she tried to assess the nature of her caller. She decided that he was attractive, not so attractive as to overwhelm, but pleasant enough in his features. He spoke with a more pronounced Southern accent than most Houstonians. She thought perhaps he was from Mississippi or Alabama. The softness of his speech was mitigated by his direct manner and his probing questions. Jeananne considered that his charm was purposeful, that she was being mesmerized into some admission of guilt.

"I appreciate that you must investigate large claims against your company, especially when robbery is the cause," Jeananne said because she found comfort in focusing attention away from herself, but she didn't like the fact that an investigator was in her home asking questions. "I am a victim of a crime, not a criminal."

"I didn't mean to imply that you are a criminal, Mrs. Wilkins. The company with which your husband does business as a routine hires me or someone like me to look into large claims. I work as an independent investigator."

"I am curious. Here you sit in my house asking me questions about a traumatic event that occurred in Monterrey, Mexico, one that I would forget if it were possible. It seems that you are here because someone doesn't believe that the robbery occurred. I can assure you that it did occur. Have you spoken with my husband?"

"First, I would like to hear your version of the robbery."

"My version? I can tell you what happened. I was there. What I experienced isn't someone's version. I can assure you that I tell the truth."

Jeananne was not a friend to her own anger and as she felt her face reddening, she fanned herself with her hand.

"We seem to have gotten off on the wrong foot, Mrs. Wilkins. I do not doubt that you were robbed. Your account of the incident would be most helpful. Your husband filed a claim for stolen property valued at $250,000."

Jeananne gasped. "That much?"

"Yes, most of it for your jewelry. Could you give me a list, even verbally, of what pieces were stolen? Do you go often to Monterrey and do you usually take valuable jewelry with you?"

"Did you say 250,000 American dollars?"

"Yes."

In a low voice, Jeananne said, "Is my jewelry worth that much? I thought I took paste with me. I didn't take the most valuable pieces."

"I should say, the claim included some pieces of men's jewelry: a top-of-the-line man's Rolex watch and a man's onyx ring."

"I never paid much attention to my husband's watches and rings. He always wore a good watch, probably a Rolex."

"Which brings me back to my request. Could you tell me which pieces of jewelry you took with you to Monterrey?"

Jeananne closed her eyes as if she could answer the question better without looking at Zach Coleman. She envisioned herself dressed for the party on the night of the robbery and saw in her mind the necklace, earrings and rings she had worn. She remembered she wore the fake Tiffany diamond ring, the one that Miriam had purchased years ago, the one Geoff had given her for their engagement. She mentioned this to Mr. Coleman. She said that she loved the ring and was grateful that the real ring was not stolen but instead was secure in the Houston safe. The same was true for the fabulous bracelet that Geoff had purchased years ago from Neiman-Marcus at a special sale held at the Oil Club. Those were her most valuable pieces, she related, and they were both secure.

Jeananne closed her eyes again and remembered placing a few odd pieces of jewelry in a flat case that Geoff placed in the backseat of the new car.

"Like most women, I love jewelry but I wasn't raised to worship material goods. If you knew my background you would understand that I was raised with values of honesty and truthfulness. My father was, is, a preacher and he taught all of us who followed him that pride was, is, a sin. I still hold those beliefs."

"As do I, Mrs. Wilkins. Perhaps our backgrounds are not dissimilar. The real problem is that I cannot account for the $250,000 that your husband claimed he is due. Can you prove me wrong? Can you prove your husband's claim accurate?" Zach Coleman, in a gesture of sincerity, leaned forward in his chair and made direct eye contact with Jeananne. An observer might have thought that he was pleading with her.

"I cannot speak against my husband, Mr. Coleman, but there is nothing else that I can say except to repeat that I am the victim here, not a criminal. Why would my husband request payment of more money than he was entitled to?"

"You surely know that I cannot answer that question."

"What will happen now? Doesn't the insurance company have a police report? Wouldn't that clarify these questions?"

"It is interesting that you think of the police in Monterrey. The police chief wrote the report. Did you give him the information about what was stolen?""

"No, my husband is an old friend of the police comandante. They knew each other as children. I was very distressed after being held at knifepoint and my husband arranged for me to return immediately to Houston. Geoff did all the talking to the police."

"And they never contacted you?"

"No."

"Mr. Coleman, why are you here? You say you are an investigator hired by the insurance company. Why are you questioning the information that my husband must have supplied? Do you have reason to believe something is amiss or is it standard practice to investigate in these situations? Help me understand, please. I may be unknowledgeable about your practices but I am not without intelligence."

"I am here, Mrs. Wilkins, as I said, because the claim was for a great deal of money and after the insurer paid out, new information was presented that has led them to suspect that something was not on the up-and-up."

"And you thought perhaps I had somehow done something dubious."

"You may be a better investigator than I, Mrs. Wilkins." Zach Coleman smiled. Although his lips were hidden by his moustache and unruly beard, by wrinkling his brow he managed to convey both irony and humor.

"I think we will end this interview. If you or the person you work for has any further desire to talk to me, we will do so in the presence of an attorney.

You know the Wilkins family is very well known in this community. I doubt they will take kindly to any false accusations." Jeananne stood indicating that she was indeed terminating discussion. She called for Rosa, sensing that Rosa was nearby, and asked her to show Mr. Coleman out.

Aware of physical sensations, her deep breathing, the touch of a wayward strand of hair on her forehead, the pressure on her right ankle where her stocking had twisted and was constricting blood flow, Jeananne blocked from her mind the content of the last hour's interchange. She sat for several minutes, time irrelevant to her, removing herself from any sense of predicament.

Rosa's entering the room shook her from her stupor. "Do you want a glass of lemonade?"

"I think brandy will do," was Jeananne's reply, "we're almost into winter."

Chapter 46

For a split second Jeananne considered whether to park her car or turn around and return home. Liz Carter's car was parked in the driveway of Sam and Miriam's home. Deciding it was better to face Liz than to avoid her, Jeananne parked in the back of the house and walked in through the kitchen. She immediately encountered Miriam and guessed that Liz was in the office with Sam.

They greeted each other warmly but behind Miriam's calm demeanor Jeananne detected something amiss. Something about the movement of her hands, the way she continuously rubbed the back of her palm, indicated tension. Miriam smiled, all the while working her hands as though she were soothing aching joints, and gazed at Jeananne, waiting for an explanation for her visit.

"You look uneasy, child," Miriam said. "Is anything wrong?"

"Yes. I should probably talk with both you and Sam. Are you well, Miriam? We haven't had much of a chance to talk since I've been back, especially since Martha and I had to be away." Jeananne omitted the reason she had not had much time to visit Miriam because she did not want to bring up the topic of Faye's dying. Sitting near Miriam, Jeananne could sense Miriam's discomfort. Jeananne reached over and placed her hand on Miriam's arm.

"It's good to see you. I just wish I had good news."

"Here he is," said Miriam noting that Sam had come into the room. Skirting around him to enter first was Liz Carter.

"I didn't know you were here," Liz said to Jeananne and remembering her manners directed her attention to Miriam. "Sam and I have just completed our business and I am on my way out. It was nice seeing you as well."

"Sit, dear, and tell me about Monterrey. I understand you stayed there after the unfortunate event that kept Geoff there." Miriam rubbed her hand more rapidly. "How was Geoff? Did he seem to be handling matters well? I imagine he was pretty upset. As you can see Jeananne has done very well here on her own but I'm sure she has missed her husband."

Jeananne smiled innocently as though she were in elementary school and receiving praise from a teacher.

"I had commitments in Monterrey and wasn't ready to return home as quickly as Harold." To Jeananne, "I'm sure you missed your husband. When I left, he was feeling upbeat. I believe the business with the police and the insurance company had all come to a conclusion."

"Did he say when he will be coming back home to Houston?" asked Miriam.

"Now that you are here, Liz, perhaps he will return," Jeananne said.

"I don't know about that. More likely, having the mess behind him will be the reason he returns to Houston. And you, of course. I really have to go. Sam and I finished our business and I need to move on to the next thing on my list. Errands have stacked up. Poor Harold is such a nose-to-the-grindstone kind of man that he doesn't pay attention to household matters."

"We'll excuse you, Liz. I'm sure you have lots to do to keep Harold happy," Miriam said. "Sam, after you show Liz out, would you join us, please."

"You don't need to be formal with me. I'll be back in two shakes," Sam said.

"I feel much better with that woman out of the house. What did she want, Sam?" asked Miriam.

"I'm surprised at you, Miriam. Have you taken against her?" asked Sam.

"I don't think she can be trusted."

"She wanted to tell me that we should look closely at the Wilcarco books. She suspects something is out of whack."

"Like what?" Jeananne asked.

"Like maybe funds missing. She seems to be questioning our son's honesty, Miriam."

Miriam gasped.

"I don't know the truth of it," said Sam, "but we'll have to include Martha in this discussion. I think the next step might be an audit of their books, if for no other reason than to stop Liz Carter from spreading falsehoods and ruining our reputation."

During the silence that followed all three seemed lost in thought about the impact of a financial problem that could lead to a business disaster. Loss of reputation in the oil industry was akin to end of days. Jeananne broke the silence.

"I have a matter to discuss that is pretty bad, maybe devastating. Can you take more bad news?" Jeananne asked.

Both Miriam and Sam looked at Jeananne in alarm. Almost in unison, they repeated in disbelief and fear, "More bad news?"

"Yes."

Once Jeananne began telling them about the investigator and his insinuations, she could hardly stop to breathe. She poured out her concerns about Geoff's gambling debts and her fear that he had falsified the robbery and insurance claims. She didn't mention her certainty that Geoff was unfaithful to her, that Liz was the object of his affections, that the two had enjoyed the pleasures of each other's company in Mexico City. She focused on the possibility of fraud.

"Are you sure you have the original valuable jewelry in your safe, Jeananne? Maybe you took that Tiffany diamond with you. Are you absolutely sure you have the real stuff in your safe?" Sam asked.

"I'm pretty sure. I never take that ring to Monterrey. I'm always very careful with it and with all my jewelry. You know I never had such beautiful things in my younger life and now that you all have gifted me with rings and necklaces and bracelets worth fortunes, I have been grateful and careful." Jeananne said, her voice cracking.

"We'll go together to your house, get the jewelry out of the safe. I'm calling that jeweler we've dealt with. He'll see us right away, all the business we've given him. I'll have him take a good look at everything. We'll find out what's what. Now, why would Geoff need $250,000? I've always helped him out. If he is guilty of doing what this investigator says, then why didn't he come to me?" Sam said.

"Surely he hasn't done anything illegal. Not Geoff," Miriam said. She began to cry softly. "Do you think he is gambling again?"

"Don't upset yourself," Sam said. "I'll look into it. We've always found ways to solve our problems."

Chapter 47

Sam Wilkins was a man who rationed his energy. Always appearing easy-going, he could move as "slow as molasses" (so said his mother in years past) and could appear like he was in a stupor or enjoying an internal reverie. He could sit at his desk with an open newspaper in front of him and not turn the page for an hour. He rarely sped anywhere in his life, but to those who knew him, he was the depth of still waters.

Miriam observed to Jeananne early in their acquaintanceship, that Sam had a devious side, that he could look like a slow-moving closed-to-the-world turtle but his mind was a rapidly moving hare.

"Generally," she said, "when he is sitting quietly and not moving, he is deep in thought, probably solving a knotty problem. He keeps the problems to himself and I may never know about the problems or his solutions. And I never ask."

Jeananne knew Sam Wilkins was clever and sharp, despite his appearance. She appreciated Sam's quiet times. She thought he was more talkative among men. After all he had managed to build an oil empire, the world of men. It took a smart man to do that, a man of decision and resolve.

Jeananne respected Sam but she also worried about him. His entire family was involved in Wilkins Enterprises but Sam never gave up control. Martha said that her husband Wendell was the more out-going of the two.

"My Win never knew a stranger," Martha had told Jeananne. "With those two men, the sky was the limit. They built Wilkins Enterprises from the ground up. When Win died, naturally Sam stepped up and filled the boots of both men. I don't know what we would do if anything happened to Sam."

"Wouldn't Geoff take over?" Jeananne had asked.

"I'm not so sure," Martha had answered.

Jeananne remembered these conversations as she watched Sam sitting quietly on a leather sofa in the private customer room at Neiman Marcus. Sam was holding in his hands a finely cut Baccarat crystal glass of whiskey, swirling the tiny bit left so that the one small cube of ice clinked sounding like a clear high-pitched bell. Jeananne sat beside him, a tiny space separating their two bodies. Neither spoke.

"It's time I took you home," Sam said and stood.

Jeananne picked up the large tote bag containing all the jewelry, hers and Geoff's, most of it in boxes or cases, and arranged the straps over her shoulder.

"At least we found out that the ring is the ring and the bracelet is the bracelet, none of it is paste. That's what I thought but I don't feel any better for having been right."

"Sam, maybe Geoff had two Rolex watches. Maybe he bought one that I didn't know about. He didn't always tell me what he bought. Maybe the Rolex in the safe is his second Rolex."

"Sweet Jeananne. I know you want that to be true."

Sam cleared his throat and made a slight coughing noise. He placed a hand under Jeananne's elbow and guided her out of the store. Neither spoke until they were alone together in the car.

"What do we do now, Sam?" Jeananne asked breathlessly.

"Do you know when Geoff's coming back to Houston?"

"No, I don't. It isn't like him to stay this long down in Monterrey by himself. Thank God Edo is down there."

Sam was quiet.

Jeananne filled the void. "Geoff hasn't been easy to reach lately. I've called several times and either no one answered or Edo answered and had nothing to tell me. Edo did say that Geoff went to Mexico City but I think Geoff is back in Monterrey. Liz said Geoff is in Monterrey and she would know."

Sam raised his eyebrow but said nothing.

"If Geoff is in Monterrey and has $250,000 that he got from the insurance company…" Jeananne didn't finish the sentence.

"Don't finish that thought," warned Sam. "I'll take care of it."

"By doing what, Sam?"

"I have to go to Galveston."

"Now?"

"Yes. I'll drop you off first."

"I'd like to come with you. What can I do at home?" Jeananne asked.

"Let's stop at your house first and telephone Geoff."

191

"Maybe if we knew what was going on, we would feel better," Jeananne said with hope in her voice.

Sam did not respond.

Sam talked with Edo who informed him that Geoff was not at Las Palmas. Standing close enough to hear Sam's end of the conversation did not enlighten Jeananne because Sam said very little. When he hung up, Sam told Jeananne he was heading to Galveston.

"I'm coming with you. What did Edo say?"

"That Geoff is in trouble."

Sam and Jeananne entered Island Casino and told the concierge they wanted to talk with Eddie Barga. Within minutes Eddie, the Touch, appeared, offered his hand to Sam, and after establishing that Sam wanted a private conversation, Eddie invited Sam and Jeananne to his office.

The office was basic, a desk, a chair, a lamp, and a telephone but through a door at the rear they found a more comfortable space where they could sit down and talk face to face. The group in the room included Eddie, Sam, Jeananne and two of Eddie's men who were not introduced.

"I'll get straight to the point," Sam said. "How much money does my son owe you?"

"Almost two hundred fifty thousand dollars. I can get the exact figure, if you want," Eddie said and nodded to one of his men.

"Where do things stand?"

"As of right now, as you know, your son is in Monterrey and as you may not know, he has made no effort to pay me. Where do things stand? Your son stands in quicksand."

"I don't want him hurt. Let me pay you and get him off the hook. I'll need to make a couple of calls to get the money but you know my word is gold."

"Sam, your word is gold with me but this time I am not letting anyone bail Geoff out of this mess. This debt is between Geoff Wilkins and Eddie Barga. Understand?"

"It's only money, Eddie. I'll pay and clear the slate."

Jeananne sat unmoving. She had never seen Sam in a negotiation and she could sense that he was eager, maybe even desperate. She was feeling desperate.

"You may not think I am honorable, Sam, but this debt is between your son and me. Your son owes me the money. Nothing you can say will make me take money from you."

"As an honorable man, Eddie, tell me you will let me pay if Geoff does not satisfy the debt. Don't take it out on him."

"And if I let you pay again and again and Geoff comes in to gamble again and again, what do you think will happen? I am making no deal with you Sam."

Eddie rose from his seated position and walked out of the room leaving Sam and Jeananne behind. One of Eddie's men nodded toward the door and Sam and Jeananne walked out into the casino which was filled with noises of machines and coins clanking on metal.

For the first time, Jeananne noticed the lines on Sam's face.

Chapter 48

"Come in and shut the door behind you," Señor Manuel ordered the man lurking in the hallway outside his office. "What do you have to report?" Senor Manuel did not look up from the papers on his desk. He continued examining them, his face revealing no sign of his thoughts or feelings.

"Wilkins's got the money, cash direct from the bank and he's heading this way, just like you said he would. That man can't keep money, can he?" The speaker was a nondescript Mexican, a man whom any witness would call "average" in his looks and dress. He was one of several men who worked odd jobs for Señor Manuel.

"How did you get your information, Jose?" Señor Manuel sat, unmoving.

"I watched him with my own eyes."

"How do you know he has the money?"

"I tipped the manager. He gave me the sign. Wilkins has all the money, half in US dollars and half in pesos."

"Go downstairs and get the gringo. Name's Ernie G. Bring him up here."

Jose did as he was ordered and returned with Ernie Greer who was breathless after the effort of climbing up the stairs.

"Where we are is this: Wilkins is heading to the bar and will want to show off and of course, he's a gambler, so we'll have to accommodate him. I want your assurance that you speak for Eddie. Sit down and look me in the face," Manuel reached into the center drawer of his desk and pulled out a revolver that he gently placed atop the papers in front of him.

Ernie G said, "There's no need for that. We're in total agreement. You have my word and the word of The Touch. We are in it for 50% split."

"Wilkins has made it easy for us. He's asked for 125000 in pesos. That's Manuel money. The rest in the US currency. That's yours, or Eddie's or however you've arranged that split." Manuel kept his hands on his lap but the gun remained on the desk.

Ernie G, not to be outdone by Manuel, unbuttoned his jacket and revealed the gun he was carrying in a shoulder harness. "I think we're ready. All we ask is that we get our cut."

A young boy knocked on Señor Manuel's door and when he was told to enter, he went straight to the man behind the desk and whispered in his ear. He left the room smiling, a peso held tightly in his right hand. "Get outa here," Manuel hollered after him.

To Ernie G, "Wilkins is in the house. He's at the bar. We start now."

"My man will show you out the back way. Jose, you'll return through the front and join Wilkins, like we planned. Out with you." Ernie G and Manuel's man disappeared through a side door.

Geoff Wilkins stood at the bar drinking Mexican beer, his booted foot on the railing, peanut shells strewn on the floor at his feet. He looked around the room and nodded to several men in acknowledgement of acquaintance. In truth he recognized the faces of only one or two of the men but he was in a friendly mood. It was late in the afternoon and most of the patrons in the Barra de Juegos were men. Geoff thought it was too bad because he always liked to look at a pretty face.

The bartender placed a bottle of whiskey on the bar about the same time as Jose stepped up beside Geoff.

"Offer you a drink?" Jose said to Geoff.

"Sure. I'm never one to turn down whiskey. It goes well with the beer."

A few shots later, the men were laughing and, having been joined by two or three others, the talk had turned to sharing a game or two of poker. Jose said he knew the club owner would give them the use of the back room.

"Yeah, I know Señor Manuel. He'll do it for me, but I need some reassurance that you fellows are in my league."

"Who are you doubting?" asked one of the men.

"I've never seen you fellows before. I'm ready to play big-boy games. Poker is fine by me, but I prefer craps." Geoff raised his whiskey glass toward Jose. "Do you think Manuel could set us up?"

"I don't know. I can ask."

Minutes later, Jose reported that Manuel invited them to join him at the site of the new casino which was still under construction.

"Most of the building is complete. Not all the slots are set up but we can play craps in one of the rooms. The table is already more or less ready for play and Señor Manuel is prepared to be the House. He says if we want to play, we should get ourselves over there now."

"Yeah. Sounds good to me. Really good. I am having a lucky day anyway so I might as well have a lucky night. I'm ready to go now. I know where to go. Does anyone want to ride along with me?"

"Yeah, I'll come with you," offered Jose.

"Wow. I can't believe Manuel got this place set up so quickly." Geoff parked his car in a graveled lot behind the building that was not yet open to the public. A single bulb lit a service door and Jose unlocked it with a key that he said Manuel had just given him. The two men walked in and were greeted by Señor Manuel who showed them to a large gaming room, bar on one side and two or three craps tables in place.

Drinks were served and Geoff and several of the men purchased chips and examined the dice. The currency was Mexican and Geoff used his pesos. He kept his US dollars in a bank envelope inside his wallet and he kept his wallet in his back pocket.

Soon the room was in full action.

As the booze flowed, the dice were blown on, blessed, thrown, blessed and cursed. For the first two hours, Geoff won more than he lost. He used his winnings to purchase more chips, higher denomination chips. By the third hour, he had consumed at least half a bottle of whiskey and several glasses of beer. He was seeing with difficulty the numbers on the dice. He began to lose.

In the fourth hour, he began making greater bets in an effort to win back what he had lost. He approached Señor Manuel and asked to buy chips using US dollars. Manuel sold him $10,000 in chips, an amount that Geoff loudly claimed was an insult.

Manuel stood firm. Geoff began flailing about in anger, kicking the nearest barstools.

"Time for the game to end. It is my call. The night is over," Manuel announced.

Jose and two other men grabbed Geoff and carried him screaming out to his truck. They placed him behind the wheel and started the ignition for Geoff.

"Go home, Wilkins. Go home. You've had your night," Jose said and stepped away from the truck as Geoff peeled out, gravel flying.

Hardly able to see the road, Geoff told himself that he was lucky that the truck knew the way home. The road out of town was dark but when Geoff made a wild turn onto his family's property, he thought he saw lights.

Chapter 49

"Turn the flashlight off, you idiot. I hear a truck. I think he's pulled into the property."

The two men were standing near the entry gate where they had staged the robbery. Missing was their leader, Jorge Manuel. He had been laid to rest in the Manuel section of the cemetery near the taqueria where he had been murdered.

His men were intent on revenge. The deal that Jorge made with Geoff Wilkins, rich white man, was supposed to leave them with an expensive car and several pieces of fine jewelry. Instead, they got a car so identifiable that they couldn't drive it anywhere, and a bunch of junk rings and trinkets. The car had to be broken down for parts. The trinkets were worthless. The men made enough money to pay for new boots and two nights of booze and women. They had expected a great deal more and they had not anticipated the loss of Jorge Manuel.

Conchi, the owner of the taqueria where Jorge was killed, was a friend to all. She kept quiet when Jorge and his men drank and talked loudly about their exploits. She served good food that she prepared herself, food that stuck to the ribs and made the young men remember their mothers. She knew the power of Jorge's father and innately knew her duty to her neighbors. When she saw the blonde gringo from Las Palmas kill Jorge, she had known what to do. She told the police that terror had prevented her from seeing anything.

She shook and shivered as she relayed the full story to her husband, then she went directly to Señor Manuel and told him everything. Her intent was to maintain her reputation. Other consequences, she determined, were not her responsibility and even if pressed, she would not have admitted that Señor Manuel's honor was at stake and that, in grief, he would seek retribution. She left Manuel's presence with her conscience clear.

Filled with alcohol, angry about losing his money to Manuel, Geoff, talked to himself as he drove. He cursed the shock absorbers on his father's truck as it bounced along the dirt road on the ranch, the very road where he had a few weeks earlier driven his new convertible. He cursed the craps table and told himself that the dice were loaded. He cursed the men who had gathered around the table and cheered for him. He cursed Monterrey and he cursed Mexico.

Ahead was the gate and he told the truck to stop. With difficulty his foot managed to find the brake and press it toward the floor to bring the large vehicle to a stop.

Geoff's vision was dubious and his balance unpredictable. He nevertheless opened the door and ventured out holding on first to the edge of the door then propping himself up on the truck's cab. He inched his way toward the gate but was stopped in his tracks by a bright light shining directly into his eyes. The light enhanced the queasy feeling in his stomach and he thought he might throw up.

Slurring his speech, he spat out, "Is that you? Edo? I'm home."

But it wasn't Edo.

"Edo is dead, morte. It won't do you any good to call for your friend now," said one of the men. "Do you know who we are?"

"Edo is dead?" Geoff staggered but corrected his balance by placing both hands on the hood of the truck. "I think I'm going to be sick." Geoff leaned forward and threw up, falling to his knees. He wiped his mouth with his shirtsleeve but didn't try to stand up.

"Look at me." The voice was strong, loud, and decisive. "Look at me, you murderer, you weakling, you sorry excuse for a man."

"Do I know that voice?"

Geoff raised his head and looked into the eyes of Manuel.

"You double-crossed my son and his men and you killed Jorge for a ring that you could have bought ten times over. A man like you doesn't deserve to be called a man. Where is your honor?"

"I'm rich, Manuel. You know money isn't a problem. I'll pay. I'll pay Jorge's men. I'll pay you. Look in my wallet. In my back pocket."

"There is nothing in your back pocket," said Manuel. "You don't even have the ability to hold on to your own wallet."

Gingerly Geoff reached for his wallet and confirmed that it was not in his back pocket.

"But I have money. My family has money." Geoff's mouth was dry and the whiskey and beer were gurgling around in his stomach. He swallowed to try to keep himself from vomiting again.

"Your family may have money and your father and mother may even love you like I loved my son. I am sorry for your parents. They will have to grieve as I am grieving, but such is the way of the world."

Geoff's efforts to keep down the contents of his stomach failed, and he began to vomit again. When he lifted his head again, the world around him was dark. He started to crawl intending to make his way back to the truck.

Geoff Wilkins's body was found by Comandante Gonzalez. Geoff was lying face down on the ground a few feet from the gate to the inner property of Las Palmas. He had no identification on his body and there was no car or truck in sight.

Gonzalez was following up on a call from Sam Wilkins. Sam said he had been trying for two days to reach Geoff. "Would Gonzalez check the property, do what he could to see if Geoff, and Edo, were around?"

"I'm afraid that Geoff is in trouble. Edo told me a few days ago that Geoff was in trouble. I'm at my wit's end and my wife is crying and sure something is wrong. I hate to ask for favors, Diego, but would you go out to the ranch and make sure nothing is wrong?" Sam had tried to make it sound benign but his voice was shaky as he spoke.

From the phone in the main house of Las Palmas, Comandante Gonzalez called his office to report two murders. Geoff's body was on the road and Edo's was found in the kitchen at the back of the hacienda.

Gonzalez also called Sam and delivered the bad news.

Part 5
1962

Chapter 50

Jeananne removed the gold compact from her evening purse, opened it and looked at herself in the tiny mirror. She applied a fresh coat of coral lipstick, smiled at her image, and quickly daubed a bit of pressed powder on her nose. As she closed the purse and turned her body to hang it by its long chain strap over the back of her chair, her right arm brushed against the forearm of the man seated next to her. He immediately reacted by repositioning his chair so that he could face her.

The room was candle-lit and smelled of flowers and expensive perfume. The tables were set in cobalt and cream china. Crystal sparkled. Beautifully dressed guests sat at round tables distributed around the Oil Club's largest dining room in celebration of President John F. Kennedy's speech that day at Rice University.

In the room were wealthy and influential Houstonians known for their support of the President's space program as well as key scientists and NASA officials.

"I'm one of the lucky men here tonight. John Kennedy is here with Jackie but I am seated next to arguably the most gorgeous Texan in the room," said the red-headed man seated next to Jeananne.

"I'm accustomed to flattery, Dr. James Rowan," Jeananne replied, aware of her good looks. "I would expect an original greeting from someone as intelligent as you are reported to be."

"Don't be so hard on me. Where is that Texas hospitality I have heard so much about?"

"We are hospitable, Dr. Rowan, and generous. My company is very interested in this new space venture although I can't claim to understand much about your field. Astrophysics, is it?"

"And, how did you know that?"

"We each have a place card, Dr. Rowan."

"And you are Jeananne Wilkins, President of Wilkins Enterprises." Dr. Rowan grinned and raised his eyebrows as he looked at Jeananne. "I read yours, too," he added, his eyes twinkling.

"Yes, it's more or less an honorary title. I still consider myself a student of the business." Jeananne smiled and looked directly into the eyes of Dr. Rowan. Green they were and set fairly close together. She studied his face, noting his long nose and crooked smile, his red hair long in front and short in back, cut badly, she thought.

She liked what she saw but she wasn't sure why. It had been five years since her husband had died in Monterrey. Five years during which she had devoted herself to learning about Wilkins Enterprises. Thank God, she told herself, for Martha who had taken her under her wing, had gotten her through the rough times and had stuck by her.

First Jeananne had had to deal with the circumstances of Geoff's death. She wasn't alone in her grief and anger. Poor Sam had been hit the hardest. His beloved Miriam had not been able to accept the death of her darling son. Miriam's health declined rapidly and Sam had taken her to every reputable doctor in Houston to no avail. When she died, Sam had to convince himself that he had done everything possible to save her.

Left alone to pick up the pieces, Sam had repaid the insurance company in an effort to keep the scandal of Geoff's fraudulent behavior from becoming public knowledge. He refused to participate in the Mexican investigation of his son's death and was never interested in knowing who had killed Geoff. He was afraid of what he could find if he dug deep.

Sam also mourned the death of his faithful Edo. When Marva left Houston for Monterrey to be with their mother, Sam gave her an envelope stuffed with money and told her that he knew money wouldn't bring Edo back, but maybe it would help the family in difficult times. Marva took the money and said she would give it to her mother but it would not be sufficient to make up for the loss of Edo. Sam also gave a mysterious instruction to Marva, one that she didn't understand. He told her that he expected to die sometime in the future, and he wanted Marva to contact his attorney in Monterrey after he was gone. Marva told him that everyone dies in the future. Sam ignored her attitude and when she questioned him about the need for an attorney, Sam had nothing more to say on the subject, other than to admonish her to keep the piece of paper with the name of the attorney on it.

Caught up in his personal tragedy, Sam began to withdraw from his duties at the company he and his brother had founded. By the time Sam was consumed by dementia, his sister-in-law Martha had taken over full control of the privately-owned company.

Martha had advised Jeananne not to make any dramatic changes in her life at first. She said she had experience as a widow and knew that it was easy to make rapid poorly-considered decisions during grief. Jeananne later said that she had more or less turned her decision-making over to Martha during the first year of her widowhood and that Martha had guided her down a solid path.

Martha insisted later that Jeananne herself had displayed maturity and good judgment. It was true that their relationship was strengthened by the tragedy that they both labelled, "that night in Monterrey." Neither clarified which night they meant but it wasn't important to them. Forevermore in both their minds, "that night in Monterrey" referred to tragedy, a frightening occurrence, a nightmare and an experience one hoped never to repeat.

After Faye died and Martha and Jeananne returned to Houston and Sam had begun his mission first to prevent scandal, then to save Miriam, then to save himself, Jeananne threw herself into helping Rosa start her business. She also began spending more time in the downtown offices of Wilkins Enterprises, following Martha's lead as Martha began increasing her role day by day.

Poor Harold Carter. Shortly after Liz returned from Monterrey back in the fall of 1957, Harold had started divorce proceedings. Jeananne found it difficult to think of Liz as "poor Liz Carter" because after all, she had openly had an affair with Jeananne's husband. After the divorce, Liz had packed up and moved to whereabouts unknown. Harold had stayed on. Reliable Harold. Steady Harold. Thank goodness for Harold, Jeananne had told Martha, because he held up, the subsidiary company originally founded by Harold and Geoff. Technically, the subsidiary now belonged to Harold and Jeananne.

Jeananne was not poor, not poor in regards to finance, and not poor as in pathetic. She considered herself fortunate because Geoff's death had made her confront her own strengths and future. Lemon into lemonade, she told herself. Like Sam and Martha, Jeananne didn't want to know more about the circumstances of Geoff's demise. She just wanted to build a life that had some meaning.

Martha had suggested that Jeananne could find meaning in work. Up until that night at the Oil Club, Jeananne had had no interest in men. She told her acquaintances that she wouldn't mind being in a happy marriage, but anything less than happy, well, she would rather stay single.

Yet here she was, sitting next to a man more highly educated, surely more intelligent (and in a field she knew nothing about). She knew little about him, and she was intrigued.

Chapter 51

The mirror attached to the door was crooked and there was a small crack across the top. The edge of the bed was about two feet from the door, too close to the mirror for Marva to get a full view of herself. She tried to straighten the mirror but the door wasn't quite right.

She had slept late that morning. It must be at least nine o'clock. Usually, she and Ricky awoke at the same time and were up and about their daily routines at seven o'clock. Usually, they were in Houston but today things were different: they were in Monterrey, Mexico.

She could hear Ricky's voice. He was in the kitchen with Juanita and they were talking. She was alone in the bedroom.

Marva felt giddy with excitement. She had the feeling of displacement that comes from waking up in someone else's home and not knowing what the day would bring. At least the home was not totally unfamiliar to her. It had been her grandmother's house, before her grandmother died. Now it belonged to Marva's mother, Juanita.

The house had two bedrooms and a bathroom with a bathtub, indoor toilet and sink. The kitchen boasted a hot water heater and a stove and modern refrigerator. When the grandmother died in 1957, the same year as Edo, Juanita used the money Sam sent her to put a new roof on the house and she proudly told her daughter that she was going to live in the house for the rest of her life. If Marva wanted, she could visit, but Juanita said she never would leave her home.

Juanita kept her word. She never travelled more than the distance from her house on the downtown side of Monterrey to the other side of the barrio and even then, she only made the trip on market days.

Two years earlier, when Marva and Ricky got married in Houston, Juanita had sent her love and her blessings. She said she was too poorly to travel. When Marva told her employer, Martha Wilkins, that she and Ricky were going to get married, Martha had worried about how they would manage, but it didn't take long for a plan to develop. Ricky and Marva would live in the house with Sam. Martha would hire another housemaid, "a day girl" to help at her house. Ever practical, Martha worked out a schedule for Ricky, Marva and the day girl and it seemed to have worked.

Marva thought Juanita's health had declined because of Edo's death. Losing him had been difficult for everyone in the family. Sam Wilkins had suffered too after Edo died. He suffered because his own son Geoff died and he seemed to feel equally sorrowful about the death of Edo.

Marva had witnessed Sam go from invincible to unrecognizable. She could hardly believe as she sat looking at what she could see of herself in the mirror, that Sam was dead. Time was passing quickly. Sam died in late September, 1962. He was seventy years old. His death was a release, she thought. Ricky had looked after him and his house after Miriam died and after the dementia had worsened.

Watching Ricky as he helped Sam had made Marva love him more. She saw how gentle and kind he was. He made sure Sam always was cleaned up and dressed smartly and even when Sam couldn't walk, Ricky pushed him around in the wheelchair.

After Sam died, Ricky and Marva moved into the apartment over the garage in the back of Sam's property. They considered the move temporary because they thought Martha would oversee the sale of the house that had been Sam and Miriam's home. They weren't even settled in the apartment when Martha told them to take a vacation. That's what she called it, a vacation. Both Marva and Ricky were surprised at the word. They had had afternoons off, or days off, and once or twice Marva or Ricky had shuttled back and forth between Mexico and Houston as employees. Marva had spent a few days with her mother after Edo died, but a vacation. The word was not in either Marva's or Ricky's vocabulary.

Encouraged by Martha, no, actually instructed by Martha, after Sam's death, Marva and Ricky drove to Monterrey for a vacation. Now Marva sat on the side of the bed in her grandmother's house, listening to her husband and mother talking in the kitchen.

She wasn't quite ready to make a start on the day. She sat, holding the sheet of paper Sam had given her after Edo's death. He told her to keep the paper and after his death to contact the attorney whose name was written on the paper. "But wait until after I'm gone," Sam had said.

It had been tempting to Marva to ignore Sam's instruction. She was curious and fantasized about why Sam would want her to see an attorney in Monterrey after he died. Maybe he wanted to give her a present for her loyalty. She knew other housemaids, employees of rich people, who received presents or who were mentioned in wills. She didn't think she was that important to Sam Wilkins. Maybe she had done something wrong and Sam was sending her to the lawyer who would tell her she owed money. But that was ridiculous because she didn't have any money and she shouldn't have to pay Sam anything because she couldn't think of anything wrong that she had done.

Once after they were married, Marva had told the story to her husband and had shown him the name of the lawyer. Ricky had shrugged and said he didn't know about attorneys. He had added that it was too bad they couldn't get more information from Sam but Sam's mind had gone and he wouldn't be able to tell them why he wanted Marva to talk to the lawyer after he died. Eventually, Marva put it out of her mind and focused on marriage and then on her pregnancy.

Sitting on the edge of the bed, seeing only a part of her pregnant body in the mirror, Marva held the paper Sam had given her and told herself that she was finally going to get an answer to the mystery. It was peculiar that Martha had encouraged Ricky and Marva to make this trip to Monterrey. Martha only said that the trip was important and that she didn't want to stand in their way, a statement that only added to the mystery.

The sun was already sending its warmth to Monterrey. Marva wore a sleeveless shift and hoped that she wouldn't perspire. She and Ricky were due at the lawyer's office at eleven o'clock. They decided to walk because the lawyer's office was next door to the town hall, just on the east side of the barrio. They could leave Juanita's house at a quarter to eleven and still be on time but they decided to leave at ten-thirty to be sure they weren't late.

They left Juanita in her kitchen, smoking and drinking coffee while reading a daily newspaper popular in the neighborhood. She wished them luck.

The two were enamored with each other and with the thought of the new life growing inside Marva's body. They held hands as they walked through the narrow streets lined with tobacco shops, confectionaries, and cafes. Ricky stopped to look into the window of a hardware store, but Marva pulled him away.

Chapter 52

The attorney sat at his desk with his hands placed over a large file folder. Marva and Ricky entered the office and sat down opposite him.

"I hope you don't mind. Comandante Gonzalez wants to join us. Do you know him?" The attorney spoke in a manner that made disagreement difficult.

Marva shook her head but Ricky spoke up, "We know who he is. He's the head of the police."

Hearing that the police were interested made Marva's anxiety increase. She wondered if she had done something that would lead to her arrest. She squeezed Ricky's hand and the look in his eyes indicated he too was nervous.

Ricky spoke, "Does he have to be here?"

"No," said the attorney. "He wants to talk to you. Why don't we ask him to continue to wait outside until we finish our business?"

Marva and Ricky looked at each other and nodded slightly in agreement.

The attorney rose and closed the door to the office.

"First, I understand you do not know why we are meeting and I want to assure you that I am here to inform and to help you. I have a number of documents to read to you and to explain, if you require an explanation." He opened the folder and removed a folded document. "This is a document written by Sam Wilkins, stating his wishes concerning his property and interests in Monterrey. I knew Sam Wilkins very well and prepared this document for him. As a matter of record, I also represented your brother Edo."

"Edo had an attorney?"

"Yes. This is going to sound complicated. I will begin with this first document, as I said, written by Sam Wilkins." He read the document then offered an explanation to Marva and Ricky. "What I read was an agreement between Sam Wilkins and Edo Wilkins. Sam purchased Las Palmas and placed the deed under Edo's name. You were a minor at the time. Sam agreed to provide all maintenance and operation costs and assumed all responsibilities and benefits of ownership."

At this point the attorney stopped and gave Marva a chance to fan herself. He called out to his secretary to bring in water both for Ricky and for Marva.

"I don't understand," Marva said.

"You may not know the history of Mexico but all property, with a few exceptions, must be owned by Mexican citizens. Sam was loved in Monterrey and no one questioned whether or not he actually owned Las Palmas. The state didn't get involved because the taxes were paid and the deed was in the name of a Mexican citizen."

"What did you say Edo's name was?" Marva asked.

"Wilkins. More about that later."

Marva turned to Ricky. "We never knew our father. Mother always said she met him at church so we just assumed he was Mexican. Why would Sam say that Edo's last name was Wilkins?"

"Back to business, Marva. When Edo wrote his will, he assigned all his property to you. You were, and are, his heir. When Edo died, the ownership of Las Palmas passed to you."

"I owned Las Palmas? Edo died five year ago. Do I still own Las Palmas? I've owned Las Palmas for five years? I don't believe this." Marva was sitting very still but her eyes were darting from the attorney to Ricky and back. Ricky grabbed her hand but was speechless.

"It is all true. These are the legal papers to prove it. After Edo died, Sam sat in this very room, where you are sitting and told me that you were his only remaining child and he wanted you to have Las Palmas, but he didn't think you were ready to take on the responsibility. I tried to convince him to turn the property over to you at the time. You were after all the rightful owner, but Sam said no. When I look back at it, it is my judgment that he was trying to protect you. He thought it would be too much for you to cope with Edo's death and this news."

"He didn't want to tell me himself that I was the owner of the ranch?"

"No, I don't think he did and I don't think he wanted to tell you himself that he was your father. He thought it would be too big a shock."

"Shock. Mio dio, I am feeling shock." Marva began making slow, methodical movements with the palm of her left hand around her belly. "Sam Wilkins was my father."

"These other documents are your brother's will, the property deeds, your birth certificate and other documents that pertain to the business of the ranch."

"I don't want to go through all of those right now, unless I have to. This is all so overwhelming. You are saying I own that ranch? I've only been there a couple of times. It's huge. I can't run a ranch like that. What are we going to do?"

Marva turned to Ricky who said, "I'm in shock too. Marva, we need to talk to your mother. She never told you about any of this?"

The attorney said, "Sam didn't tell Juanita everything. She probably doesn't know about the ranch ownership. Edo was pretty quiet about his business too. Does your mother know that you are here today?"

"Yes, but she didn't say anything about any of this. Did Sam leave anything for her?"

"You should talk with your mother. Sam has taken good care of her."

"What about when we were children?"

"I don't know about your childhood. Did you want for anything?"

"No, but I didn't have a father." Marva shook her head in disbelief. "I didn't have a father and now you tell me I did have a father and I've spent over ten years working as a maid for his sister? What kind of man does that to his daughter?"

"I can't answer your questions, Marva. Your father did leave an envelope here for you. Maybe he has answered some of your questions. Do you want me to read it to you? It's sealed. He wrote it by hand, I believe."

"No, no, no. I'll take the envelope and, well, I don't know what I will do."

Ricky said, "You're right, Marva. Take the letter and read it later."

"I own Las Palmas?"

"Yes, Marva. You own Las Palmas. I have the deed here with the property in your name."

"What if I don't want it? We're not fancy people. I wouldn't want to live in that house now that I know about Sam."

"My best advice to you, Marva, is not to make any decisions immediately. I will hold all these documents for you, if you want. You don't have any urgent decisions to make about the property. We've got a property manager out there who is taking care of the day-to-day running of the place. I've overseen every transaction as Sam wanted. Why don't you come back tomorrow and we can go through the rest of these papers? We can do this over several sessions."

"You are my attorney, then?"

"I was Sam's attorney and Edo's attorney. Do you want me to work for you? I come well-recommended." He smiled.

"Yes. I don't know what else I could do and you are familiar with the history. Why is the Comandante here? Have I done something wrong?"

"Nothing wrong. Sam knew his father and helped the Comandante in a number of ways. I believe he wants to buy Las Palmas from you."

Chapter 53

December, 1957

Dear Marva,

If you are reading this letter, you are aware of our true relationship. I hope you can forgive me for keeping secrets from you. Your brother and I both thought it best so that we could protect you.

A man can love more than one person. I met your mother when I was a young buck. I had just struck it rich in the oil fields and had so much money I didn't know what to do with all of it. One of my buddies told me I should buy property and I did. Of course, I set up my business with my brother Wendell. I bought the house in Houston and made sure my wife and son Geoff had a home. Then a friend told me about Monterrey. He was going to move his company to Mexico. I was game for exploring possibilities, so I went to Monterrey with him just to see the lay of the land. That was a long time ago, but writing about it reminds of me of being young when the world was my oyster.

To make a long story short, I told my friend I wasn't educated enough to be a part of the university crowd in Monterrey and I am 100% USA and couldn't possibly move my new company to Mexico which is another country.

But I liked Monterrey. I liked the mountains and the colors and the people and the food. I met your mother by accident. It was a holiday, I think Independence Day in Mexico, and people were celebrating in the streets. Your mother was part of a group that was dancing. I was walking around just enjoying myself when I saw her. She had long black hair and when she danced her hair flew over her shoulders and I was in love the minute I saw her. She had a flower in her hair and wore a skirt that she swirled around.

She also had a chaperone. In those days young girls were guarded closely but I managed to get her attention. The chaperone wouldn't let me get close to her and I had the devil's own time getting her name.

To get to the main part of my story, we fell in love. At first, I didn't tell her about my life in Houston. She just thought I was some cowboy from Texas but I finally did tell her. I told her about everything including Miriam and Geoff. At first, she was angry with me but I convinced her that I loved her and when Edo came along and then you, I still loved her and I kept my word that I would take care of all of you.

Your mother was a proud person, probably still is. She wanted to stay in Monterrey but I wanted you and Edo where I could see you so I moved all of you to Houston. It was a hard time for your mother. She wanted to go back to Monterrey.

We agreed never to tell Miriam or Martha or Geoff about our being together. If I were a sentimental man, I would say we loved each other and in our own way, we tried to be a family.

I believe your mother will tell you she has had a happy life. I tried to do my best by her and to do my best for you and Edo.

My heart was broken when I lost both my sons at the same time. Edo was a fine man, loyal and capable of taking care of all kinds of problems. He had good sense. I trusted him with my life.

I trusted you to my sister-in-law, Martha. I knew she would treat you well. She never knew you were my daughter. She will not learn the truth until I die and she reads my will. She is in good health and I think she will outlive me.

The fact that you are reading this now confirms that Miriam and I are both dead. Martha, if she is living, will be shocked but will be a help to you. If you need her, I am sure she will do whatever it takes to help you.

As to my wishes, Martha and my daughter-in-law Jeananne will inherit Wilkins Enterprises. Jeananne already owns half of Wilcarco. Since you are my only direct heir, I have deeded the property in Houston to you. Sell it or keep it. It is yours to decide.

Edo has all along owned Las Palmas. That may be shocking to you. It was my intent for him to have the running and benefits of the ranch after my death but sadly that could not happen.

Geoff would have had Wilcarco and the oil business to run but sadly that didn't happen.

You, Marva, are now in a position to make the most of your life as a wealthy woman. Las Palmas has been well-taken care of and its profits can support you. My advice is that you should let the attorney help you with all the business of running the ranch.

I think I have said everything I need to say. I don't know if you will ever feel any love for me, but I have watched you grow up and I have been proud of you.

Signed: Sam Wilkins

Chapter 54

The plaza was filled with children playing on tricycles and skating and running. Mothers and grandmothers sat on benches placed to allow them close scrutiny of the play scene in front of them. No one paid attention to Marva and Ricky who were seated under a palm tree off to the side of the main action. If they had, they would have seen her sobbing and they would have seen Ricky trying to console her.

"What's in the letter? Is it so bad?" Ricky asked.

"Read it for yourself," Marva said through her tears. She gestured to the sheets of paper in her lap.

When Ricky finished reading, Marva spoke. "He never explained why he had me work as a maid. All those years, I cooked and cleaned for the Wilkins family and I was a Wilkins."

"It doesn't make sense. I wouldn't do anything like that."

"No. Of course, you wouldn't. I married you because you are kind and gentle and caring. And what about Edo? My dear brother. He deceived me. He knew we were Wilkins." Her voice got higher in pitch. "And, he never told me that he owned Las Palmas and that someday it would be mine."

"Maybe they had good reasons," Ricky said, trying to make sense of the situation.

"Maybe it just doesn't make sense. Maybe they were just looking out for themselves. Not Edo, though. He would never have hurt me."

"I think Edo was doing what he thought was right. I know he must have loved you and wanted the best for you."

"And mother, how could she have accepted the life Sam Wilkins offered her?"

"I guess she thought it was better than the life she had before."

"And what did he mean when he said he wanted to have me close so he could protect me. What was he protecting me from?"

"I think I know the answer to that one but maybe I shouldn't say. It isn't nice."

"Ricky, I have to know. Protect me from what?" Marva glared at Ricky.

"I think from Geoff. Can you imagine what Geoff might have done if he had known he had a Mexican half-brother and half-sister?"

"You think he might have hurt us?"

"I don't know. He was capable of some pretty bad stuff, and he drank, and he gambled and knew some dangerous people."

"Sam Wilkins had two families. Poor Miss Miriam. I guess she never knew. You better not do anything like that to me." Marva's eyes were wide.

"I'm not at all like Sam Wilkins. I promise you I'll never be like him. We have lots to think about. You own Las Palmas and you own the big house in Houston. Can you see us living in either place? We don't have to make any decisions today. Like the lawyer said, don't make any quick decisions but I can't help but think about it, imagine a different life."

"I am in such a state of shock that I can't think of anything like that right now. I don't want to live in any place that Sam Wilkins lived in. To me, he thought he did right by me but where was he when I was growing up? Where was he when I was lifting those heavy wet sheets out of the laundry tub and carrying them out to the clothesline? No, I don't want to live anyplace he lived. I don't have to spend any time thinking about getting rid of those two properties."

Ricky and Marva sat silently, their hands clutching each other.

Marva said, "I want to live in Monterrey. We'll buy a little house somewhere close to Mama so we can look after her. I want a yard so our daughter (I know it must be a girl) can play outside. We'll buy a car or a truck and if we have any money left over, we can buy a small ranch where you can look after some cattle or we can buy a garage for you to work on motors."

"Sounds good to me. I'd like a garage. I don't want to fool with cattle and a farm. What about the house in Houston?"

"Like I said, I don't want to live in that house. It belonged to Sam and Miriam and in my mind, it will always be theirs. I don't even want to go back to Houston. Maybe the lawyer can manage everything, sell the house for us. It will be worth a lot of money. Only rich people live in that neighborhood. I have no idea how much money it will bring, but enough to buy a place here and the garage. I'm beginning to see how this could work for us."

"That would leave us with Las Palmas. The ranch is a huge enterprise. If we kept it, you could be the richest woman in Monterrey. Do you want to be the rich Mexican woman in town?" Ricky grinned.

"You're teasing me. If we kept the ranch, we could give work to a lot of people. We would have to live there all the time, I think, instead of living in a house in town near Mama. We would need to hire more people to take care of the house. Then there are the horses and the cattle and the gardens and…" Marva was talking so fast she had to stop to catch her breath.

"The attorney said there is a manager on the ranch now. We could keep the manager. He would take care of hiring and looking after all the people who would work there. The more I think about our living at the ranch, the more complicated it seems. What would we do with our time if we lived there? I could work out in the back garage like I did when Sam was alive but at night, I'd come into the big house and sit in the front room smoking cigars. What would you do all day? Would we want to sit and watch everyone else work? I'm beginning to think I wouldn't like to live like that. It's really going to be up to you, though. You are the one who has the money." Ricky stuck out his lower lip.

"As long as I have money, we both have money. We're married, remember?" Marva poked Ricky in the ribs. "I'm not sure what we should do. I do know this though: we have to talk to my mother. Let's walk for a while. She'll want to know what happened at the attorney's office."

"You don't seem surprised," Marva and Ricky were sitting on a stuffed sofa holding hands. Across from them was Juanita.

"Surprised? I was never surprised about anything Sam Wilkins did."

"What can you tell me, Mama, about why you worked as a maid, why you let me work like that? How could you live in Miss Martha's house knowing that you were like the wife of her sister's husband? I just don't understand it."

"Don't judge me, Marva. I made the best decisions I knew how to make and Sam Wilkins took pretty good care of me and of you and Edo. It was a better life than I could have made on my own."

"Mama, don't you think you could have done better if you'd raised us up in Monterrey?"

"No. I had no way to earn a living. We would have been poor. This way, look at what Sam has done for you."

"You mean because he left me these properties, everything else he did is okay?"

"Marva, he has left you land and money and you are set for life. What more could you want?"

"Something is missing from this picture, Mama." Marva began to cry.

"Marva, you can cry if you want, but I have everything I need to live out the rest of my life and you and Ricky are rich and will be able to do anything you want. If you live here in Monterrey, you'll probably be the richest Mexican in town. You can be hoity-toity, too good for the rest of us if you want."

"Mama, you make me ashamed."

Chapter 55

Jeananne placed the telephone receiver in place and said to Martha, "The lawyer says it is all decided."

"Tell me everything. This has been such a shock. Nothing can surprise me now. What is our Marva going to do now?"

"It seems she isn't eager to see us again."

"Who could blame her for that, but none of this was our fault. Give me the update so I can get back to business. I still have a meeting on my schedule." The two women were sitting in Jeananne's office adjacent to Martha's. The sign on the door said, JEANANNE WILKINS, PRESIDENT.

"Marva is selling everything, the house and the ranch. I tried to get the attorney to tell me what she plans to do with all that money but the most he would say is that she and Ricky plan to live in Monterrey."

"I can understand that. Juanita is there. You know the funny thing is that Juanita was a great housekeeper. I can't believe I had her in my house all that time and didn't know she was sleeping with Sam. I guess Sam must have taken her to a hotel. On second thought, I don't want to think about it."

"And Miriam didn't know anything about it."

"Are you asking me or telling me? Miriam told me everything and since she never said a word about Sam's having a mistress and children, for God's sake, I think I can safely believe that Miriam never knew about it and I am glad for that. It was a blessing that she never knew."

"She would have been devastated," offered Jeananne.

"Absolutely devastated," repeated Martha.

"It is the end of an era," said Jeananne shuffling the papers on her desk, moving the top sheet and placing it into a file.

"You have work to do?" asked Miriam.

"Don't we all? I want to get through this stack of papers before heading to the airport."

"Have you already packed?"

"Yes, I've packed. Dr. Rowan is picking me up here in about three hours. I'm not all that excited about going to London for New Year's. You'd think we could have picked some place warm. But he wanted to visit his cousin and I guess he wanted to introduce them to me. I'm curious about his family, maybe a little nervous to meet them."

"Why?" asked Martha.

"I think they are very sophisticated. I don't know how I will fit in."

"You are sophisticated, my dear. Just don't tell them you are from Arkansas. They won't understand."

"That's what has me worried. Shall I lie? I'm not very good at lying. I'll tell them I'm from Texas. I don't know what they think of Texans."

"Be proud of yourself, Jeananne. You are becoming a major force in the oil business in Texas. That's a big deal."

"Proud. We all know about pride."

Chapter 56

"What time are we due at the attorney's office?" Ricky lifted his head from the pillow and saw himself in the cracked mirror at the foot of the bed.

"Not until eleven," Marva responded. With some effort and with Ricky's help, she rolled onto her side, facing Ricky.

"Do you still love me, now that I am growing bigger?"

"Don't be silly. I think you are beautiful."

"Do you still love me, now that we are rich?" Marva looked plaintively at Ricky.

"You must be joking, my sweet," Ricky replied.

"Don't touch me. We have to get up and get dressed and Mama is just outside in the kitchen." Marva pushed Ricky to the edge of the bed.

"You are one strong woman," Ricky joked.

The two made their way again to the office they had visited several times in the past few days. As usual, Ricky's attention was diverted when they reached the hardware store. Its windows were decorated with tinsel.

"Maybe you want to buy that store," said Marva, and to clarify, she added, "if it is for sale."

"No, I still want a garage. I like to get myself all covered up with grease. You'll like me getting grease all over our new house, right?"

"Not right. We don't even have a new house, yet."

"We will. We haven't had enough time to do everything we want to do. Remember how we talked about being patient?"

"You talked about being patient. I'm not so sure I feel like I want to be patient."

"But you do want exactly the right house, so you have to be patient until we find it."

The two reached the office building at the same time as Comandante Gonzalez who was holding hands with a woman unknown to Ricky and Marva.

As the four walked up the stairs together, the police chief introduced his wife. Anyone observing these four would have said they were old friends because they seemed comfortable in each other's company, laughing and joking as they moved along.

Once inside the attorney's office, they tried to be serious because the business between them was serious. In exchange for a great deal more money than Marva had ever imagined she would see in her lifetime, she signed over the ownership of Las Palmas to Comandante Gonzalez and his wife. There was no discussion about where his money came from. No one in the office cared. He offered to walk with Ricky and Marva to the bank to deposit the check and they accepted. As they walked Marva asked him why he wanted the property.

He replied, "When I was a boy, Geoff Wilkins always told me he was better than me. I was just a little Mexican boy and he was the son of the great, rich Texan. He always said he was the king and I said I would be President of Mexico. Well, he never became a king, but I still think I will be President of Mexico."